A DARKER PLACE

JACK HIGGINS

A DARKER PLACE

HarperCollins*Publishers*

HarperCollins*Publishers*
77–85 Fulham Palace Road,
Hammersmith, London W6 8JB

www.harpercollins.co.uk

Published by HarperCollins*Publishers* 2009
1

A catalogue record for this book
is available from the British Library

ISBN: 978 0 00 729493 0 (hbk)
ISBN: 978 0 00 729494 7 (tpk)

Set in Aldus by Palimpsest Book Production Limited,
Grangemouth, Stirlingshire

Printed and bound in Great Britain by
Clays Ltd, St Ives plc

Mixed Sources
Product group from well-managed
forests and other controlled sources
www.fsc.org Cert no. SW-COC-1806
© 1996 Forest Stewardship Council

FSC

FSC is a non-profit international organisation established to promote the
responsible management of the world's forests. Products carrying the FSC
label are independently certified to assure consumers that they come
from forests that are managed to meet the social, economic and
ecological needs of present and future generations.

Find out more about HarperCollins and the environment at
www.harpercollins.co.uk/green

Once again, for Denise
and
Brewer Street

Avoid looking into an open grave.
You may see yourself there.

—Russian proverb

NEW YORK

1

Fresh from the shower, Monica Starling sat at the dressing table in her suite at the Pierre and applied her make-up carefully. She'd dried and arranged her streaked blonde hair in her favourite style as she always did, and now sat back and gave herself the once-over. Not bad for forty and she didn't look that ancient, even she had to admit that. She smiled, remembering the remark Sean Dillon had made on the first occasion they had met. 'Lady Starling, as Jane Austen would have Darcy say, it's always a pleasure to meet a truly handsome woman.'

The rogue, she thought, wondering what he was up to, this ex-enforcer with the Provisional IRA and now an operative in what everyone referred to as the 'Prime Minister's private Army'. He was a thoroughly dangerous man, and yet he was her lover. Look at you, Monica, she thought, shaking her head – a Cambridge don with three doctorates, falling for a man like that. Yet there it was.

She put on a snow-white blouse, beautifully cut in fine Egyptian cotton, and buttoned it carefully. Next came a trouser suit as black as night, one of Valentino's master-pieces. Simple diamond studs for the ears. Manolo Blahnik shoes, and she was finished.

'Yes, excellent, girl,' she said. 'Full marks.'

She smiled, thinking of her escort, dear, sweet old George Dunkley, Professor Emeritus in European Literature at Corpus Christi College, Cambridge, bless his cotton socks and all seventy years of him, and thrilled out of his mind to be here tonight. Not that she wasn't a little thrilled herself. When she'd accepted the United Nations' invitation to this international scholars' weekend, she'd had no idea who the guest of honour would turn out to be.

Alexander Kurbsky – the greatest novelist of his generation, as far as she was concerned. *On the Death of Men* and *Moscow Nights* – astonishing achievements, born out of his experiences as a paratrooper in Afghanistan and then the years of hell during the first and second Chechen wars. And he was only, what? Thirty-four, thirty-five? Hardly anyone outside Russia had actually met him since the publication of those books, the government kept him on such a short leash, and yet here he was, in New York. It was going to be quite an evening.

She turned from the mirror and the phone rang.

Dillon said, 'I thought I'd catch you.'

4

'What time is it there?'

'Just after midnight. Looking forward to meeting Kurbsky?'

'I must admit I am. I've never seen George so excited.'

'For good reason. Kurbsky's an interesting guy in lots of ways. His father was KGB, you know. When his mother died giving birth to his sister, an aunt raised them both for several years, and then one day, Kurbsky just up and ran away to London. The aunt was living there by then, and he stayed with her, studied at the London School of Economics for two years, and then – gone again. Went back, joined the paratroops, and the rest is history or myth, call it what you like.'

'I know all that, Sean, it's in his publisher's handout. Still, it should be quite an evening.'

'I imagine so. How do you look?'

'Bloody marvellous.'

'That's my girl. Slay the people. I'll go now.'

'Love you,' she said, but he was gone. Men, she thought wryly, they're from a different planet, and she got her purse and went to do battle.

In a room on the floor below, Alexander Kurbsky examined himself in the mirror and ran a comb through his shoulder-length dark hair. The tangled beard suggested a medieval bravo, a roisterer promising a kiss for a woman and a blow for a man. It was his personal statement, a turning against any kind of control after his years in the Army. He was a shade under five ten, much of his face covered by the beard, and his eyes were grey, like water over stone.

He was dressed totally in black: a kind of jersey with a collar fastened by a single button at the neck, black jacket and trousers, obviously Brioni. Even his pocket handkerchief was black.

His mobile phone, encrypted, buzzed. Bounine said, 'Turn left out of the entrance, fifty metres and I'm waiting. Black Volvo.'

Kurbsky didn't reply, simply switched off, went out, found the nearest lift and descended. He went out of the entrance of the hotel, ignoring the staff on duty, walked his fifty metres, found the Volvo and got in.

'How far?' he asked.

Bounine glanced briefly at him and smiled through gold-rimmed glasses. He had thinning hair, and the look of somebody's favourite uncle about him, except that he was GRU.

'Fifteen minutes. I've checked it.'

'Let's get on with it then.'

Kurbsky leaned back and closed his eyes.

Igor Vronsky was thirty-five and looked ten years older, but that was his drug habit. His hair was black and a little too long, verging on the unkempt. The skin was stretched too tightly across a narrow face with pointed chin. A paisley neckerchief at his throat and a midnight-blue velvet jacket combined, by intention, to give him a theatrical look. His notoriety in Moscow these days didn't worry him. The government loathed him for his book on Putin's time in the

KGB, but this was America, he had a new job writing for the *New York Times*, and they couldn't touch him. The book had brought him fame, money, women – to hell with Moscow.

He smiled at himself in the bathroom mirror, then leaned down to inhale the first of two lines of cocaine that waited. It was good stuff, absolutely spot on, and he followed it with the second line. He was dizzy for a moment, then slightly chilled in the brain and suddenly very sharp and ready for the great Alexander Kurbsky.

There was an old Russian saying: there was room for only one cock on any dunghill. He had no illusions that Kurbsky would be the star attraction at this soirée, but it might be amusing to knock him off his pedestal. He moved into the untidy living room of the small fifth-floor apartment, found a raincoat and let himself out.

'He never books a cab,' Bounine had said. 'It's only a step into Columbus Avenue, where he can have them by the dozen.'

So Kurbsky waited in the shadows for Vronsky to emerge, stand for a moment under the light of the doorway to his apartment building, then advance to the left, pulling up his collar against the rain. As he passed, Kurbsky reached out and pulled him close with considerable strength, his left arm sliding round the neck in a chokehold, the blade of his bone-handled gutting knife springing into action at the touch of the button. Vronsky was aware of the needlepoint nudging in through his clothing, the hand now clamped over his mouth, the blade seeming to know exactly what it was doing as it probed for the heart.

He slid down in a corner of the doorway and died very quickly on his knees. Kurbsky took out a fresh handkerchief, wiped the knife clean and closed it, then he leaned over the body, found a wallet and mobile phone, turned and walked to where Bounine waited. He got in to the Volvo and they drove away.

'It's done,' Bounine said.

Kurbsky opened the glove compartment and put the wallet inside, plus the mobile phone. 'You'll get rid of those.'

'Just another street mugging.'

'He was on coke.'

'Are you sure?'

'I'm sure.' He took out a pack of Marlboros.

Bounine said, 'Does it bother you?'

Kurbsky said calmly, 'Did Chechnya bother you?' He lit a cigarette. 'Anyway I'm not in the mood for discussion. I've got a performance to give. Let's get the great Alexander Kurbsky on stage.'

As they moved along Columbus Avenue, Bounine said, 'Is that all it is to you, Alex?'

'Yuri, old friend, I'm not into Freud at the start of a dark winter's evening in good old New York. Just get me to the Pierre where my fans are waiting.'

He leaned back, staring out at the sleet, and smoked his cigarette.

*   *   *

When Monica Starling and Professor Dunkley went into the reception at the Pierre, it was awash with people, the surroundings magnificent, the great and the good well in evidence. The US Ambassador to the United Nations was there, and his Russian counterpart. The champagne flowed. Monica and Dunkley took a glass each, moved to one side and simply observed the scene.

'There seem to be a few film stars,' Dunkley said.

'There would be, George, they like to be seen. There seems to be a pop star or two, as well. I suppose they feel an affair like this touches them with a certain . . . gravitas.'

'He's there,' Dunkley said. 'Talking to the French Ambassador, Henri Guyon, and the Russian – what's his name again?'

'Ivan Makeev,' Monica told him.

'They seem very enthusiastic about something, their heads together, except for Kurbsky.'

'He looks bored, if anything,' Monica said.

'We'll be lucky to get anywhere near him,' Dunkley told her mournfully. 'Look at all those people hovering like vultures, waiting for the ambassadors to finish with him so they can move in. We've had it.'

'Oh, I don't know.' She stood there, her left hand on her hip, her black suede purse dangling from it, and as he turned, she caught his eye and toasted him, glass raised, and emptied it. He knew her, of course, but she didn't know that, and he gave her a lazy and insolent smile as he walked over.

'Lady Starling, a pleasure long overdue.' He relieved her of her empty glass and waved for a passing waiter. 'How are things in Cambridge these days? And this will be Professor George Dunkley, am I correct? I've read your book on the other Alexander.'

Dunkley was stunned. 'My dear chap.' He shook hands, obviously deeply affected.

'The other Alexander?' Monica inquired.

'An early work,' Dunkley told her. '"An analysis of Alexandre Dumas and his writing salon."'

'All those assistants and Dumas prowling up and down the aisles like a schoolmaster in a black frock coat,' Kurbsky said.

He resonated charm, throwing it off as if it was of no account, his voice pleasantly deep, only a hint of a Russian accent.

'Was it really like that?' Monica asked.

'But of course, and look what it produced. *The Three Musketeers, The Man in the Iron Mask, The Count of Monte Cristo.*'

Dunkley said, breathless with enthusiasm, 'The literary establishment in Paris in his day treated him abominably.'

'I agree. On the other hand, they really got their faces rubbed in it when his son turned out one of the greatest of French plays, *La Dame aux Camellias.*'

'And then Verdi used the story for *La Traviata*!' Dunkley said.

Kurbsky smiled. 'One would hope Dumas got a royalty.'

They laughed and Dunkley said, 'Oh, my goodness, Captain Kurbsky, my seminars would be so crowded if my students knew you were going to attend.'

'That's an enticing prospect, but Cambridge is not possible, I'm afraid – and Captain Kurbsky belongs to a time long gone. I'm plain Alexander now.' He smiled at Monica. 'Or Alex, if you prefer.'

She returned his smile, slightly breathless, and an aide approached and said formally, 'The Ambassador is ready. If you would form the party, dinner is served.'

'Yes, of course,' Kurbsky said. 'These two will be sitting with me.'

The aide faltered, 'But, sir, I don't think that would be possible. It's all arranged.'

'Then rearrange it.' He shrugged. 'Of course, if there is a problem, we could sit at another table.'

'No, of course not, sir,' the aide said hastily. 'No need – no need at all. I'll go and make the necessary changes.'

He departed. Dunkley said, 'I say, old chap, we seem to be causing a bit of a problem.'

'Not at all. I'm their Russian Frankenstein, the great Alexander Kurbsky led out like a bear on a chain to astonish the world and help make Mother Russia seem great again.'

All this was delivered with no apparent bitterness, and those cold grey eyes gave nothing away. They reminded Monica uncomfortably of Dillon's, as Kurbsky continued, taking Monica's hand and raising it to his lips; 'If you glance over my shoulder you may see the Russian Ambassador approaching to see what the fuss is about.'

'Quite right,' Monica told him. 'Is he going to be angry?'

'Not at all. The moment he claps eyes on the most beautiful woman in the room, he's going to scramble to make sure you grace his table and no one else's.' He turned to Dunkley. 'Isn't that so, Professor?'

'Don't ask me, dear boy, I'm just going with the flow. I haven't enjoyed myself so much in years.'

And then the Ambassador arrived.

The diplomat ended up with his wife seated on his right, Monica on his left, and Kurbsky opposite. Dunkley beamed away lower down the table, facing the French Ambassador and proving that an Englishman could speak the language perfectly. The whole thing was thoroughly enjoyable, but glancing across the table, Monica was conscious that Kurbsky had withdrawn into himself. He reminded her once again of Dillon in a way. For one thing the champagne intake was considerable, but there was an air of slight detachment. He observed, not really taking part, but then that was the writer in him, judging people, constantly assessing the situation in which he found himself.

He caught her eye, smiled slightly and raised his eyebrows, as if saying what fools they all were, and then silence was called for speeches and the Russian Ambassador led the way. It was as if it were international friendship week, nothing unpleasant was happening in the world, the wars in Iraq and Afghanistan faded into obscurity, the only thing of any significance being this dinner in one of New York's greatest hotels, with wonderful food, champagne, and beautiful women. Everyone applauded, and when Monica glanced again at Kurbsky, he had joined in, but with the same weary detachment there. As the applause died, the French Ambassador rose.

He kept it brief and succinct. He was pleased to announce that if Alexander Kurbsky would make himself available in Paris in two weeks' time, the President of France would have great pleasure in decorating him with the *Légion d'Honneur*. Tumultuous acclaim, and Kurbsky stood and thanked the Ambassador of France in a graceful little speech delivered in fluent French. It was a fitting ending to a wonderful evening.

Later, as people dispersed, Monica and Dunkley hovered. There was no sign of Kurbsky. 'What an evening,' Dunkley said. 'I haven't enjoyed myself so much in years.' They were on a Virgin flight to London in the morning, leaving at ten-thirty local time. 'We've got an early start, so I'm for bed.'

'I'll see you in the morning,' she said.

As he walked away to the lifts, Monica paused, still seeking a sign of Kurbsky, but there wasn't one. In fact, he was outside the hotel sitting in the Volvo talking to Bounine.

'This Legion of Honour nonsense. Did you know about it?'

'Absolutely not, but what's wrong, Alex? The Legion of Honour – it's the greatest of all French decorations.'

'Do you ever get a so-what feeling, Yuri? I've been there, done that.'

'Are you saying no? You can't, Alex. Putin wants it, the country wants it. You'll be there in Paris in two weeks. So will I. God help us, you've got your own Falcon back to

Moscow in the morning, and a Falcon's as good as a Gulfstream.'

'Is that a fact?'

'Yes, old son. I'll pick you up at ten sharp.'

Kurbsky shrugged. 'Yes, I suppose you will.'

He got out and Bounine drove away. Kurbsky watched him go, turned and went back into the Pierre. The first thing he saw was Monica waiting for a lift and he approached, catching her just in time.

'Fancy a nightcap, lady?'

She smiled, pleased that he'd turned up. 'Why not?'

He took her arm and they went to the bar.

There weren't too many people. They sat in the corner and he had Russian vodka, ice cold, and she contented herself with green tea.

'Very healthy of you,' he told her.

'I wish I could say the same to you, but I'm not sure about that stuff.'

'You have to be born to it.'

'Doesn't it rot the brain?'

'Not really. Drunk this way, from a glass taken from crushed ice, it freezes the brain, clears it when problems loom.'

'If you believe that, you'll believe anything.'

'No, it's true. Now, tell me. I know about your academic accomplishments – the Ministry of Arts in Moscow is very thorough when one is attending affairs like this – but nothing about you. I'm puzzled that such a woman would not be married.'

'I'm a widow, Alex, have been for some years. My husband was a professor at Cambridge, rather older than me and a knight of the realm.'

'So, no children?'

'No, a brother, if that helps.' Her smile faltered for a moment, as she remembered her brother, Harry, recuperating from the terrible knife wounds he had so recently suffered, and, even more, the terrible psychological wounds. To see his wife assassinated in mistake for him – the healing process would take a long time . . .

She brought the smile back. 'He's a Member of Parliament,' she said, making no mention of what he really did for the Prime Minister.

Of course, Kurbsky actually knew all that, but he kept up the subterfuge.

'But there must be a man in your life, a woman like you.'

She wasn't offended in the slightest. 'Yes, there is such a man.'

'Then he must count himself lucky.'

He poured another vodka and she said, 'What about you?'

'Good heavens, no. The occasional relationship, but it never lasts. I'm a very difficult man, but then, I've had a difficult life. You know about me?'

'A bit. Your aunt raised you, right?'

'Svetlana was everything. I loved her dearly, but life in Moscow under Communism was difficult. When I was seventeen she got a chance to travel with a theatre group to

London – she was an actress – and she met a professor named Patrick Kelly, a good man. For once she had found something for herself, so she refused to return to Moscow, stayed in London and married him.'

'How was it you managed to join her?'

'That was my father. As a KGB colonel, he had influence. He arranged for me to visit Svetlana, hoping she'd change her mind.'

'And your sister?'

'Tania was at high school and only fifteen. She'd never been close to Svetlana and so she stayed with my father. There were servants, a couple living in my father's house, to care for her.'

'And where did the London School of Economics come in?'

He grinned, looking different, like a boy. 'I always had a love of books and literature, so I didn't need to study it. I found a new world at the LSE. Svetlana and Kelly had a wonderful Victorian house in Belsize Park, and they felt I should fill my time for a few months, so I took courses. Sociology, psychology, philosophy. The months stretched out.'

'Two years. What made you return to Moscow?'

'News from home, bad news. Over fifty-five thousand dead in Afghanistan. Too many body bags. Broken-hearted mothers protesting in the streets. Student groups fighting with the police. Tania was only seventeen, but up to her neck in it. Pitched battles, riot police, many casualties.' He paused, his face bleak. 'And Tania among them.'

Her response was so instinctive as to be almost banal. She put a hand on his. 'I'm so sorry.'

'I returned at once. A waste of time, of course, it was all over. Just a headstone in Minsky Park Military Cemetery. My father used his influence to make things look respectable. She was already dead when he'd got in touch with me in London, so he'd trapped me into returning. I got my revenge on him when I went downtown and joined the paratroopers. He was stuck with that. To pull me out would have looked bad in Communist Party circles.'

'Then what?'

'If you've read the opening chapters of *On the Death of Men*, you already know. There was no time to learn how to jump out of a plane with a parachute. I got three months' basic training, then I was off to Afghanistan. It was eighty-nine, the year everything fell apart, the year we scrambled to get out, and lucky to make it.'

'It must have been hell.'

'Something like that, only we didn't appreciate that Chechnya was to come. Two years of that, and that was just the first war.'

There was a long pause and he poured another vodka with a steady hand. She said, 'What now – what next?'

'I'm not sure. Only a handful of writers can achieve great success, and any writer lucky enough to write the special book will tell you the most urgent question is whether you can do it again or it was just some gigantic fluke.'

'But you answered that question for yourself with *Moscow Nights*.'

'I suppose, but . . . I don't know. I just feel so . . . claustrophobic now. Hemmed in by my minders.'

She laughed. 'You mean the bear-on-the-chain thing? Surely that's up to you. When Svetlana cast off her chains and refused to return to Moscow, she had to defect. But things are different now. The Russian Federation is not dominated by Communism any longer.'

'No, but it is dominated by Vladimir Putin. I am just as controlled as I would have been in the old days. I travel in a jet provided by the Ministry of Arts. I am in the hands of GRU minders, wherever I go. I don't even handle my own passport. They would never let me go willingly.'

'A terrible pity. Any of the great universities would love to get their hands on you. I'm biased, of course, but Cambridge would lay out the red carpet for you.'

'An enticing prospect.'

He sat there, frowning slightly, as if considering it. She said, 'Is there anything particular to hold you in Moscow?'

'Not a thing. Cancer took my father some years ago, there are cousins here and there. Svetlana is my closest relative. No woman in my life.' He smiled and shrugged, 'Not at the moment anyway.'

'So?' she said.

'They watch me closely. If they knew I was even talking this way to you, they'd lock me up.' He nodded. 'Anyway, we'll see. Paris in a fortnight.'

'Something to look forward to. You should be proud.'

She opened her purse and produced a card. 'Take this. My mobile phone number is on it. It's a Codex, encrypted and classified. You can call me on it whenever you like.'

'Encrypted! I'm impressed. You must be well connected.'

'You could say that.' She stood up and said, 'I mean it. Call me. Paris isn't too far from Cambridge, when you think of it.'

He smiled. 'If it ever happened . . . I wouldn't want an academic career. I'd prefer to leave the stage for a while, escape my present masters perhaps, but vanish. I'd like to think that my escape would be total, so Moscow had no clue as to where I had gone. I wouldn't appreciate the British press knocking on my door, wherever I was.'

'I see what you mean, but that could be difficult.'

'Not if I were able to leave quietly, no fuss at all. Moscow would know I'd gone, but the last thing they'd want would be for it to be public knowledge, which would create a scandal. They'd keep quiet, say I was working in the country or something on a new book, and try to hunt me down.'

'I take the point and will pass it on to my friends. Take care.'

He caught her arm. 'These friends of yours. They would have to be very special people who knew how to handle this kind of thing.'

She smiled. 'Oh, they are. Call me, Alex, when you've had time to think.'

She went to the lifts, a door opened at once, she stepped in and it closed.

Four o'clock in the morning in London, but in the Holland Park safe house in London, Giles Roper sat as usual in his wheelchair, his screens active as he probed cyberspace, his bomb-scarred face restless. He'd slept in the chair for a couple of hours, now Doyle, the night sergeant, had provided him with a bacon sandwich and a mug of tea. He ate the sandwich and was pouring a shot of Scotch when Monica's voice came over the speaker.

'Are you there, Roper?'

'Where else would I be?'

'You're the only fixed point in a troubled universe. That's one thing I've learned since getting involved with you people. Is Sean spending the night?'

'Returned to a bed in staff quarters ages ago. How was your evening? Did Kurbsky impress?'

'Just listen and see what you think.'

It didn't take long in the telling, and when she was finished, Roper said, 'If he's serious, I can't see why we couldn't arrange something. I'll speak to Sean and General Ferguson first thing in the morning. You, we should be seeing some time in the early evening.'

'Exactly.'

She switched off. He sat there thinking about it for a while. Alexander Kurbsky doing a runner to England. My God, Vladimir Putin will be furious. He put Kurbsky up on the screen. Too good-looking for his own good, he decided morosely, then brought up his record and started going through it carefully.

Kurbsky had found Bounine in the Volvo outside the Pierre and brought him up to speed. He smoked a cigarette.

Bounine said, 'So far, so good. It's worked. She must be quite a lady.'

'That's an understatement.'

'So, if they take the bait, we have Paris to look forward to. Colonel Luhzkov will be pleased.'

'Only because he wants to please Putin, and if Paris works, you mustn't be a part of it, Yuri. No one should know who you are. Luhzkov will work out something for you. Cultural attaché, for instance, would do you very well. Someone I can trust personally when I'm in London.'

'I'm glad you still do,' Bounine said.

'It's been a long time, Yuri. You're the only GRU man I know who looks like an accountant. No one would ever dream you were in Afghanistan and Chechnya with the paratroopers.'

'Whereas you, old friend, look like they found you in central casting. The smiler with the knife, they used to call you from that first year, remember?'

'Quite right.' Kurbsky got out and turned, holding the door. 'I also write good books.'

'Great books.' Bounine smiled. 'One thing is certain, Putin will be happy the way things have gone.'

'Putin has many reasons to be happy with the way things are going these days,' Kurbsky said. 'Night, Yuri.' He closed the door and went back into the hotel.

Moscow
London

2

It had all started three weeks before with Colonel Boris Luhzkov, Head of Station for the GRU at the Embassy of the Russian Federation in London, being called. The summons to Moscow had come from Putin himself and could not be denied, although it had surprised Luhzkov that it had come from him and not from General Ivan Volkov of the GRU, Putin's security adviser.

The reason became clear when he was driven to Berkley Down outside London, and found a Falcon jet waiting to fly him to Moscow, a luxury which should have warned him to expect the worst.

Two pilots were on board, the aircraft ready to go, and a steward, who introduced himself as Sikov, was waiting as he boarded. Luhzkov seated himself and belted in.

Sikov said, 'A great pleasure, Colonel. The flight time is approximately seven hours. I was instructed to give you this from Prime Minister Putin's office as soon as you arrived. May I offer you a drink?'

'A large vodka, I hate takeoffs. I once crashed in Chechnya.' Sikov had given him what looked like a legal file.

Sikov did it old-style, a bottle in one hand, a glass in the other. Luhzkov tossed it back and coughed, holding out his glass. Sikov poured another, then moved up to the small galley. Luhzkov swallowed the vodka and, as the plane started to roll, examined the file: several typed sheets stapled together, and an envelope addressed to him, which he opened.

The letter was headed: *From the Office of the Prime Minister of the Russian Federation.* It carried on: 'Attention of Colonel Boris Luhzkov. You will familiarize yourself with the material contained in the enclosed report and be prepared to discuss it with the Prime Minister on your arrival.'

Luhzkov sat there, staring down at the report, a bad feeling in the pit of his stomach. The Falcon had risen fast to thirty thousand feet and the flight so far was very smooth. Sikov returned.

'Would you like to order, Colonel?'

Business first. Better get it over with. More vodka was indicated. He suspected he was going to need it. In fact, it was worse than he could have imagined, although some of it was already familiar to him.

* * *

The report detailed an operation gone bad. General Volkov had hired a group of IRA heavies to strike at Ferguson and his associates, but instead it was Ferguson who had struck at them, killing them all at their base in Drumore in the Irish Republic. If that wasn't bad enough, General Volkov himself and two GRU men had disappeared. It could only mean one thing.

On top of that, the attempted assassination of Harry Miller, the individual known as the Prime Minister's Rottweiler, had been a botched job from the beginning and had only succeeded in killing his wife in error. And – the greatest shock of all – Volkov's connection to Osama bin Laden, the shadowy man known only as the Broker, had been unmasked. It had turned out to be Simon Carter, the Deputy Director of the British Security Services. Luhzkov could hardly believe his eyes – he had known Carter for years! Needless to say, Carter was no longer in the picture, either.

Miller's sister, Lady Monica Starling, had apparently played a part in the Drumore affair, too, and now she had an apparent relationship with Dillon. GRU agents, of whom there were twenty-four at the London Embassy, had sighted them together on a number of occasions.

It was all a bit too much for Luhzkov's whirling brain, but he turned the page and found the next one was headed 'Solutions'. He started to read, pouring himself another vodka, and gagged on it as his own name came up. He read the paper several times, phrases like 'the Prime Minister's final decision in this matter' floating before him. Finally, he came to the last page, headed 'Alexander Kurbsky'. It began:

'Kurbsky is a man of extraordinary talents, who has served his country well in time of war. To use these talents again in the present situation would be of great use to the State. If he objects in any way, the enclosed DVD and the additional attached information should persuade him.'

There was a small DVD screen on the back of the seat in front of Luhzkov, and after reading the information, he inserted the DVD and switched on. It only lasted five minutes or so, and when it was finished, he switched off and removed it.

'Holy Mother of God,' he said softly and there was sweat on his brow. He took out a handkerchief and mopped it. Sikov approached. 'Something to eat, Colonel?'

'Why not?' Boris Luhzkov said wearily. 'Why not.'

They landed on time, and a limousine with a uniformed GRU driver at the wheel was waiting. The streets were dark, frostbound, a city of ghosts, snow drifting down – angel's wings, his mother used to call them when he was little – and he sat there, thinking of what awaited him as they passed the great entrance of the Kremlin and moved through narrow streets to the rear, came to a halt in a paved yard. Steps up to an entrance, a blue light over it. The door swung open and a young lieutenant in GRU uniform admitted him.

'Please to follow me, Colonel.'

Luhzkov had never in his entire career been to Putin's suite and he followed in a kind of awed trance, one gloomy corridor after another, the decorations finally becoming more ornate, oil paintings in gold frames on walls. Everything was subdued, no sign of people, not even an echoing voice. And then they turned left and discovered two individuals in good suits seated in high chairs one on either side of a large gilded door. Each of them had a machine pistol by their right hand on a small table. They showed not the slightest emotion as the lieutenant opened the door and ushered Luhzkov through.

The room was a delight: panelled walls painted in seventeenth-century style, heavily gilded furniture of the correct period, portraits of what were probably obscure Tsars confronting each other across the room, a large ornate desk in the centre.

'It's very beautiful,' Luhzkov said. 'Astonishing.'

'This was General Volkov's private office,' the lieutenant informed him. The use of the past tense confirmed Luhzkov's misgivings. 'The Prime Minister will be with you directly. Help yourself to a drink.'

He withdrew and Luhzkov, in a slight daze, moved to the sideboard bearing a collection of bottles and vodka in an ice bucket. He opened the bottle, filled a glass and drank it.

'It's going to be all right,' he murmured. 'Just hang on to that thought.' He turned, glass in hand, as a secret door in the wall behind the desk opened and Vladimir Putin entered. 'Comrade Prime Minister,' Luhzkov stammered.

'Very old-fashioned of you, Colonel. Sit down. My time is limited.' He sat himself and Luhzkov faced him. 'You've read my report.'

'Every word.'

'A great tragedy, the loss of General Volkov. My most valued security adviser.'

'Can he be replaced, Comrade Prime Minister?'

'I shall handle as much as I can myself, but on the ground, I need a safe pair of hands, particularly in London. You will now be reporting directly to me. You agree?'

'It's . . . it's an honour,' Luhzkov stammered.

'More and more, London is our greatest stumbling block in intelligence matters. We must do something about it. These people – Ferguson, Dillon, those London gangsters of theirs, the Salters. What is your opinion of them?'

'The London gangster as a species is true to himself alone, Comrade Prime Minister. I've employed them myself although they wrap themselves in the Union Jack and praise the Queen at the drop of a hat.'

'This Miller has suddenly become a major player. Do you think they'll appoint him to Carter's post?'

'I don't see him wanting the job. More likely, it'll be Lord Arthur Tilsey. He held that post years ago, and was awarded his peerage for it. He's seventy-two, but still very sharp, and he's old friends with Ferguson. He'll do for the interim at least.'

'And Miller's sister, Lady Starling. You think there is something in this attachment with Dillon?'

'It could be so.'

Putin nodded. 'All right. It is clear we need to infiltrate this group, people at the highest level of security in the British system. You've read my suggestion. What do you think?'

'Alexander Kurbsky? An astonishing idea, Comrade Prime Minister. He is so . . . infamous.'

'Exactly. Just like in the Cold War days, he defects. Who on earth would doubt him? It fits like a glove. The UN wants him for some gathering in New York. Lady Starling will also be there. All Kurbsky has to do is approach her and turn on the charm. A colossal talent, a much-decorated war hero and handsome to boot – he can't go wrong. She's the key – her links to her brother and Ferguson and now Dillon – they make everything possible. If she passes the information to her friends, they'll think of Paris, and the right arrangements will be put in hand, I'm certain of it.'

'But Luhzkov – make sure you don't tell his GRU minders in Paris what's going on. His escape must at all times appear genuine to the British. If the minders fall by the wayside, so be it.'

'Of course,' Luhzkov said hastily.

'Finally, Kurbsky makes it a clear condition that his defection attracts no publicity. He will demand a guarantee of that. Otherwise he won't do it.'

'And you think Ferguson and company will accept that?'

'Absolutely, because he knows what jackals the British press are. We stay quiet about the whole matter, but all our security systems go through the motions of trying to recover him. As far as the general public knows, he's working away somewhere, faded from view. Any questions?'

'I was just wondering . . . this suggestion regarding the journalist Igor Vronsky in New York? That Kurbsky eliminate him?'

'Is there a problem?'

'No,' Luhzkov said hastily. 'I was just wondering, would

this set a precedent? I mean would that kind of thing be part of his remit?'

'If you mean would I expect him to assassinate the Queen of England, I doubt it. On the other hand, should a more tempting target present itself, who knows? I doubt it would bother him too much. He was in the death business for long enough, and in my experience few people really change in this life. Was there anything else?'

'Only that everything hinges on him actually agreeing to this plan, Comrade Prime Minister.'

Putin smiled. 'Oh, I don't think that will be a problem, Luhzkov. In fact, I expect him any minute now. I'll leave him to you.'

And he disappeared back behind the secret door. Moments later, the door behind Luhzkov opened and Alexander Kurbsky entered, the GRU lieutenant hard on his heels.

An hour earlier, Kurbsky had been delivered to the same door at the rear of the Kremlin by Military Police. Although he had been drinking when they picked him up at his hotel, he'd been enough in control to realize that when the Kremlin was mentioned, it meant serious business. He'd been led into a small anteroom next to the main office, with chairs and a TV in the corner.

He said, 'All right, I bore easily, so what is this about?'

The lieutenant gave him the DVD. 'Watch this. I'll be back.' He opened the door and paused. 'I'm a great fan.'

The door closed behind him. Kurbsky frowned, examining

the DVD, then he went and inserted it, produced a pack of cigarettes, lit one and sat down. The screen flickered. A voice quoted a lengthy number and then said *Subject Tania Kurbsky, aged 17, born Moscow.* He straightened, stunned, as he saw Tania, his beloved sister, but not as he remembered her. She was gaunt, hair close cropped, with sunken cheeks. The voice droned on about a court case, five dead policemen in a riot, seven students charged and shot.

Then came the bombshell, Tania Kurbsky had been given a special dispensation obtained by her father, Colonel Ivan Kurbsky of the KGB. Instead of execution, she'd been sentenced to life, irrevocable, to be served at Station Gorky in Siberia, about as far from civilization as it was possible to get. She was still living, aged thirty-six. There followed a picture that barely resembled her, a gaunt careworn woman old before her time. The screen went dark. Kurbsky got up slowly, ejected the DVD and stood looking at it, then he turned, went to the door and kicked it.

After a while, it was unlocked and the lieutenant appeared. One of the guards stood there, machine pistol ready. Kurbsky said, 'Where do I go?'

'Follow me.' Which Kurbsky did.

In the next room, he looked Luhzkov over. 'And who would you be?' Behind him, the lieutenant smiled.

'Colonel Boris Luhzkov, GRU. I'm acting under Prime Minister Putin's orders. You've just missed him. How are you?'

'For a man who's just discovered that the dead can walk,

I'm doing all right. I'll be better if I have a drink.' He went to the cabinet and had two large vodka shots, then he cursed. 'So, get on with it. I presume there's a purpose to all this.'

'Sit down and read this.' Luhzkov pushed the file across the desk, and Kurbsky started.

Fifteen minutes later, he sat back. 'I don't write thrillers.'

'It certainly reads like one.'

'And this is from the Prime Minister?'

'Yes.'

'And what's the payoff?'

'Your sister's release. She will be restored to life.'

'That's one way of putting it. How do I know it will be honoured?'

'The Prime Minister's word.'

'Don't make me laugh, he's a politician. Since when did those guys keep their word?'

And Luhzkov said exactly the right thing. 'She's your sister. If that means anything, this is all you can do. It's as simple as that. Better than nothing. You have to travel hopefully.'

'Fuck you,' Kurbsky said, 'and fuck him,' but there was the hint of despair of a man who knew he had little choice. 'Anything else?'

'Yes. Igor Vronsky. Does the name mean anything to you?'

'Absolutely. The stinking bastard was in Chechnya and ran a story about my outfit. The 5th Paratroop Company, the Black Tigers. We were pathfinders and special forces. He did radio from the front line, blew the whistle on a special op we were on, and the Chechens ambushed us. Fifteen good men dead. It's in my book.'

'He's working as a journalist in New York now. We want you to eliminate him, just to prove you mean business.'

'Just like that.'

'I believe you enjoyed a certain reputation in Chechnya. "The smiler with the knife"? An accomplished sniper and assassin who specialized in that kind of thing. A lone wolf, as they say. At least three high-ranking Chechen generals could testify to that.'

'If the dead could speak.'

'That story in *On the Death of Men* when the hero is parachuted behind the lines though he had never had training as a parachutist. Was it true? Did you?' Luhzkov was troubled in some strange way. 'What kind of man would do such a thing?'

'One who at the age of nineteen in the hell that was Afghanistan decided he was dead already, a walking zombie, who survived to go home and found himself a year later knee deep in blood in Chechnya. You can make of that what you will.'

'I'll need to think about it. I'm not sure I understand.'

Kurbsky laughed. 'Remember the old saying, "Avoid looking into an open grave because you may see yourself in there". In those old Cold War spy books, you always had to have a controller. Would that be you?'

'Yes. I'm Head of Station for GRU at the London Embassy.'

'That's good. I'll like that. I had an old comrade in Chechnya who transferred to the GRU when I was coming to the end of my army time. Yuri Bounine. Could you find him and bring him in on this?'

'I'm sure that will be possible.'

'Excellent. So if you're available, let's get out of here and go and get something to eat.'

'An excellent idea.' Luhzkov led the way and said to the lieutenant, 'The limousine is waiting, I presume? We'll go back to my hotel.'

'Of course, Colonel.'

He led them along the interminable corridors.

'They seem to go on forever,' Luhzkov observed. 'A fascinating place, the Kremlin.'

'A rabbit warren,' Kurbsky said. 'A man could lose himself here. A smiler with the knife could do well here.' He turned as they reached the door. 'Perhaps the Prime Minister should consider that.'

He followed the lieutenant down the steps to the limousine and Luhzkov, troubled, went after them.

But over the three weeks that followed, things flowed with surprising ease. They moved him into a GRU safe house with training facilities outside Moscow. On the firing range, Kurbsky proved his skill and proficiency with every kind of weapon the sergeant major in charge could throw at him. Kurbsky had forgotten none of his old skills.

Yuri Bounine, by now a GRU captain, was plucked from the monotony of posing as a commercial attaché at the Russian Embassy in Dublin and returned to Moscow, where he was promoted to major and assigned to London, delighted to be reunited with his old friend.

Kurbsky embraced him warmly when he arrived. 'You've put on weight, you bastard.' He turned to Luhzkov. 'Look at him. Gold spectacles, always smiling, the look of an aging cherub. Yet we survived Afghanistan and Chechnya together. He's got medals.'

Again he hugged Bounine, who said, 'And you got famous. I read *On the Death of Men* five times and tried to work out who was me.'

'In a way, they all were, Yuri.'

Bounine flushed, suddenly awkward. 'So what's going on?'

'That's for Colonel Luhzkov to tell you.'

Which Luhzkov did in a private interview. Later that day, Bounine found Kurbsky in a corner booth in the officers' bar and joined him. A bottle of vodka was on the table and several glasses in crushed ice. He helped himself.

'Luhzkov has filled me in.'

'So what do you think?' Kurbsky asked.

'Who am I to argue with the Prime Minister of the Russian Federation?'

'You know everything? About my sister?'

Bounine nodded. 'May I say one thing on Putin's behalf? He wasn't responsible for what happened to your sister. It was before his time. He sees an advantage in it, that's all.'

'A point of view. And Vronsky?'

'A pig. I'd cut his throat myself if I had the chance.'

'And you look such a kind man.'

'I am a kind man.'

'So tell me, Yuri, how's your wife?'

'Ah.' Bounine hesitated. 'She died, Alex. Leukemia.'

'I'm so sorry to hear that! She was a good woman.'

'Yes, she was. But it's been a while now, Alex, and my sister has produced two lovely girls – so I'm an uncle!'

'Excellent. Let's drink to them. And to New York.' They clinked glasses. 'And to the Black Tigers, may they rest in peace,' Kurbsky said. 'We're probably the only two left.'

New York came and New York went. The death of Igor Vronsky received prominent notice in the *New York Times* and other papers, but in spite of his books and his vigorous anti-Kremlin stance, there was no suspicion that this was a dissident's death. It seemed the normal kind of mugging, a knife to the chest, the body stripped of everything worth having.

On the day following Vronsky's death, Monica Starling and George Dunkley flew back to Heathrow, where Dunkley had a limousine waiting to take them back to Cambridge. She hadn't breathed a word about what had happened between her and Kurbsky, but Dunkley hadn't stopped talking about him during the flight. It had obviously affected him deeply. She kissed him on the cheek.

'Off you go, George. Try and make it for High Table. They'll all be full of envy when they hear of your exploits.'

There was no sign of her brother's official limousine from the Cabinet Office or of Dillon. She wasn't pleased, and then Billy Salter's scarlet Alfa Romeo swerved into the kerb and he slid from behind the wheel while Dillon got out of the passenger seat.

He came round and embraced her, kissing her lightly on the mouth. 'My goodness, girl, there's a sparkle to you. You've obviously had a good time.'

Billy was putting her bags in the boot. 'A hell of a time, from what I heard.'

'You know?' she said to Dillon. 'About my conversation with Kurbsky?'

'What Roper knows, we all end up knowing.' He ushered her into the back seat of the Alfa and followed her. 'Dover Street, Billy.'

It was the family house in Mayfair where her brother lived. 'Is Harry okay?' she asked as they drove away.

'Nothing to worry about, but he's been overdoing it, so the doctor has given him his marching orders. He's gone down to the country to Stokely Hall to stay with Aunt Mary for a while. Anyway, this Kurbsky business has got Ferguson all fired up. He'd like to hear it all from your own fair lips, so we're going to take you home, wait for you to freshen up, then join Ferguson for dinner at the Reform Club. Seven thirty, but if we're late, we're late.'

'So go on, tell us all about it,' Billy said over his shoulder.

'Alexander Kurbsky was one of the most fascinating men I've ever met,' she said. 'End of story. You'll have to wait.'

'Get out of it. You're just trying to make Dillon jealous.'

'Just carry on, driver, and watch the road.' She pulled Dillon's right arm around her and eased into him, smiling.

* * *

39

It was a quiet evening at the Reform Club, the restaurant only half full. Ferguson had secured a corner table next to a window, with no one close, which gave them privacy. Ferguson wore the usual Guards tie and pinstriped suit, his age still a closely kept secret, his hair white, face still handsome.

The surprise was Roper in his wheelchair, wearing a black velvet jacket and a white shirt with a knotted paisley scarf at the neck.

'Well, this is nice, I must say.' She kissed Roper on the forehead and rumpled his tousled hair. 'Are you well?'

'All the better for seeing you.'

She wore the Valentino suit from New York and Ferguson obviously approved. 'My word, you must have gone down well at the Pierre.' He kissed her extravagantly on both cheeks.

'You're a charmer, Charles. A trifle glib on occasion, but I like it.'

'And you'll like the champagne. It's Dom Perignon – Dillon can argue about his Krug another time.'

The wine waiter poured, remembering from previous experience to supply Billy with ginger ale laced with lime. Ferguson raised his glass and toasted her. 'To you, my dear, and to what seems to have been a job well done.' He emptied his glass and motioned the wine waiter to refill it. 'Now, for God's sake, tell us what happened.'

When Monica was finished, there were a few moments of silence and it was Billy who spoke first. 'What's he want, and I mean really want? This guy's got everything, I'd have thought. Fame, money, genuine respect.'

'But is that enough?' Dillon said. 'From what Monica says, he's lacking genuine freedom. So the system's different from the Cold War days, but is it really? I liked his description of himself to you, Monica, about being like a bear on a chain. In Russia he's trapped by his fame, by who he is. In the cage, if you like. The Ministry of Arts controls his every move because they themselves are controlled right up to the top. From a political point of view, he's a national symbol.'

Ferguson said, 'Obviously I've read his work and I'm familiar with his exploits. It all adds up to a human being who hasn't the slightest interest in being a symbol to anyone.'

'He just wants to be free,' Monica agreed. 'At present, every move he makes is dictated by others. He's flown privately when visiting abroad, he's carefully watched by GRU minders, his every move is monitored.'

'So let him claim asylum here,' Billy said. 'Would he be denied?'

'Of course not,' Ferguson said. 'But he's got to get here first. This Paris affair, the Legion of Honour presentation, presents an interesting possibility.'

'They'd be watching him like a hawk,' Dillon said. 'And there's another problem. You know what the French are like. Very fussy about foreigners causing a problem on their patch, and that applies big-time to Brit intelligence.'

'Still, it looks to me like a straightforward kidnap job with a willing victim,' Billy said. 'It's once he's here that he'd need looking after. They'd do something even if they couldn't get him back. How many Russian dissidents have come to a bad end in London? Litvinenko poisoned and two cases of guys falling from the terraces of apartment blocks, and that was in the same year.'

Roper beckoned the wine waiter. 'A very large single malt. I leave the choice to your own good judgment.' He smiled at the others. 'Sorry, but the joys of champagne soon pall for me.'

'Feel free, Major,' Ferguson said. 'I notice that you haven't made a contribution in this matter.'

'Concerning Kurbsky?' Roper held out his hand and accepted the waiter's gift of the single malt. He savoured it for a moment, then swallowed it down. 'Excellent. I'll have another.'

'Don't you have any comment?' Monica asked.

'Oh, I do. I'd like to meet his aunt, this Svetlana Kelly. Yes, that's what I'd like to do. Chamber Court, a late-Victorian house in Belsize Park. I looked it up.'

'Any particular reason?' Ferguson said.

'To find out what he's like.'

'Don't you mean was like?' Monica asked. 'As I understand it, she last saw him in 1989. When you think of what he's gone through since then, I'd suppose him to be completely different.'

'On the contrary. I've always been of the opinion that people don't really change, not in any fundamental way. Anyway, I'll go to see her tomorrow, if you approve, General?'

'Whatever you say.'

Monica jumped in. 'Would it be all right if I came with you? I don't need to be back in Cambridge till Friday.'

'No, that's fine. I don't think we should overwhelm her.'

Dillon said, 'Old Victorian houses aren't particularly wheelchair friendly.'

'I'll phone in advance. If there's a problem, perhaps we can meet somewhere else.'

'Fine. I'll leave it in your hands,' Ferguson said. 'Now I don't know about you lot, but I'm starving, so let's get down to the eating part of the business.'

Later, they went their separate ways. Sergeant Doyle had waited for Roper in the van that had the rear lift for the wheelchair. Ferguson had his driver, and Billy gave Dillon and Monica a lift to Dover Street in the Alfa.

'Very useful,' Monica told him, as they moved through Mayfair. 'You being a non-drinker.'

'I get stopped now and then,' Billy said. 'Young guy in a flash motor like this. I've been breathalysed plenty. It's great to see the look on their faces when they check the reading.' He pulled up outside the Dover Street house. 'Here we are, folks. You're staying, right?' he asked Dillon.

'What do you think?'

'You're staying.'

He cleared off, they paused at the top of the steps for Monica to find her key, and went in. She didn't put the light on, simply waited for him to lock the door, then put her arms around his neck and kissed him quite hard.

'Oh my goodness, I've missed you.'

'You've only been away four days.'

'Don't you dare,' she said. 'Ten minutes, and if you take more, there'll be trouble,' and she turned and ran up the stairs.

He changed in one of the spare bedrooms, put on a terrycloth robe and joined her in her suite. He'd found a tenderness with her that he'd never known he had – he'd surprised himself as their relationship blossomed – and they made slow careful love together.

Afterwards she drifted into sleep and he lay there, a chink of light coming through the curtains from a lamp in the street. On impulse, he slipped out of the bed, put on the robe, padded downstairs to the drawing room, took a cigarette from a box on the table, lit it, then sat by the bow window, looking out and thinking about Kurbsky. After a while, Monica slipped in, wearing a robe.

'So there you are. Give me one.'

'You're supposed to have stopped,' he said, but gave her one anyway.

'What are you thinking of?' she said. 'Kurbsky?'

'That's right.'

'I thought you might. He reminded me of you.'

'You liked him, I think?'

'An easy man to like, just as you are an easy man to love, Sean, but like you, there's the feeling of the other self always there, like a crouching tiger just waiting to spring.'

'Thanks very much.'

'What were you thinking?'

'What on earth would we do with him if we got him?'
He stubbed his cigarette out and got up. 'Come on, back to
bed with you.' He put a hand round her waist and they went
out.

It was ten thirty when Roper found himself back in his chair
in the computer room at Holland Park. Sergeant Doyle said,
'You've everything you need to hand, Major, so I think I'll
have a lie down in the duty room.'

'You should be entitled to a night off, Tony. What about
Sergeant Henderson?'

'He's on ten days' leave.'

'And the Royal Military Police can't find a replacement?'

'But we wouldn't want that, would we, sir? A stranger in
the system? I'll get a bit of shut-eye. If you need me, give
me a bell.'

Roper lit a cigarette and set his main screen alive, bringing
up Svetlana Kelly. In her early years, she'd been a member
of the Chekhov Theatre in Moscow, which meant she was
well grounded in classical theatre. She hadn't been much of
a beauty, even when young, but he saw handsomeness and
strength there. There was a selection of photos from the
early years, and then London in 1981. *A Month in the
Country* at the Theatre Royal, Haymarket. Fifty-five and
never married, and then she'd met Patrick Kelly, an Irish
widower and professor of literature at London University.
Roper looked at Kelly's photos – he was strong, too, undoubt-
edly and yet there was a touch of humour about his mouth.

Whatever the attraction, it was strong enough for them to marry at Westminster Register Office within a month of meeting and for Svetlana to cut herself free of the Soviet Union. She would be seventy-one now. It was eleven o'clock, and yet on sheer impulse, Roper phoned her. He stayed on speakerphone, he always did, and there was an instant answer.

'Who is this?' It was a whisper in a way, and yet clear enough, the Russian accent undeniable.

'Mrs Kelly, my name is Giles Roper – Major Giles Roper.' He spoke fair Russian, product of an Army total-immersion course just after Sandhurst, and he'd kept it up since. 'Forgive the intrusion at such a time of night. You don't know me.'

She cut in. 'But I do. I attended a charity dinner for the Great Ormond Street Children's Hospital last year. You spoke from your wheelchair. You are the bomb disposal expert, aren't you? The queen herself pinned the George Cross to your lapel. You're a hero.'

It was amazing the effect of that voice, so soft, like a breeze whispering through the leaves on an autumn evening. Roper's throat turned dry, incredibly touched. It was like being a child again.

He said in English, 'You're too kind.'

'What can I do for you?'

'May I come to see you tomorrow morning?'

'For what reason?'

'I'd like to discuss a matter affecting your nephew. I'd have a woman with me, a Cambridge don who has just met Alexander in New York.'

'Major Roper, be honest with me. What is your interest

in my nephew? You must know I haven't seen him in sixteen years.'

To this woman, one could only tell the truth. Roper knew that nothing else would do. 'I'm with the British Security Services.'

There was a faint chuckle. 'Ah, what they call a spook these days.'

'Only on television.'

'You intrigue me. Tell me of your companion.' Roper did. She said, 'The lady sounds quite interesting. If you're a spook, you know where I live.'

'Chamber Court, Belsize Park.'

'Quite right. My husband died ten years ago and left me well provided for. Here, I live in Victorian splendour supported by my dear friend and fellow Russian, Katya Sorin, who takes care of the house and me and manages to find time to teach painting at the Slade as well. I'll see you at ten thirty. Your chair will not prove a problem. The garden is walled, but the entrance in the side mews has a path that will give you access to French windows leading into a conservatory. I'll be waiting.'

'Thank you very much, Mrs. Kelly. I must say, you seem to be taking me totally on trust.'

'You fascinated me at that luncheon. Your speech was excellent, but modest, and so afterwards I looked you up on the internet. It was all there. Belfast in 1991, the Portland Hotel, the huge bomb in the foyer. It took you nine hours to render it harmless. Nine hours on your own. How can I not take such a man on trust? I'll see you in the morning.'

It was quiet sitting there, staring up at his screens, and he put on some background music. Just like comfort food, only this was Cole Porter playing softly, just as it had been all those years ago in the Belfast safe house not far from the Royal Victoria Hospital. It was a long time ago, a hell of a long time ago, and he lit a cigarette and poured a Bushmills Irish whiskey for a change and remembered.

ROPER

BELFAST

1991

3

___

Roper remembered that year well and not just because of his nine hours dismantling the Portland Hotel bomb. There had also been the mortar attack on Number Ten Downing Street. The Gulf War had been at its height, and the target had been the War Cabinet meeting at 10.00 a.m. on February seventh – an audacious attack, and the missiles had landed in the garden, just narrowly missing the house. It bore all the hallmarks of a classic IRA operation, although nobody ever claimed responsibility for the attack.

In Belfast, meanwhile, the war of the bomb continued remorselessly, and in spite of all the politicians could do, sectarian violence ploughed on, people butchering each other in the name of religion, the British Army inured by twenty-two years to the Irish Troubles as a way of life.

For Giles Roper, scientific interest in the field of weaponry and explosives had drawn him in even during his training days as an officer cadet at Sandhurst, and on graduation, it had led to an immediate posting to the Ordnance Corps. In ninety-one, he was entering his third year as a disposal officer, a captain in rank and several hundred explosive devices of one kind or another behind him.

Most people didn't realize that he was married. A summer affair with his second cousin, a schoolteacher named Elizabeth Howard, during his first year out of Sandhurst had turned into a total disaster. It was a prime example of going to bed on your wedding night with someone you thought you knew and waking up with a stranger. A Catholic, she didn't believe in divorce and indeed visited his mother on a regular basis. He hadn't seen her in years.

The ever-present risk of death, and the casualty rate amongst his fellows in the bomb disposal business, precluded any kind of relationship elsewhere. He smoked heavily, like most of his kind, and drank heavily at the appropriate time, like most of his kind.

It was a strange bizarre existence which produced obsessive patterns of behaviour. On many occasions, he'd found himself dealing with a bomb and indulging in conversation, obviously one-sided, demanding answers which weren't there. It was an extreme example of talking to yourself. A bomb, after all, couldn't talk back except when it exploded, and that would probably be the last thing you heard. However, he still talked to them. There seemed some sort of comfort in that.

His father had died when he was sixteen. It was his uncle who had arranged for his schooling and Sandhurst, and maintained his mother at the extended family home in Shropshire. She was basically there as unpaid help as far as Roper could see, but on army pay there wasn't much he could do about it, until the unexpected happened. His mother's brother, Uncle Arthur, a homosexual by nature and a broker in the City with a fortune to prove it, had died of AIDS and, lacking any faith in his sister's ability to handle money, left a considerable fortune to Roper.

He could have left the army, but found that he didn't want to, and when he tried to get his mother her own place, it turned out she was perfectly happy where she was. It had also become apparent that the perils of bomb disposal were beyond her understanding, so he settled a hundred thousand pounds on her, and the same on his wife, and left them to the joys of the countryside.

Before the Portland Hotel, he had been decorated with the Military Cross for gallantry, although the events surrounding it had only a tenuous link with his ordinary duties.

On standby, he had been based in a small market town in County Down where there had been a spate of bomb alerts, mostly false, though one in four was the real thing. The unit had five jeeps, a driver and guard and a disposal expert. On that particular day, a call came in over the radio, and the jeeps disappeared, leaving only Roper and his driver, the unit being a man short. The first call was false, also the second.

There was another, this time for Roper by name. There was something about it, the speaker had a cockney accent that sounded wrong.

Terry, his driver, started up, and Roper said, 'No, just hang on. I'm not happy. Something smells.' He had a Browning Hi-Power pistol stuffed in his camouflage blouse. He was also wearing, courtesy of his newfound wealth, a nylon and titanium vest capable of stopping a .44 Magnum at point blank range.

Terry eased up an Uzi machine pistol on his knees. There was a nurses' hostel to the side of the old folks' home across the street and as the voice sounded over the radio again, still calling for Roper, a milk wagon came round the corner. It braked to a halt outside the hostel. Two men were in the cab in dairy company uniform.

The one on the passenger side dropped out, turning suddenly as Roper started forward, pulled out a pistol and fired. He was good, the bullet striking Roper in the chest and knocking him back against the jeep. The man fired again, catching Terry in the shoulder as he scrambled out with the Uzi, then fired again at Roper as he tried to get up, catching him in the left arm before turning and starting to run. Roper shot him twice in the back, shattering his spine.

The vest had performed perfectly. He picked up the Uzi Terry had dropped, got to his feet and walked towards the milk truck. The driver had slipped from behind the wheel and was firing through the cab where the passenger door was partially open. A bullet plucked Roper's shoulder. He dropped down on his face and could see directly under the truck where the driver's legs were exposed from the knees down. He held the Uzi out in front of him and fired two sustained bursts, the man screaming in agony and falling back against the hostel wall.

Roper found him there, sobbing. He tapped the muzzle of the Uzi against the man's face. 'Where is it, in the cab?'

'Yes,' the man groaned.

'What kind? Pencil timer, detonators or what?'

'Go fuck yourself.'

'Have it your own way. We'll go to hell together.'

He grimaced at the pain of his wounded arm, but managed to pull the man up and push him half into the cab. There was a large Crawford's biscuit tin. 'You could get a Christmas cake in there or a hell of a lot of Semtex. Anyway, let's try again. Pencil timer, detonator?'

He turned the man's face and pushed the muzzle of the Uzi between his lips. The man wriggled and jerked away. 'Pencils.'

'Let's hope you're right, for both our sakes.'

He pulled off the lid and exposed the contents. Three pencils – the extras just to make sure. 'Oh, dear,' he said. 'Fifteen minutes. I'd better move sharpish.' He pulled them out and tossed them away and eased the man down as he fainted.

People were emerging from the houses and the local bar, now a couple of dogs barked, and then there was a sudden roaring of engines as two jeeps appeared, moving fast.

'Here we go, the bloody cavalry arriving late as usual.' He slid down on the pavement, his back to the hostel wall, scrabbled a pack of cigarettes from his pocket, fumbled to get one out, and failed.

It didn't make him notable in any way beyond military circles. The national newspapers didn't make a fuss simply because death and destruction were so much a part of everyday life in Northern Ireland that, as the old army saying went, it was old news before it was news. But the Portland Hotel a year later, the lone man face-to-face with a terrible death for nine hours, really was news, even before the decision had been taken to reward him with the George Cross. He'd continued to meet the daily demands of his calling, working out of an old state school in Byron Road which the army had taken over on the safe house principle, fortifying it against any kind of attack, the many rooms providing accommodation for officers and men, with a bar and catering facilities. There were places like it all over Belfast, safe, but bleak.

Local women fought for the privilege of working there in the canteen, the laundry or as cleaners. That many would be Republican sympathizers was clear, and a rough and ready way of sorting the problem was to try to employ only Protestant women. On the other hand, it was obviously a temptation for Catholics who needed work to pretend to be other than they were. Such women lived locally, and came and went through the heavily-fortified gates with identity cards, often so false they could be bought for a couple of pounds in any local bar.

Roper had been posted to Byron Street for nine months,

and in that time had caused something of a stir with his Military Cross and good looks, but his gentlemanly behaviour towards the younger women, which was conspicuously absent in his fellows, had provoked a suggestion that, as the local girls put it, there had to be something wrong with him.

On the other hand, his incredible bravery was a fact, and so was the fact that in those nine months, some of his comrades had paid the final price and others had been terribly injured.

The Portland Hotel caused many people to look at him differently, as if there was something otherworldly about him, and there were those who felt uncomfortable in his presence, hurrying past him. One who did not was a new young cleaner who replaced an older woman who'd moved away. The girl's name was Jean Murray and she was from a Protestant Orange background.

Roper's room was on her list and she was resolutely cheerful from the moment she started and knew all his business within two days. Her mother had been killed in a bombing four years earlier, for which she blamed the fugging Fenians, as she called them. Her father was a member of the local Orange Lodge and had a plum job at the Port Authority. There was also a brother of twenty-one named Kenny in his final year at Queens University.

She extracted as much personal information from Roper as she could. As long as it wasn't military, he didn't mind. The truth was that to a certain extent he rather fancied her, which gave him pause for thought, because it meant the defensive wall he'd built around himself was weakening.

'What's it get yer, Captain, the hero bit? You're a lonely

man, that's the truth of it, and you've stared death in the face for so long, it's dried up any juice that's in you.'

'Well, thank you, Dr Freud,' he said. 'I mean, you would know.'

'Why do you do it? It's a known fact in this dump that you're well-fixed financially.'

'Okay, look at it this way. When the Troubles started in sixty-nine, the bomb thing was in its infancy. Very crude, no big deal. Over the years, as the Provisional IRA has grown in power, bombs have become very sophisticated indeed. The public image of the IRA as a bunch of shaven-headed yobs off a building site is well off the mark. Plenty of solid middle class professionals are in the movement. Schoolteachers, lawyers, accountants, a whole range of ordinary people.'

'So what are you saying?'

'That the bombmakers these days have got university degrees and they're very clever and sophisticated. Consider the Portland bomb. I'm an expert and I've dealt with hundreds of bombs over the years, but that one took me nine hours, and shall I tell you something? He'll be back, that bomb-maker. He'll come with something just a little bit different, just for me. He can't afford to have me beat him. It's as simple as that.'

She stared at him, pretty and rumpled in her blue uniform dress, leaning on her broom, no makeup on at all, and there was something in her eyes that could have been pity.

'That's terrible, what you say. Still, it can't go on, things change.'

'What do you mean things change?'

'The whole system. My Kenny says the bombs won't need people like you soon. He's read about you in the papers. He knows I work for you.'

'What does he mean things change?'

'He's taking his finals in his degree soon. Electronics. He makes gadgets. These days you have a hand control to work your television, open your garage doors, unlock your car, switch on security systems in your house. We've only got an ordinary terrace, but the gadgets he's created in it are brilliant.'

'Very interesting, but what's this got to do with bombs?'

'Well, it's too technical for me, but he's been working on a thing he calls a Howler. It looks like a standard television control, but it's really different. He can turn off security systems, and I mean really important ones. He demonstrated on our local bank. He kept locking the doors as we walked past. They didn't know whether they were coming or going. Does it to people's cars as we go by, turns on store alarms, even big shops in town.'

'Very interesting,' Roper said. 'Fascinating, but I still don't see the relevance to bombs.'

'Well, that's what he's really been working on. He said he can maybe adapt the Howler so that even a big sophisticated bomb like your Portland Hotel job could simply be switched off. That's the only way I can describe it.' She smiled. 'Anyway, I can't stand around here chattering. I've got five other rooms to do.'

'No, just a minute,' Roper said. 'Let me get this straight. Has Kenny really gotten anywhere with his invention?'

'He's working at it all the time at the moment. He was talking about bombs at the time because of that Paradise Street bomb the day before yesterday, the one in the car that killed the sergeant. He said the Howler could have switched it off at the touch of a button, that was what he was working towards.'

Roper was cold with excitement. 'He said that, did he?'

She laughed. 'I said could it work the other way, could what was switched off be switched on? He said a Howler has two faces. What could be switched off could be switched on again.' She picked up her bucket. 'Anyway, I'll be away now. Work to do.'

'Just one more thing. Could I meet Kenny?'

She had moved to the door and turned. 'I don't know about that. I mean, soldiers are targets at the best of times and you never know who's who these days. Fenians everywhere.'

'I wouldn't be in uniform, Jean. I'd just like to meet him and discuss his work if he'd let me. It sounds very interesting. And he might find it rewarding to discuss his ideas with someone like me who has spent so much time at the coalface, so to speak.'

She looked serious. 'You've got a point. I can't speak for him, but I'll give him a phone call, see what he has to say. I've got to get moving. I'll let you know.'

She was away and Roper sat on the bed and thought about it. It wasn't as crazy as it sounded. Most really sophisticated bombs had multiple electrical circuits of one kind or another, intertwining in complicated puzzles, feeding into each other, often in the most bizarre way. The theory behind this Howler device of Kenny's was a kind of Holy Grail. After all, if the most complicated of security systems could be neutered at the touch of a button, it seemed logical that the right touch of genius could do the same thing to bomb circuits.

It was a thought that wouldn't go away and he went down to the bar and ordered a large whiskey since he was off duty, took a newspaper to a corner table and sat there, pretending to read it, but thinking.

Major Sanderson, the commanding officer, glanced in. 'I see you've got a night off, Giles. Lucky you. I've got a general staff meeting at the Grand Hotel. Your leave's been approved, by the way. Starts Sunday. Two weeks, so make the most of it.'

He went, and for a moment there was no one else in the bar except the corporal behind the counter busying himself cleaning glasses. Jean Murray peered in at the door.

The corporal said, 'You can't come in here, you know that.'

'It's all right,' Roper told him. 'She wants me.' He swallowed his whiskey, got up and joined her in the corridor. 'What have you got for me?'

'I've spoken to Kenny, and he says he'll see you, but it's got to be tonight, because he's starting the practical side of his finals for his degree at Queens University tomorrow.'

'That's fine by me.'

'I'm finished in an hour. I'll meet you on the corner by Cohan's Bar, and no uniform, like I said.'

'No problem. Where are we going?'

'Not far. Half a mile maybe. You know where the Union Canal is? He has a room he uses for his work in what used to be a flour mill. You'll need a raincoat. It's pouring out there.'

'Sounds good to me,' Roper told her.

He returned to the bar, ordered another whiskey and sat in the corner, thinking about it. His boss was out of the way at his staff meeting, there was no point in discussing his intended adventure on the streets of Belfast after dark with anyone else. There were risks, but risk of any kind had been so much a part of his life for years now that it was second nature.

He would go armed, of course, his usual Browning Hi-Power, but a backup would be a sensible precaution, and he drank his whiskey and went along to the weapons store, where he found a Sergeant Clark on duty.

'I'm going on the town tonight, out of uniform, Special Op. I'll have the Hi-Power, but is there anything else you could suggest?'

Clark, who regarded Roper as a true hero, was happy to oblige. 'Colt .25, Captain, with hollow-point cartridges. It's hard to beat. There you go.' He placed one on the counter and a box of ten cartridges.

'So that will do it?' Roper enquired.

'With this.' Clark produced an ankle holder in soft leather. 'Nothing's perfect, but in a body search, when somebody finds an item like a Browning, they tend to assume that's it.' He smiled cheerfully. 'You just have to live in hope. Sign here, sir.'

He pushed a ledger across and offered a pen. Roper said, 'I knew I could rely on you, Sergeant.'

'Take care, sir.'

In his room, Roper changed into a pair of old comfortable trousers, not jeans, because it made the ankle holder more accessible. He carefully loaded the Colt with six of the hollow-points and checked that he could reach it easily. He wore the bulletproof vest, a dark polo-neck sweater and a navy blue slip-on raincoat he'd had for years. He didn't wear a shoulder holster and simply put the Browning in his right-hand pocket. He peered out of the windows, old-fashioned street lights aglow now in the early evening darkness, rain hammering down, although when didn't it in Belfast? He went through his narrow wardrobe, found an old tweed cap, pulled it on and went downstairs.

The guards on either side of the gate stayed in their sentry boxes. They knew him well. After all, everyone did. 'A hell of a night for it, sir,' one of them called cheerfully as he raised the bar. 'Whatever it is.'

Roper smiled back just as cheerfully, pausing for a moment, looking out into that Belfast street that as far as he was concerned was like no other street in any city in the world.

'All right,' he murmured to himself. 'Let's get moving.' He slipped out and turned towards Cohan's.

*   *   *

Jean Murray stood in the entrance of the bar, sheltering from the rain. She had a large old-fashioned umbrella ready and seemed impatient. 'So there you are. I was beginning to think you weren't coming.'

'Will I do?' Roper asked.

She looked him over. 'I suppose so. But keep that gob of yours shut. You sound as if you've been to Eton or somewhere like that.' She opened the umbrella. 'Let's get moving.'

He fell into step beside her as she walked rapidly. 'A rotten night for it.'

'Don't rub it in. I've only had a sandwich all day and I'm starving.'

He kept up with her obediently, passing through one mean street after another, the river not far away. 'A hard life, living in a place like this.'

'Well, the British government in London never gave a damn about Belfast, that's for sure. The forgotten city. Did you know the Luftwaffe blitzed it worse than Liverpool during the war?'

'I suppose they were after Harland & Wolff and the shipyards. They built the *Titanic* here, didn't they?'

'Jesus and Mary, that's history, mister,' she said. 'It's what happens now that's real and the future of this country.'

Jesus and Mary. Strange on the lips of a young Protestant girl, and he slipped a hand in his pocket and found the butt of the Browning, and then she laughed harshly. 'What in the hell is getting into me, talking like a fugging Fenian? It must be the weather.'

They had moved into an area of decaying warehouses and

a place where the Union Canal emptied into the river. There were narrow decaying Victorian buildings, like something out of Dickens, an old iron footbridge and a sign saying *Conroy's Flour Mill*. An old-fashioned lamp was bracketed above the door, illuminating the area, and there was a light at the window above it.

'Here we are,' she said, and led the way up a narrow wooden stairway. The door at the top stood open, light shining down. 'Kenny, we're here,' she called, paused for a moment so that Roper could see the table in the centre of a sizeable room, littered with a variety of technical equipment, tools and vices. She stepped forward, Roper following, his hand in his pocket on the butt of the Browning.

The door slammed behind him, the muzzle of a pistol was rammed against the side of Roper's skull, and a hard Ulster voice said, 'Easy, now, or I'll blow your brains out. Hands high.' Roper did exactly as he was told. He was patted, the Browning soon found. 'A Hi-Power? You've got taste.' He was pushed towards the table. 'Over there and turn.'

Roper did and found himself facing a small wiry young man, hair almost shoulder length, a Beretta automatic in his left hand. He wore an old reefer jacket, dropped the Browning into his right pocket and grinned, making him look quite amicable.

'The great man himself.'

'And you'll be Kenny Murray?'

'As ever was.'

'And there's no Howler?'

Murray laughed. 'Not here, bomb man, not here. It exists, though. I'm working to perfect it all the time.'

'I'm impressed you'd bother,' Roper said. 'After all, your purpose is to make bombs explode.'

'It is indeed, but the scientist in me can't resist a challenge.'

Roper turned to Jean, who had taken a pack of cigarettes out of her pocket and was lighting one. 'Oh, Jean, you disappoint me, turning out to be a decent Catholic girl after all.'

'And you thinking I was some Prod bitch. All the worse for you.' There was anger there, but perhaps at herself.

'So what's the reason for all this? If you'd wanted to shoot me, you would have,' he said to Kenny.

'You're absolutely right. I'd love to have taken care of that, but I'm under orders. There are those who would like to have words with you. Information's the name of the game. Our bombmakers would appreciate the chance to squeeze you dry. So let's get going. You first.'

'If you say so.'

Roper opened the door and stood for a moment at the top of those dark stairs. He found the rail with his left hand and started down. There was only one thing to do and he'd only get one chance, so halfway down he slipped deliberately in the shadows, cursing and gripping the rail, reaching for the Colt in the ankle holder. In the ensuing scramble, he dropped it in his raincoat pocket.

'Watch it, for Christ's sake,' Kenny ordered.

'It's not my fault. The place is a death trap.' Roper hauled himself up and continued.

Kenny laughed. 'Did you hear that, Jean?' he said to his sister behind him. 'The man's a bloody comic.'

Roper went out, his right hand in his pocket, and started over the bridge. Halfway across, he paused and turned. 'There's just one thing you should know, you Fenian bastard.'

Kenny stood facing him, holding the Beretta against his right thigh. 'And what would that be, bomb man?' he asked amicably.

'You made a mistake. You should have killed me when you had the chance.'

His hand swung up, he shot Kenny between the eyes twice, the hollow-point cartridges fragmenting the back of his skull. Kenny spun round and half fell across the iron rail of the bridge. Jean screamed, Roper leaned down, caught the body by one ankle and heaved it over into the fast moving canal.

'There you go,' Roper said. 'Are you satisfied now, Jean?'

She started to back away. 'Ah, sweet Jesus and Mother Mary. What have I done?'

'You'll be asking yourself that till your dying day,' Roper told her.

She seemed to suddenly pull herself together. 'You're not going to kill me?' she whispered.

He didn't say a word, turned and walked away across the bridge, and behind him she started to sob bitterly, the sound echoing across the waters of the canal that had swept her brother into the River Lagan and out to sea.

He walked all the way back through mean rainwashed streets, the sound of shooting in the distance, walking carefully on pavements scattered with broken glass, passing bombed-out buildings boarded up. All of a sudden, it had all caught up with him, too many long and weary years, too much killing, too much death.

He made it to Byron Street without getting stopped once, which was something of a surprise, and ended up back in the bar. It was empty, the corporal behind the counter fussing around, stacking bottles.

'Just in time, sir, I'm closing in fifteen minutes. What can I get you?'

'A large Scotch, that'll do it.'

He sat in the corner, his raincoat open, thinking of the nice girl who'd sold him out and the man he'd killed, and it didn't worry him like it should have. The corporal had the radio on, some late-night show, and someone was singing a Cole Porter number, *They Can't Take That Away From Me*, filled with heartbreaking and melancholic nostalgia, and Giles Roper knew that whatever happened, he was through with Belfast beyond any argument. First he had to return the Colt .25 to Sergeant Clark and report the loss of a Browning Hi-Power, but not now, not tonight. He needed sleep. He needed peace, and he said goodnight to the corporal and went to bed.

From his emergency kit he took a pill that knocked him out, slept deeply and came to life again at seven. He lay there for a while, thinking about things, and went and had a hot shower. He had a tea-maker in his room and made a cup and stood in his robe thinking of the events of the previous night, moving to the window and looking out.

The rain was worse than ever, absolutely pouring, and the women coming in for the day shift down below crowded through the entrance, many of them with umbrellas. He started to turn away and paused, to look down there again, for a brief moment convinced that he'd seen Jean Murray, but he was mistaken, had to be. The last place she'd show her face, Byron Street. On the other hand, it would be a long time before he forgot the sight of her standing under the lamp after he'd killed her brother.

He had the day shift starting at nine and was just about to get dressed in camouflage overalls when he had a phone call from the orderly room. 'Message from Major Sanderson, sir. He wants you to join him as soon as possible at the Grand Hotel. General Marple flew in from London last night. Special ways-and-means conference.'

'I'll see to it.'

He groaned. Marple from London, which meant full uniform. He dressed quickly, taking it from the dry cleaning bag, grateful it hadn't been worn. It looked rather good when he checked himself in the mirror, and the ribbons for Ireland and the Military Cross set things off nicely. He adjusted his cap, nodded to himself, took a military trenchcoat from the wardrobe and went out.

He had his own vehicle on allocation, a Ford pick-up painted khaki green. It was parked in the officers' sector in the corner of the old schoolyard. Vehicles there were never locked in case of emergencies, and the gate sentries were deemed security enough. He opened the driver's seat, tossed his trenchcoat into the rear, and got behind the wheel.

He reached the gate and slowed as the sentry stepped out, raising the bar. 'You know Jean Murray, don't you, Fletcher? I thought I saw her earlier.'

'You did, Captain, but she wasn't around for long and left again. In fact, I think that's her over there in the church doorway.'

Roper was aware of a sudden chill, drove out slowly towards the other side of the road, and saw her standing there, soaked to the skin, hair plastered to her skull. She was like a corpse walking.

The moment she saw him, she started down the steps. He pulled up at the kerb and lowered his window. 'What are you doing here, Jean?'

'I wanted to give you a present.' She produced a black plastic control unit about nine inches long. 'The Howler, Captain. Kenny did finish it, but this isn't your present. That's under the passenger seat and, remember, the Howler has two faces. It can switch on as well as switch off.'

She laughed, and it was like no laugh Giles Roper had ever heard in his life, and as he scrabbled under the seat, pulling out the white plastic shopping bag he found there, the world became an infinity of white blinding light, no pain, not at that moment, simply enormous energy as the explosion took him into the eye of the storm.

So, Jean Murray died, killed instantly, just another bomber, a statistic of those terrible years, and the Howler, the Holy Grail, the ultimate answer to the bomb, died with her. Her final act of mad revenge started Giles Roper on a road that encompassed dozens of operations, a time of incredible pain and suffering, and yet it was also a journey of self-discovery and real achievement, as he became one of the most significant figures in the world of cyberspace.

He never disclosed what took place on that last night in Belfast. To the authorities, Jean Murray had just been another bomber, and over the years Roper had come to terms with her and was no longer disturbed by the memory. After all, what she and her brother had intended for him was kidnap, torture and murder. What they had given him unintentionally, was the wheelchair, and the new life that had brought him.

The George Cross had come afterwards, although it was a year and a half before he could face the Queen for her to pin it on. By then, his mother had died, and his wife, totally unable to cope, had moved on, pleaded for a quiet divorce, even with all her Catholic convictions, and finally married a much older man.

Roper was now an indispensable part of Ferguson's security group, spending most of his time at the Holland Park safe house in front of his computer screens, frequently racked with pain which responded only to whisky and cigarettes, his comfort food, sleeping only in fits and starts and mainly in his wheelchair. Indomitable, as Dillon once said, himself alone, a force of nature.

LONDON

4

At 10.30 on the morning following his late-night conversation with Svetlana Kelly, Roper, accompanied by Monica, was delivered to the side entrance in the mews beside Chamber Court off Belsize Avenue. Roper was off-loaded, and a CCTV camera beside an ironbound gate in the high wall scanned them.

A voice, not Svetlana's, said through the speaker, 'Would that be Major Roper and Lady Starling?'

'Yes, ma'am,' Doyle told her.

'I'm Katya Sorin, Svetlana's companion. The gate will open now. Tell them to follow the path inside, and it will bring them round to the conservatory.'

'Thank you, ma'am.' The gate buzzed and opened. Doyle said, 'I'll wait. I've got a couple of newspapers.'

Roper went through into a quiet, ordered world of rhododendron bushes, poplars and cypress trees, a weeping willow. Not much colour around, but it was, after all, February. The path was York stone, but expertly laid so that the going was smooth. They approached a fountain in granite stone, moved on to the large Victorian house, and there was the terrace of the conservatory. A glass door stood open and Katya Sorin waited.

Roper had looked her up. She was forty and unmarried, born in Brighton to a Russian immigrant who had married an English woman. A senior lecturer at the Slade, where she taught painting, she was a successful portrait painter and had even had the Queen Mother sit for her. She also had a considerable reputation in the theatre as a set designer.

She had cropped hair, a kind of Ingrid Bergman look, and wore khaki overalls. 'It's lovely to meet you.' Her handshake was firm. 'Just follow me.'

She led the way into a delightful conservatory which was a sort of miniature Kew, crammed with plants of every description. Internal folding doors were open, disclosing a large drawing room, fashioned in period Victorian splendour, but Svetlana Kelly sat in the centre of the conservatory in a high wicker chair, a curved wicker table before her, two wicker chairs on the other side of it, obviously waiting for them.

'My dear Lady Starling, how nice to meet you. Katya and I looked you up on the internet. Brains and beauty, such a wonderful combination.'

Monica had been well prepared by Roper. In a way, she felt she knew them already.

'And such good bone structure.' Katya actually put a hand under Monica's chin. 'I must do a drawing at least.'

Svetlana said, 'And Major Roper. A true hero, a noble man.'

'Yes,' said Katya. 'Now, please let me apologize, I must run off to the Slade for a seminar, so if you would accompany me, Lady Starling, I will show you the kitchen, and if there's anything you'd like – coffee, tea, something stronger – I'm sure you won't be shy about helping yourselves. We don't keep a maid.'

'Of course.' Monica wasn't in the least put out. 'Anything I can do.'

Katya kissed Svetlana on the forehead. 'Later, you may tell me all about whatever it is. Now I must go.'

She and Monica went out. There was a sideboard loaded with drinks and glasses. 'Have a drink, my dear. What is your pleasure?' asked Svetlana.

'Scotch whisky in large quantities, I'm afraid.'

'Which helps with the pain? You have had so many years of it that many drugs have lost their ability to cope, I imagine.'

'How on earth do you know that?'

'I'm a sensitive, my dear, I know the most intimate things about people. God blessed me as a child. Two gifts. To act – my abiding joy, my passion – and to heal. Come close.' He eased the chair round and she took his face in her hands. 'You have the pain in your head, am I right?'

'Always.'

'My hands are cool.'

'Very.'

'Now, my fingers on each side of your temples.' The surge of heat was profound enough to shock him, and the usual tension subsided. 'See, I told you so. Now go and get your whisky and a vodka for me.'

He went to the sideboard, poured the drinks, and brought them back. She raised her glass. 'To life, my dear.'

They tossed it down and Monica returned. 'Katya's coming back. We got as far as her Mini Cooper and her mobile rang. It was the Slade cancelling her seminar, a water pipe burst or something. Anyway, I'm glad. I must say I like her enormously.'

'And I like you, my dear. You are happy at the moment, you are in love, I think?'

'Well, it certainly isn't with me,' Roper told her.

'She will tell me in her own time, for we shall be good friends. Back to business and my nephew. I know his story, you know it, so does the whole world. So, let us start with you, my dear, having only just seen him, as I understand, at the gala cultural affair in New York for the United Nations.'

Katya, entering at that moment, heard her, and Monica hesitated, glancing at Roper. 'Look, do I tell her where all this is leading? I mean, the most important thing he's looking for if everything works out is total secrecy.'

Svetlana said, 'If you hesitate over Katya, there's no need. She is my most faithful friend and I trust her with my life.'

'Excellent. I hope we haven't offended you, Katya.'

'Of course not. Please continue.' She went to an easel by a window, removed a cloth, revealing a painting she was obviously working on, picked up a palette and brush and started to work.

Roper leaned over and took Svetlana's hand. 'When Kurbsky was seventeen, you came to London to do some Chekhov, met Patrick Kelly and decided to defect, which was a hell of a decision in Communist days. Did you ever regret it?'

'Never. I fell in love with a good man, I fell in love with London. Life blossomed incredibly, but I see the direction you're taking here. Alexander wishes to leap over the wall, too?'

Monica said, 'They control his every move. He told me he feels like a bear on a chain.'

'I see,' Svetlana said calmly. 'Then I suggest you tell me everything, my dear, exactly what he said and what happened.'

When she was finished Svetlana smiled. 'You perform well, my dear, but then you are an academic, an actor in a way. I feel I know all the people you have mentioned. This General Ferguson and his people, you and your brother, the Member of Parliament. Such a tragic figure. And my nephew – how he feels, what he wants. It's been sixteen years since he last sat with me, here where you are sitting now. For years, nothing, and then later on, the books, a photo on a cover, appearances on television. The falsity of the internet. To watch him was like watching someone playing him in a movie. In fact, that's what he looked like to me with that absurdly long hair and that tangled beard.'

'Tell me about him, please. You raised him, after all.'

'My brother was KGB all his life, so for his family, things were okay in the Soviet Union. His wife was not a healthy woman. I came to Moscow hoping to act, but he agreed to let me come only if I lived with them and supported her. She shouldn't have had another child after Alexander, but my brother insisted. Two years later, Tania was born and her mother died. We were all trapped. I was allowed to act with Moscow companies. He used his influence, but always I had to be a mother to the children, not that I objected. I loved Alex dearly.'

Monica said, 'And Tania?'

'Never cared for me, but she could do no wrong in her father's eyes. The years passed, he became a colonel in the KGB, very important. We had a couple living in at the house, so I had more freedom. When the Chekhov Theatre was invited to London to perform, I was one of their lead players, so he agreed I could go. It was a prestige thing. The rest is history. I married Kelly and refused to return.'

'And the children?'

'Tania wasn't bothered. She was fifteen, a wild child, and as always he doted on her. Alexander was a brilliant student, already at Moscow University at seventeen. I took a chance and wrote asking that he be permitted to visit. His father, knowing how close I was to Alexander, allowed him to come on holiday, but ordered him to persuade me to return.'

'Are you certain of that?' Roper asked.

'Yes, Alexander told me, and Kelly. He liked Kelly. They practised Judo together. Kelly was a black belt.'

'All this fits not only with what I've found, but with what he told Monica,' Roper said. 'About being so happy here with you and Kelly, but then came the serious unrest, the battles with the police and student groups over Afghanistan, hundreds dead in street fighting in Moscow.'

'And amongst them Tania,' Monica said.

'Her father contacted us saying she was wounded. That's what made Alexander return instantly.'

Monica said, 'He told me that he arrived too late for the farewell. He said she had a headstone at Minsky Park Military Cemetery because his father used his influence to somehow make her death respectable.'

'That sounds like my brother. He lied about her only being wounded just to draw Alexander back.'

'And when he joined the paratroopers, what did you think of that?'

'I was horrified, but by then we'd lost touch. All mail was censored, so I didn't know about it for a long time.'

'He told me he thought he'd done it to punish his father, who couldn't do anything about it because it would have made him look bad, a man of his standing.'

'I can believe that, but I don't really know. Everything after that, all his army time, Afghanistan and Chechnya, I know only from his books. I had no contact during all those years, and the years after that he covers in *Moscow Nights*, the years of his anti-establishment activities. I envy you for having been in his company and I'm grateful for what you have told me.'

Roper said, 'What do you think about his insistence on total secrecy?'

'That it might present difficulties for him. But that is a

bridge to be crossed at a later date.' She smiled and said to Katya, who had been working away quietly, 'Have you anything to say?'

Katya put down her painting things and wiped her hands. 'Let me just mention this. Svetlana and I first became friends when I was thirty – I've never met Alex, but I'm a play designer; a total concept specialist. Not just sets, but people, clothes, appearance, and one thing I can tell you: any problem, however difficult, has a solution.'

'As she's proved at the National Theatre on many occasions,' Svetlana put in.

Katya found a pack of cigarettes in her smock and lit one. 'Think of this whole affair as a theatrical performance. Alex flies from Paris, you and your people get him to England in one piece, Major, and then what do you do with him?'

'Help him vanish,' Roper said. 'That's what he wants.'

'And what would you do with someone you really needed to keep safe?'

'We have safe houses for situations like that. But for Kurbsky, it would just be a temporary solution.'

'Here would be an impossibility,' Svetlana said. 'I'm sure they'd look for him here. He couldn't possibly show his face.'

Katya went to the sideboard, poured a vodka and passed it to Svetlana. 'True – if it was his face.'

Svetlana looked at her. 'Thank you, my dear. I presume you mean plastic surgery?'

'Not as such, although it's a long-term possibility. Making him a new person, totally different in every way, that's how I would approach it. What is a postman or a policeman?

A uniform is what we see and accept, not so much the individual. Take Alex. His persona is like a Hollywood costume actor's – the hair, the beard, so extravagant. Svetlana has told me of his love as a boy for *The Three Musketeers* and *Captain Blood*, the swagger, the boldness inherent in such costume dramas. That is what he projects and what people see in him.'

'So how would you change him? By cutting his hair?' Monica said.

'If you did that and removed the beard, I think you would be amazed.'

They all thought about it and Svetlana said, 'He couldn't live in the house, of course. But Kelly used to use the apartment over the garage as a study. They practised judo up there.'

'Do you still use it?' Roper asked.

It was Katya who answered. 'Until three months ago, we had a young Pole named Marek living there, taking care of the garden. He had a sociology degree, but in Warsaw that only brought him two pounds an hour as a teacher. We let him live in the apartment, and as long as he saw to the garden, we never queried what else he did. He was with us for almost a year before he decided to go home again.'

'There's another possibility, too,' Svetlana said. 'I have a cottage way down by the Thames estuary beyond Dartford looking out towards Sheerness and the Isle of Sheppey. Holly End the place is called, marshland, wildfowl, birds, shingle beaches. You can breathe there.'

'It sounds nice. Could Alex hide himself there?' Monica asked Katya.

'It's lonely and desolate enough. The problem is if it's *too* lonely.'

'We'll take a look at it, too,' Monica said. 'We wouldn't want Alex going stir-crazy, though.'

'There's an old Russian saying,' Katya put in. 'If you want to hide a pine tree, put it in a forest of pines.'

'What's your point?' Roper asked.

'I may be wrong, but I recall a story about an important letter that was the object of a heated search.'

'I think I know the one you mean. The letter was in plain view all along, just another letter,' Roper said. 'And you think that might work for Kurbsky?'

'Yes,' Katya told him. 'Let me give it some thought. But now, it's time for lunch.' She smiled at Monica. 'If you'd mind helping me?'

'Only if you call me Monica.' They went out together and Svetlana reached and put a hand on Roper's knee.

'There is much more going on with Alex than it seems, I'm sure of it. I don't know what it is, but I will find out, I promise you, my dear.'

'So you and Katya will come on board, help us to find a solution?'

'What else would I do? Alexander is my blood, and blood is everything. Now – I'm an old woman now and haven't time to waste, so forgive my directness. When Monica was telling us the story, she mentioned General Ferguson and one of his closest associates, a Sean Dillon, who used to be with the IRA.'

'Yes. When the General persuaded him, if you could call

it that, to join the organization, he said it was because he needed someone who could be worse than the bad guys.'

'I see. And it is this man whom Monica favours?'

'You could put it that way.'

'I look forward to meeting him. Kelly flirted with the IRA when he was a student in Dublin. He once said it brought out the romantic in him.'

'There wasn't anything in the least romantic about the IRA in Belfast in the years I was there,' he told her.

'But that is all over now, my dear, a long, long time ago.'

That evening, there was a council of war at Holland Park. Ferguson was there, Roper, Monica, Dillon, and Harry and Billy Salter.

'This is absolutely top security, this Kurbsky affair,' Ferguson said. 'I'm not even informing Lord Arthur Tilsey of the matter. He's got enough on his plate running the Security Services in place of the late and unlamented Simon Carter.' He turned to Monica. 'You haven't seen your brother since you got back?'

'No, his doctor wasn't too happy with him. He's gone down to Stokely Hall to take it easy for a while.'

'I must ask you to keep the Kurbsky matter to yourself. It's absolutely essential if we're to carry out this operation not only successfully, but with total secrecy, as Kurbsky told you he wants.'

'So I don't tell my brother?'

'It's the name of the game, love,' Dillon said.

'So we're it,' Ferguson said. 'A nice tight crew, the six of us, and that's the way we keep it. We handle it, no one else.'

'What about Svetlana and Katya Sorin?'

'I classify them as technical backup. I'm particularly interested in the Sorin woman and what she's said to you. I look forward to hearing from her. You gave Kurbsky your Codex number?'

'I thought that was okay. I was told it was encrypted.'

'It is and you did right, but it puts you on the end of the wire. We're already only twelve days away from when Kurbsky will enter the Elysée Palace to have the Legion of Honour pinned to his manly breast by the French President. When he calls you, Monica, find out when the ceremony is, morning or evening – they do both – how much protection he has, and whether he's staying at the Russian Embassy or a hotel.'

'I'll give you a check list. What are your movements?'

'Back to Cambridge tomorrow, long weekend, necessary business. I could be back in three days, I think.'

'I'll feel more secure when you're back with us. There's a real element of danger here.'

'Look, you don't need to worry about me, Charles. I'm involved by chance, but this isn't the first time I've been in a dangerous situation. I was at Drumore, remember, during the shootout with those IRA thugs. And I killed a man. You were there. He needed killing and I got over it. End of story.'

'Very civil of you,' Ferguson said. 'I think that will do for the moment, people.'

Harry got up. 'Anybody want a bite to eat at the Dark Man? It's only eight o'clock. Best pub grub in London and on me.'

Monica nudged Dillon. He said, 'Thanks, Harry, another time. Monica's got an early start in the morning.'

'All right, lovebirds. Come on, Billy,' and they left.

Ferguson was writing away. 'There's your check list.' He handed it to Monica and she put it in her purse.

'We could stop in at that French restaurant in Shepherd's Market on the way back,' she said to Dillon.

'Why not.' He turned to Roper, 'Are you okay?'

'I've done enough travel for one day, Sean. A sandwich and the Scotch and I'll catch up on cyberspace.'

Monica said, 'What about you, Charles?'

He hesitated, 'Oh, you don't want an old fogey like me at the table.'

Her Codex went, she flicked to see where the call originated, her eyes widened and she held it out to Roper. He took it from her, making an adjustment that linked it to his speakers.

She said, 'Who's that?'

'Monica? It's Alex Kurbsky.'

Roper put a finger to his lips and waved the others to silence. Monica said, 'What a surprise, Alex, to hear from you so soon. Where are you?'

'A special hotel the Ministry of Arts runs, but I move soon to a safe house outside Moscow, where the GRU will keep an eye on me until Paris.'

'Where are you staying when you go there?'

'They haven't decided yet, but I've been thinking about what we discussed. I'd like to proceed.'

'That's wonderful.'

'But on the terms I discussed with you. Total secrecy. You said you knew people in the British Secret Service at the highest level.'

'I do and I've spoken to them.' She took a chance now. 'You can speak to my controller right now. I happen to be visiting the London safe house. Major Giles Roper.'

'Put him on.'

Roper said, 'Mr Kurbsky. It's a great honour, one soldier to another.'

'Monica said her phone was encrypted. Is that so?'

'A work of technical genius. What can I do for you?'

'As Monica knows, I wish to fly my cage, but my terms are strict. I prefer total anonymity, certainly for a while.'

Roper glanced at Ferguson, who nodded. 'That's a given. Totally guaranteed.' He also took a chance now. 'I spoke with Svetlana today. Monica and I visited her. She was thrilled to hear about New York and now Paris.'

'God in heaven,' Kurbsky said. 'Is she well?'

'She lives with a woman friend, Katya Sorin, in Chamber Court. Kelly died years ago, but I suppose you knew that.'

'Not until afterwards. So, if you talked to my aunt, I presume the question of my desire to flee was raised?'

'She made an assumption it was impossible to deny. So, she and her friend are aware of what's intended, but obviously they're trustworthy.'

'I accept that. I would trust Svetlana with my life, but I

don't want her involved in this business in any way. She's an old woman. I would not wish to bring any kind of threat to her. So, you think you can snatch me in Paris? I fly in privately with three GRU minders and they'll dog my every step.'

'We'll think of something.'

'Is your boss there?'

'Yes, General Charles Ferguson.'

'I sensed there might be somebody. Put him on.'

Ferguson said, 'Kurbsky, what a pleasure.'

'I must go, but titbits for you. I spoke to Putin person-ally. He made it clear how important I am to dear old Mother Russia. I used to be handled by a General Volkov who was in charge of security. Does that mean anything to you?'

'It does indeed.'

'It seems Volkov is no more and Putin intends to handle the security side himself. Does that interest you?'

'Very much.'

'And does the name Luhzkov strike a chord?'

'Certainly. Station Head of GRU at the London Embassy.'

'Putin spoke to him in my presence. Told him that London was the top hot spot and he was promoting him to full colonel and sending him back there.'

'That is interesting.'

'I must go. I've been hiding in the toilet too long. I'll be in touch. I won't give you my number this time. I don't want you calling me at an inconvenient moment.'

He was gone, and Roper was smiling all over his ravaged face. 'Well, how about that then?'

'How about that indeed?' Ferguson turned to Dillon and

Monica. 'Thank you, and I'd love to join you for dinner in Shepherd's Market.'

It was eleven o'clock at the Minsky Hotel in Moscow, and Kurbsky was sitting with Bounine and Luhzkov in a corner by the bar.

'Wonderful things, mobile phones.'

'Well, if they're not encrypted, they can be a stone in the shoe,' Luhzkov said, 'but ours are good. Play the recording back.'

Kurbsky did as he was told and turned the sound up. Afterwards, Bounine said, 'Hah, you must be pleased to hear about your aunt. Christ, you used to talk about her in Afghanistan.'

'She was the only mother I knew, a wonderful person. Was I okay?' he asked Luhzkov.

'Amazing to hear Roper and Ferguson. I know them so well. And the information you gave them was harmless – they'd find out anyway, and every little bit helps to establish your credentials. The magic name of Putin will certainly excite them.' He turned to Bounine. 'I go back to London on Thursday night – you come with me. If Ferguson's people are keeping an eye on Alexander in Paris, we can't have you anywhere near him.'

'Who have you selected for the minders team?'

'Ivanov, Kokonin and Burlaka.'

'I'm surprised. I'd say they've got a lot to learn,' Bounine commented.

'And they aren't in on the plot. That's definite?' Kurbsky asked.

'Whatever Ferguson's people do, they'll expect your minders to defend you. If they didn't, they'd smell a rat.'

'So they could get killed?'

'My dear Alexander, they're expendable. That's the name of the game.'

'So they play their part and die for the Motherland?'

'A great honour,' Bounine said. 'I thought you'd have learned that by now.' He got up. 'It's late. Let's turn in. It's been a long day.'

The day Bounine and Luhzkov boarded their flight for London, Monica returned from Cambridge to Dover Street. Her brother was still unwell and remained at Stokely in the care of Aunt Mary and the servants. She phoned Roper at Holland Park.

'I'm back. No further word from Kurbsky. How's Sean?'

'He's here somewhere. I've had a message from Katya Sorin. She wants us to call. Apparently she's got something she wants to run by us. Are you doing anything at the moment?'

'Absolutely not. I'll come straight round. Ask Sean if he wants to come with us. I think he should meet them.'

An hour later, Tony Doyle delivered them to Chamber Mews, three of them this time, and they followed the path and found Katya waiting on the terrace at the open door. Inside, Svetlana sat in her wicker chair like a queen on a throne.

'So this is your Irishman?' she said to Monica and held out her hand to Dillon, holding it for a long moment. 'A good man, but two men are inside you and one fights the other. However, you are better than you think, my friend, in spite of yourself. I should do a Tarot reading.'

'Jesus, Joseph and Mary, spare me that, ma'am.' He turned to Katya. 'Miss Sorin.' He shook hands. 'I went to RADA as a boy and was an actor for a while. I admire your work. The *Macbeth* you designed, the Nazi one. Jesus, if ever there was a *tour de force*, it was that.'

'We were just having tea Russian-style. Everyone join in.' She gestured to the samovar, the cups. Svetlana said, 'What is your birthday, Mr Dillon?'

'January the thirteenth.'

'Capricorn. Among your aspects, you have Jupiter in the House of Marriage and the Moon in good aspect with Venus.' She turned to Monica. 'And yet he isn't married. This is most unusual.'

'Perhaps he's just been waiting for me?' Monica said.

There was general laughter. Katya said, 'If you'd all come in to the drawing room, I'd like to show you something which may interest you.'

Dillon helped Svetlana up and gave her his arm. They went through and Katya settled them in front of the large television screen. She had a keyboard control in one hand.

Roper said, 'Before you start I should tell you that Alex

92

phoned Monica the other night. He's confirmed that he wants us to help him defect in Paris.'

Katya said, 'Then it is even more important that I explain what I intend. Pay attention, please.'

She pointed the control, pressed a button and the large screen was filled with a full length picture of Alexander Kurbsky in a bomber jacket and jeans, hands in his pockets, face calm, smiling slightly.

'So here we have the man as he is, the man the world knows, for appearance is everything in this life. A gallant soldier, a star, if you like to put it that way, with a swagger to him. A sort of Renaissance man, with the hair almost to his shoulders, the beard, as if basing himself on the heroes of those books by Alexandre Dumas we are told he so loved as a boy. Everything about him says: look at me.'

'I take your point,' Monica said. 'But couldn't he really be hiding his real self? The extravagant appearance would argue that to me.'

'Possibly, there are two sides to any coin, but the important thing here is to change him into something else.'

'Change his appearance?' Dillon said.

'Yes, but not just that. We must change the inner man as well. It will require a performance. But first, the other man.'

She tapped on her keyboard, the head moved into full screen, and within moments the beard had gone – the mouth area, the chin, clear of all facial hair.

There was silence for a moment, then Dillon said, 'Amazing. How accurate is this?'

'Well into the ninety per cent range,' Katya said.

'How different to see the firm chin, the mouth,' Svetlana said. 'And the cheeks so hollow, a hint of the boy I knew.'

'It's a revelation,' Monica whispered.

'One can make further adjustments, and remove the smile, for instance,' Katya said, and did just that. 'Now, he is much more sombre. Not quite the Alexander Kurbsky people are used to.'

Roper said, 'I'd say a great many people looking at him like that wouldn't recognize him at all.'

'Certainly not the general public,' Dillon said.

'And let's take it further. The extravagant hair.' Katya had the head image turning, the hair shortening to a neat conservative style, and stabilized it. 'Now we'll change clothes from the bomber jacket and jeans.' She punched away at the keys until the figure on the screen wore a dark single-breasted suit, white shirt and striped tie.

'My God, he could be something in the City, a banker or accountant,' Monica said.

'He certainly isn't Alexander Kurbsky,' Dillon said. 'I think you've demonstrated that.' He looked at Roper. 'What about you?'

'Katya said ninety per cent and I'd accept that, even a little more. But we're up against professionals here. I'd never underestimate Russian intelligence. The GRU are as good as it gets. That's something we have to accept.'

'So you want more?' Katya asked. 'I thought you might. I told you I would treat this as a performance and it will require Kurbsky to adopt a new identity so different from his own that anyone would accept him, even the most skilled operatives of the GRU. Remember our conversation about the best place to hide the letter, Major Roper?'

'In plain sight.'

'So, what if I suggested that Alexander Kurbsky be lodged here in plain sight? That he use the flat over the garage and work as Svetlana's gardener and odd job man just like Marek, the Pole. Observe.' Katya manipulated the screen again, stripping Kurbsky of his clothes, substituting loose hospital scrubs for them. The hair was removed totally, the image now of a gaunt human being with sunken cheeks and a shaved skull.

'That's how chemotherapy leaves you when you have treatment for lung cancer, which is why he has been residing at that wonderful hospital, the Royal Marsden. He's of French extraction – through his father, perhaps? I understand he speaks excellent French, but that would be up to you people. What do you think?'

'You're a genius,' Roper said. 'I'd defy anyone to look at that man on the screen and identify it in any way with Kurbsky.'

'I agree,' Monica said. 'What about you, Sean?'

'Remarkable. I wouldn't have believed it if I hadn't seen it myself.' He turned to Svetlana. 'And you?'

'I want him safe, I want him close to me again, and if this is the only way, so be it.'

'That's it, then,' Roper said. 'We'll report back. Is there anything else?'

'Now we wait,' Svetlana said. 'The rest, I suppose, is up to you.'

'I've got time off from the university.' Monica gave her a kiss. 'I'll stay in close touch.'

Katya came all the way down to the gate with them. 'Now comes the hard part, I think. Paris. They'll be guarding him closely. The Russians can be very difficult.'

'Don't worry. We can be difficult, too.' Dillon smiled and he and Monica followed Roper out.

MOSCOW

LONDON
———

5

On the firing range in the cellars of the GRU safe house outside Moscow, the three men who were to be responsible for Kurbsky's protection in Paris stood facing the target area, supervised by a hardened sergeant major with a cropped head named Lermov. Kurbsky, dressed in a track suit and woollen hat, sat on a stool, watching, and smoked a cigarette. The three GRU men were in uniform.

'Six single shots and take your time. Kokonin first. First two head shots, then four in the heart and chest area.'

The lights came on in the gloom, the target figure moved from right to left, pausing, and Kokonin loosed his shots. His first round clipped an ear, the next went through the left cheek, the chest grouping was widely dispersed.

Kokonin was a junior lieutenant in rank but Lermov didn't take prisoners. 'If that's the best you can do, I wonder how you handle your cock, sir. Stand back. Next.'

Which was Burlaka, who managed to catch the head once, but his grouping in the chest was very poor.

'Even worse,' Lermov said, and called to Burlaka, 'just fire six times at the body,' which Burlaka did, peppering the torso area.

Lermov shook his head. 'Terrible.'

Burlaka was angry and said, 'I did the job, Sergeant Major – hit whoever it was six times.'

Lermov laughed harshly. 'That's one point of view, sir.' He turned to Kurbsky. 'Afghanistan, Chechnya, it's all gone. They're sitting behind desks these days, doing everything by computer. What's happened to the world? Where did it all go?'

'We're dinosaurs, Sergeant Major.'

The three young GRU officers were angry. Ivanov put his pistol on the table after removing the clip. 'If you can do any better, show us. I'm tired of being put down like this. If you're so much better, let's see it. And what about you, Comrade?' he said to Kurbsky. 'You make a lot of claims in your books.'

Kokonin said, 'Maybe that's all they ever were.'

There was a moment's silence, Kurbsky dropped his cigarette on the floor and stood. Lermov picked up a Stechkin. 'I've got a certain affection for this. I've had it since Afghanistan. It should take you back, Comrade.'

'It certainly should,' Kurbsky said.

He held it against his right thigh. Two targets swung up. He double-tapped, shooting the left target twice in the heart, then twice in the forehead. He swung right, double tapping the heart, then a single shot through each eye. There was silence.

Kurbsky handed the Stechkin back to Lermov, who was thoroughly enjoying himself. 'I must say you keep it in perfect working order, Sergeant Major. My compliments. Now I'm going to go for my run.'

He went out and Lermov turned to the other three. 'What was it you were saying, sir?' he asked Ivanov. He shook his head. 'He's not like other people, he's a one-off, but don't let it get you down. I'm going to give you your most important lesson.' He pushed a fresh clip into the butt of the Stechkin. 'Come with me, all of you.'

He led the way down to the range and stopped three paces away from the targets. 'Watch this.' He raised the Stechkin and shot the target in the heart, then in the forehead. He handed the weapon to Ivanov. 'Now you.' The shots slammed home and he said, 'Let the others do it.'

They obeyed him one after another. 'Perfect.' He held out his hand and Burlaka passed him the pistol again. 'Now you know, get that close if possible. There's only one alternative that's better.'

'What's that, Sergeant Major?' Ivanov asked.

Lermov replaced the clip on the Stechkin, stepped close to the target, rammed the muzzle into it and fired several times.

'There you go, Comrades, a job well done. But that's

enough. I believe your task is never to leave Alexander Kurbsky for a moment, and there he is running through the orchards on his own.'

Ivanov looked hunted. 'Come on, you bastards.' He rushed out, followed by the others.

In fact, as they emerged into the entrance hall, they discovered Kurbsky talking to a man in an old-fashioned fedora and a black leather coat. Kurbsky turned. 'Ah, here they are. We were just having a little pistol practice on the range. This is Major Gregorovich from Moscow. Good boys, this lot, Major, they never leave me for a moment.'

'Following our orders, Major, that's all,' Ivanov said piously.

'As you should,' said Gregorovich. 'Now into the commanding officer's office. I need to discuss Paris with you.'

He didn't even take his coat off, but did remove his hat as he sat behind the desk and opened a briefcase and took out some documents. 'There is a copy for each of you, including you, Comrade,' he said to Kurbsky. 'Lieutenant Ivanov will be in charge.'

Kurbsky said, 'So, the ceremony? Is it afternoon or evening?'

'Seven o'clock at the Elysée Palace. There will be other honourees – scientists, academics, fifteen in all. It'll be an exclusive affair, government officials, a few ministers. A buffet will be served.'

He sounded as if he didn't approve. 'I know how it goes,' Kurbsky said. 'The worst excesses of decadent capitalism.

Great looking women in gorgeous frocks, champagne, mountains of caviar. They know how to seduce us Russians.'

His minders were struggling not to laugh, and Gregorovich
was not amused. 'Kurbsky, you have a sacred duty to the
Motherland to serve her at all times.'

'But I do, I assure you, Major.'

'Back to business. You will fly by private plane next
Tuesday afternoon, and land at Charles de Gaulle Airport.
In view of the importance of the affair to our reputation,
you will stay at the Ritz Hotel.'

The young men perked up considerably. Kurbsky said, 'My
goodness, Major, are you sure we can afford it?'

'Such levity does not become you.'

'My apologies. The Ambassador will be there, I presume.'

'No, he's needed at an important meeting in Brussels.'

'How interesting. I didn't realize we were now in the
European Union.'

'That is not amusing. You book into the Ritz immediately.
This is to guarantee your presence the next day. As I've
already made clear, the ceremony is at seven. You return to
Moscow in the jet at ten o'clock Thursday morning from
Charles de Gaulle.'

'Well, there you go, lads,' Kurbsky said. 'No chance even
to get laid.'

'Your kind of frivolity does not amuse me, Kurbsky.'
Gregorovich closed his briefcase and put his hat on. 'The
Motherland has treated you well. I would suggest you
remember that.'

'Oh, I will, I will,' Kurbsky assured him.

Gregorovich got up. 'Good morning. I can't wait to get back to Moscow and sanity.' He opened the door and paused. 'I don't like you, Kurbsky. I never approved. They spoil you too much. But, what goes around comes around. You should remember that.'

He went out. Ivanov and his friends looked troubled. Kurbsky stood up. 'Don't worry, lads, he's been a desk man all his career. Guys like that hate real soldiers for obvious reasons. Anyway, I'm going for a run. I don't know what you lot are going to do, but if you want to keep up with me, you'll have to get your running shoes on.'

He left them there, ran through the hall, and out across the car park, where he saw Gregorovich leaving in his limousine, went down the terrace steps and ran towards the orchards and the woods in the distance.

At Holland Park, Katya Sorin finished demonstrating her reconstruction of Alexander Kurbsky to the full crew, including Ferguson and the Salters.

'You've got to admit, it's brilliant,' Harry said. 'Absolute genius. I've known a lot of villains over the years who'd have paid you a fortune to have been given a make-over like that,' he told Katya.

'I'm for it completely,' Ferguson said. 'Is everyone agreed?' They all nodded. 'Good, now his identity. I'll give it to the MI-6 Office Five forgery department. A French father, an English mother, born here. Parents dead, and so on and so on. He'll need documentation from the Royal Marsden and insertion into their system. London University, English degree. Journalist. Maybe a war correspondent in the Balkans, something like that. Passport filled with all the right stamps. Henri Duval, that name sound about right?'

'You're enjoying this, aren't you?' Monica said. 'You should have been a writer yourself.'

'Leave it to that nice lady at Office Five,' Dillon urged him. 'So can we get down to how we lift him?'

Ferguson said, 'A fast flight out, I'd say. Nothing official. If Parry and Lacey do it, it's got to be out of the way somewhere. Certainly no airport in the Paris area. There are plenty of small airfields in Brittany that deal with business clients. I'll speak to Squadron Leader Lacey and put it in his hands.'

'And who goes to Paris?' Dillon asked.

'You and Billy.'

Billy smiled coldly. 'That suits me fine.'

At that moment, Monica's phone rang. It was Kurbsky. 'I haven't got long. Listen carefully. I fly down to Charles de Gaulle on Tuesday, arriving in the evening. The Ministry has decided to splash out, so I'll be at the Ritz with my three minders. The ceremony is at seven on Wednesday evening. We fly back from Charles de Gaulle at ten on Thursday morning.'

His voice echoed over the speakers. Roper said, 'We've got that. We'll work out how to snatch you and tell you next time you call.'

'Have you come up with a way of guaranteeing my anonymity?'

'Absolutely. Katya Sorin has come up with a most

ingenious suggestion. It will make you into a totally different person – one that no one would recognize as Alexander Kurbsky. You must trust us on this.'

'All right. But I must go now. My minders are looking for me.'

Ferguson said, 'The Ritz, by God. He should surely be able to give them the slip from there.'

'I would say so,' Dillon told him.

Katya said, 'I'll be on my way,' and left.

Ferguson said, 'There is one other matter, now that Katya's gone, so sit down again for a minute. The six of us make a nice tight crew, but it's starting to go at the edges. First Katya and Svetlana. Now I'm going to have to include Lacey and Parry.'

'Yes, Charles, but come off it. Those guys have supported us for years. We've been to the war zones with them: they brought Billy back from Hazar, shot to pieces. If you can't trust them, who can you?'

'All right, I accept that, but what I'm working my way up to saying is that I haven't informed the Prime Minister.'

'Jesus,' Billy said.

'Is that legal?' Harry put in.

'Since when have we ever been legal?' Dillon told him. 'So what exactly are you getting at, Charles?'

'If we tell the Prime Minister, we have to tell Blake Johnson.'

'The man who was in Kosovo with my brother?' Monica said.

'He does for President Cazalet what I do for the Prime Minister. We usually do things in tandem.'

'I see,' she said. 'Does that give you a problem?'

'I don't know, that's why I mention it. I'd appreciate your opinions, so just think about it. We'll leave it at that for the moment.'

Kurbsky had made his call from an old ruined chapel in the wood beyond the orchard. It had a distant view of the house to one side of the track, and he'd been able to keep an eye out for the three young men as they approached, searching for him.

'Where is the bastard?' Kokonin was saying.

'He's playing with us, I'm sure of it,' Ivanov told him.

Kurbsky let them pass and vanish into the wood and lit a cigarette. So, the enterprise was afoot. It struck Kurbsky as ironic that Ferguson and company were going to such trouble to extract him and to protect his identity when his own people were aware of everything, his new identity, where he was living.

But that, of course, would depend on him. *What if he kept his identity completely to himself?* Thanks to the mobile phone, the greatest invention of all time in some ways, he could receive encrypted calls from people who did not know where he was. He could also make calls which could not be traced.

So, he, who had been a prisoner of his own people, was now in a strange way free to do what his people wanted or to refuse. It was absolutely beautiful, and then he remembered Tania at Station Gorky, and realized that his thoughts of freedom had only been an illusion.

There were voices down below on the track and he emerged from the ruins and ran down the hill and confronted them. 'Were you looking for someone?'

They seemed put out, then Ivanov laughed. 'Damn you, you've been playing with us again.'

'Well, there isn't much else to do round here, but there's Paris to look forward to. Great chambermaids at the Ritz. You never know, you could get lucky.'

They smiled at that, but Ivanov said, 'Chance would be a fine thing. One of us has always got to be on guard in your suite.'

Kurbsky, who had expected such a thing, said amiably, 'And how are you going to manage that?'

'I have to work out a rota,' Ivanov said.

'Well, that's okay. It means that when one of you is busy watching me, the other two can play.' He grinned. 'I'm starving. Lunchtime, lads, so race me back.' He ran away from them very fast.

The one time he was assured of total privacy was when he stayed in the house, using the bar facilities or the gymnasium and swimming pool or the extensive library, which included computers. Luhzkov had provided him with codes offering access to classified GRU information, and after lunch he sat down, brought up a screen and accessed the British Security Services.

There was plenty of history there, the traitors who had worked for the KGB, for instance – Philby, Burgess, Maclean and many, many more than the general public in Britain had ever known about. One thing wasn't there, though – nowhere in the files was there any mention of General Charles Ferguson and his organization. The security force known in the trade as the Prime Minister's private army simply did not exist.

He tried another approach, accessing individuals, and struck it lucky. The George Cross Database came up with Major Giles Roper. It was all there, the George Cross and Military Cross, his service in Ireland, the Portland Hotel bomb, then the final explosion which had left him in a wheelchair. Apparently he now worked in the computer industry.

'Computer industry, my arse,' Kurbsky said softly. 'But what a man.'

But that was all he could find on Ferguson and his crew. For want of something better to do, he tapped in Monica and reviewed her life. Her photo was excellent, and he smiled. A remarkable lady, and he liked her.

Finally, he typed in Svetlana, something he had never done, and was amazed at the wealth of information. There was an early photo from the Moscow days of her and Kurbsky and Tania, his father in KGB uniform. A few lines on these early days and much more about her defection and London marriage. A list of her London stage appearances. A photo of Kelly, a mention that her companion was now the artist Katya Sorin, and then a whole page on her famous nephew.

Kurbsky clicked into Katya Sorin and discovered her

life in theatre and art. There was a photo of her and Svetlana obviously taken recently. He smiled, touched, and switched off.

Lacey and Parry appeared at Holland Park and found Roper. 'The boss has filled us in. Dillon and Billy are going to snatch somebody important in Paris Wednesday night and spirit him away,' Lacey said.

'One Henri Duval, according to the passport,' Parry added, 'though if you believe that, you'd believe anything.'

'Absolute top priority,' Lacey said.

'As big as it gets.' Roper drank a little Scotch and lit a cigarette.

'Well, if you say that, I really do believe it,' Lacey said. 'So let's look at France.'

Roper brought it up on a screen, focussing on Paris. 'It can't be Charles de Gaulle or any of the small airfields operating in the Paris area.'

'Look, aren't you being a bit overcautious?' Parry asked. 'A quick in-and-out. What's wrong with that?'

'Total anonymity. Ferguson wants this man swallowed whole. It must be as if he's never been.'

'It's not a kidnapping, is it?' Lacey asked.

'Absolutely not. He wants to disappear into the depths of France – that way, his own people might think he was still in France, simply hidden away somewhere.'

'So Dillon and Billy pick him up by car and whisk him off somewhere,' Lacey said. 'Overnight to another part of the country, where we'll be waiting at some suitable airfield to fly out to the UK.'

Roper enlarged the map. 'What about Brittany?'

'Lots of places we could use there, fly out across the Channel Islands, Isle of Wight, straight up to Farley Field. Long way to go, Brittany.'

'Not if you went by rail. There's a line all the way down to Brest marked on the map.'

'And Brest *is* a hell of a long way,' Parry said.

'I'm not suggesting you go all the way. The line goes through Rennes, for example. That's not far from St Malo, the Channel Islands, Jersey. I'll bring up flying facilities for that area.'

There were several. Lacey and Parry murmured together and finally made a choice. 'St Denis. There's an excellent flying club there. They have a tarmac runway to attract business travel, so jets can get in.' Lacey nodded. 'We could do that. We could drop Dillon and Billy at Charles de Gaulle, Wednesday morning, then fly down to St Denis and overnight.'

'Now for the train.'

Roper tapped his requirements in and sat back. 'There you are. Overnight for Brest, departing midnight. Compartments available, first class, can seat four.'

'Well, there you are,' Lacey told him.

'What plane will you use?' Roper asked.

Lacey looked at Parry. 'What do you think?'

'Gulfstream's too flashy. Let's go for the sober look. The old Chieftain turboprop. Plenty of legroom, great seats.'

'I agree.' Lacey turned to Roper. 'A done deal. You take care of your end, we'll fix up Charles de Gaulle and St Denis, and we're in business.'

Parry added, 'Could it get rough in Paris for Sean and Billy?'

'Let's put it this way. They're up against people who will do everything in their power to stop them.'

'Duval must be very important.'

'When you recognize him, remember to forget you've seen him.'

The following day, Dillon and Monica accompanied Svetlana on a day out by invitation. They went in an old Ford station wagon, Katya driving, the weather brooding.

'The time of year, my dears,' Svetlana said. 'But I wanted you to see Holly End. It meant a great deal to Alexander when he was here. He used to go down for the weekends with Kelly all the time. Katya loves to paint there.'

'When the weather is right,' Katya told them.

They went through the city to Greenwich following the river. Monica said, 'London seems never-ending.'

'It all changes quite soon now,' Katya said, and she was right, for beyond Gravesend, with the rain which had threatened starting to pour, they moved into a bleak landscape of fields and marshland edged by mudflats swallowed up by the waters of the Thames estuary.

Way beyond, half-glimpsed through the mist and rain, ships moved out to sea. Katya said, 'Look, way over there on the horizon is something you seldom see these days. A lightship, permanently moored on chains.'

'So strange, this place, and so close to the city,' Dillon said. There were reeds now higher than a man, the road a raised causeway, and they came to a village of a dozen old-fashioned seaside wood bungalows, mostly painted green, with corrugated iron roofs. It looked totally desolate, not a soul in sight.

'Who on earth lives here?' Monica asked.

'No one, my dear,' Svetlana told her. 'They are holiday homes for rent. People get their supplies from Gravesend or perhaps Rochester.'

'And you must remember to fill up with petrol there, too,' Katya said.

'But who on earth would want to holiday here?' Monica laughed.

'Oh, I don't know,' Dillon said. 'It takes all sorts. Dickens wrote about Gravesend, and Rochester as I recall.'

'Bird watchers come here all the time,' Katya said. 'For people who like that sort of thing, it's a paradise. In the old days, very ancient times, there were Saxons here, then outlaws of one kind and another hiding in the marshes. Closer to our own times, certainly in the time Dickens knew it, there were smugglers.'

They came to a track on the right, turned along it and arrived at a five-barred gate bearing a painted sign *Holly End*. They entered a large farmyard, surfaced with shingle, fronting a barn and a two-storey farmhouse that was surprisingly large. It had a slate roof and shuttered windows.

Katya turned off the engine, got out, found a key and opened the blue painted front door. 'I'm only here to check the place,' she said. 'But come in, by all means. There's a pub at All Hallows, quarter of a mile away. We'll lunch there.'

Dillon helped Svetlana out, gave her his arm and they went inside. The hall was dark, and there was a smell of damp. 'Four bedrooms upstairs,' Katya said. 'Sitting room to the left, kitchen to the right and bathroom directly ahead. It's an ugly bitch of a place during the winter, and everything's covered, so there's not much to see.'

She went upstairs and Dillon and Svetlana went into the sitting room. The furniture had all been covered by old-fashioned grey drapes. 'Like shrouds, aren't they? One could imagine a corpse on each chair,' Svetlana said.

Dillon laughed. 'It's being so cheerful keeps you going, I can see that.' He helped her across to the kitchen, which was normal enough, though old-fashioned, and she sat on one of four chairs which stood at a large wooden table. 'And Kurbsky loved this place?'

'Always, even in weather like this. It was the marsh he liked, ploughing through the reeds, he and Kelly with shotguns looking for wildfowl.'

They could hear Katya's steps upstairs through the ceiling. Monica said, 'A dead world. It makes me uneasy. Those people who came here in the past must have had little choice in the matter. Refugees, outlaws.'

'I think that's what Alexander adored about it. Perhaps the feeling that he resembled in some way all those people who had gone before,' Svetlana said.

'But nothing lives here. It's a place of shadows, quietly passing, only an illusion,' said Monica.

Katya had heard her as she came down the stairs and entered the kitchen. 'There is life here and everywhere, believe me, fish in those creeks in the marsh, crabs, shell-fish, geese in the winter from Siberia, wildfowl in plenty.'

'But not to Monica's taste, I think,' Svetlana told her. 'Is all well?'

'It would seem so.'

'Then load up and we shall visit the inn at All Hallows.'

Typically for such a place, the inn, called the Smugglers, was a relic of the early eighteenth century. Crouched on the edge of the estuary, it had a weatherbeaten look to it, but the bar was friendly enough, with a beamed ceiling and a wide open hearth and a log fire. The woman behind the bar was named Betty and she greeted Svetlana warmly, seeming to be about the same age.

Katya said, 'No visitors around then?'

'A few bird-watchers as usual, the crazy type who go out in all weathers. Now what'll it be? You know me, ladies, one dish a day is my limit and, being Monday, it's stew and dumplings.'

'Which will suit us,' Svetlana said. 'And a glass of red wine for me. I don't know what the rest of you want.'

'That's fine,' Monica said. 'His lordship here will undoubt-edly hope for Irish whiskey.'

'And I'll stick to one glass of sherry, as I'm driving,' Katya said.

They sat there, enjoying the warmth, waiting for the food, and Svetlana said, 'Do you think your visit here tells you something more about my nephew?'

'I'm not sure,' Monica said. 'The man I met in New York was a handsome devil with a swagger to him, someone who seemed to face the world and say I don't give a damn what you think of me. Take me or leave me, I couldn't care less.'

Svetlana nodded. 'You must realize, I have to see this for myself.'

Dillon said, 'What did you think of the boy from Moscow who joined you in London, but loved to come down here to this desolate world?'

She opened her large handbag, rummaged in it and produced a pack of cards. 'Tarot,' she said to Monica. 'I discovered I had a gift for these things many years ago. As I said, I am a sensitive. I won't ask you if you believe. Shuffle the pack and give it back to me with your left hand.' Monica did as she was told and Svetlana spread the pack in a half circle face down. 'Three cards, that is all you need.' Monica eased them out, still face down. They looked antique and were green and gold.

Svetlana took Monica's left hand in hers. 'You thought you knew yourself, but something has happened of late to you that has changed your life irrevocably. You are no longer the person that you thought you were. Now choose one card and turn it over.'

Monica did as she was told, her stomach hollow with excitement. The picture was a pool guarded by a wolf and a dog. Beyond it were two towers, and in the sky above, the moon.

'This is good, my dear, for it is upright. It indicates a crisis in your life. All is changed utterly. Reason and intellect have no part in resolving your new situation. Only your own instincts will bring you through. You must at all times flow with the feeling. Your own feeling. This alone will present you with the true solution.'

Monica felt drained and weak. 'Good God,' she said faintly and, reaching, found Dillon's left hand and held it tight.

'You wouldn't be giving me any answers, would you?' he asked as Svetlana picked up the cards and dropped them back in her handbag.

'One at a time is all I am capable of, my dear, it is so draining, but I can speak of the past. Sixteen years ago, I sat here with Kelly and my nephew, and Alexander asked me, and not for the first time, to do the cards. I had always refused, I always had a bad feeling.'

'But this time you agreed?' Monica asked.

'Yes, but he asked for the double, one card on another. He insisted.'

There was a long pause. Dillon said gently, 'What was the result?'

'The first card was a knight on horseback, a baton in his hand, a sign of someone who chooses the path of conflict for its own sake.'

'And the second card?' Monica felt a strange chill.

'Death. A skeleton with a scythe mowing not corn, but corpses.'

'But that's terrible, horrible.' Monica was truly upset.

Katya said, 'Even worse, when they returned to Chamber

Court that evening, it was to receive the news from Moscow about Tania.'

'You mean the false report that she was only wounded?' Dillon asked.

Katya nodded and Svetlana sighed, 'Such is life, my dears.'

Betty chose that exact moment to come in from the kitchen, a plate in each hand, and put them on the bar. 'Get it while it's hot,' she said and returned to the kitchen. Katya got them and handed them down. Betty came back with two more.

The outside door opened and three men with hooded anoraks entered, binoculars around their necks. They moved down to the other end of the bar by the fireplace and ordered beer.

'Eat up, my dears,' Svetlana said, 'and don't be depressed, for all will be resolved in the end.'

On the way back to London, Monica received another call from Kurbsky, who was in the bathroom in his apartment at the safe house.

'Can you talk?'

'Just a moment.' Monica asked Katya to pull in at the side of the road and got out of the station wagon. 'You can speak now.'

'I've enjoyed looking at you on the internet. I found your Major Roper, too. Tell him I'll call at midnight my time tonight, nine yours. This isn't a request. I need answers.'

The line went dead and Monica got back in the station wagon and told Dillon. He said, 'Well, it would be difficult to say no. Call in now and tell Roper. We'll go back to Chamber Court with the ladies and then check in at Holland Park.'

'You'll keep us posted?' Katya said.

'Absolutely. There are two important moves in this game. One, to get Kurbsky out of Paris, the second to get him safe in your hands at Holland Park so you can work your magic.' He smiled at Svetlana. 'Don't worry, my love, it's going to be just fine. Trust me.'

As it drew closer to nine o'clock at Holland Park, they all sat waiting, for Ferguson had called in the Salters, too, and at nine precisely, Kurbsky came through. Roper adjusted Monica's mobile and Kurbsky spoke.

'Have you got the plan for me? We're only three days away.'

Roper said, 'We will have two operatives arriving in Paris by private plane on Wednesday. Their names are Sean Dillon and Billy Salter. We've checked the order of events at the Elysée Palace. Seven o'clock, a glass of champagne as a welcome. Things get serious from eight, then comes the buffet meal. We figure you return to the Ritz for eleven – but it could be earlier.'

'So what happens then?'

'I'm handing you over to Dillon.'

'How do your minders see to you?' Dillon asked.

'They have a rota. One on guard at all times in my sitting room in the suite.'

'You go to bed as soon as you get back, whatever time it is. I would imagine a man of your experience would have no difficulty handling the guard in your room.'

'Then what?'

'Straight downstairs, minutes only. There are always taxis at the rank outside. Tell the driver to take you to the Gare du Nord railway station. There is a train leaving for Brest at midnight. We'll be waiting at the gate. We'll even have a passport for you. You're now Henri Duval.'

'And where does this train take me?'

'Overnight to Brittany, where a private plane waits to bring you to London.'

'It's so simple it could work.'

'It will work,' Roper cut in.

'There is only one flaw. I am egotistical enough to assume that Dillon and Salter will recognize me. However, I haven't the slightest idea what they look like.'

Ferguson, exasperated, said, 'Of course they'll recognize you. Dammit, man, they'll approach you at the gate.'

'And whisper in my ear?'

Monica said, 'Shut up, the lot of you. It's perfectly simple. I'll go with them. Will that serve, Alex?'

'Good heavens, yes.'

'That's settled then.'

Ferguson said rather lamely, 'Well, I suppose it is.'

'Excellent, I'm very grateful, Monica,' Kurbsky said. 'I'm sure your two friends will look after you well.'

'Nothing to look after. It'll be a breeze.' She felt hugely elated and glanced at Dillon, who was smiling wryly.

'One more thing, Major Roper, my future, my anonymity is assured?'

'Believe me, old man, by the time we've finished with you, even you won't recognize who you are.'

Monica said, 'Alex, can I have your mobile number?'

'No, but I would like yours, Major Roper. At this stage in the game it's essential.'

'Absolutely.' Roper gave it to him. 'Take care.'

'But I always do,' Kurbsky clicked off and there was only silence.

LONDON

PARIS

6

In London, the Embassy of the Russian Federation was situated in Kensington Palace Gardens. There was a safe house close by where Boris Luhzkov had privileged quarters, and Bounine, now a major, was also well looked after. Included in all this were the joys of Kensington High Street and the pub on the other side. It was just after noon on Tuesday when Bounine went out through the main gate, waited for a break in the traffic, and darted across to keep a lunch appointment with Luhzkov.

Luhzkov had a favourite window seat and was reading the early edition of the *Evening Standard*. 'So there you are,' he said. 'How are you finding it?'

'A posting to London at last,' Bounine said. 'I like it very well.' He turned as a young waitress approached. 'A large vodka, please.'

Luhzkov swallowed the rest of his wine and gave her the glass. 'Another for me and two shepherd's pies.' He folded the newspaper. 'Always read the *Standard*, it's an institution, and almost anything on the menu here is excellent. This city is a spy's heaven, Yuri. At least twenty-four GRU people are here, posing as something else, of course. To be frank, nobody wants to go home from a London posting. What was Dublin like?'

'Great city and great people. The problem was that the ambassador wanted me not only to act like a commercial attaché – but be one.'

'What a bore. Still, life has taken on a new meaning for you now. This Kurbsky business. Very special indeed. A great opportunity for both of us.'

'What's our next move?'

'Not ours, Kurbsky's. Right about now, his Falcon is leaving the Motherland for Paris.'

His mobile trembled in his shirt pocket and he answered. 'Alexander, my friend, how are you?'

'As good as I'll ever be. Just taking off from Moscow. How are you and Yuri settling in?'

'He can't believe his luck. We're enjoying lunch in my favourite pub across the street from the Embassy.'

'Good for you, and now to business. You're aware that idiot Gregorovich informed me we would be staying at the Ritz because the Ministry did not want to shame the Motherland by its frugality. Naturally, the lads are rather worked up at the prospect of French chambermaids.'

'To say that I seriously doubt the competence of Ivanov, Kokonin and Burlaka is putting it mildly, and the chamber-maids they lust after will probably turn out to be Polish. I've given young Ivanov my personal mobile number so that he may call me at any time, if he has a problem. So what have Ferguson's people got planned?'

'I return to the hotel after the Elysée Palace affair is over. By then it will be late, so I retire to bed, having an early start for Moscow in the morning. As usual, I'll have one of the lads sitting on guard in the sitting room by the suite. I'm to deal with him.'

'Permanently?'

'That would seem extreme. Only if it's necessary.'

'And then?' Kurbsky told him of the train to Brittany, and Luhzkov said, 'Nice and simple. Dillon and Salter are very good, but I suppose the woman could complicate things.'

'Not really. It should all be perfectly straightforward. Let's get one thing clear. When I get to London safely and find myself in Ferguson's hands, I'm going to go with the flow, step-by-step, and evaluate what they've worked out for me. I won't be calling you every five minutes, and if I turn my phone off, you'll just have to accept that. By the way, I've turned off my recording facility.'

'I'd rather you didn't do that.'

'Too bad, Colonel. I'll be in touch when I have something to say.'

The line went silent. Luhzkov said, 'The bastard.'

Bounine looked bewildered. 'Something wrong?'

'Very much so. Kurbsky is suddenly turning awkward.'

He shook his head. 'I'm beginning to get a bad feeling about this whole business.'

At Holland Park, Roper was having a sandwich around ten o'clock in the evening when Dillon and Monica called in.

'Good film?' Roper asked.

'Not bad.' Dillon helped her off with her coat.

'We thought we'd have a drink with you on the way home,' she told him.

'Home, is it?' Roper said, as she sat beside him and Dillon went to the ice box and got a bottle of champagne. 'You're almost becoming a family man, Dillon.'

'Get stuffed,' Dillon said amiably, and poured. 'What's happening?'

'Kurbsky's on the fourth floor of the Ritz, his suite interconnecting with a bedroom next door. Two other separate rooms along the corridor. I've got some interiors, restaurants, bars and so on up there.' He gestured at the screens. 'Have a look. They've been having dinner in the main dining room.'

'How do you know that?' Monica asked.

'We've got an asset at the Ritz.'

'What do you mean?'

'An asset is a reliable source whom you pay for information in our game. This one is on the concierge staff. Very junior, but okay for general information. Burlaka and Kokonin have gone to a strip joint in Montmartre. Kurbsky booked the car for them. My information is very recent. He's in the bar with Ivanov.'

'So Ivanov has missed the joys of the strip show?'

'Rules of the game. One of them must be with Kurbsky at all times.'

'What a shame.' She accepted the glass of champagne from Dillon.

'Just to complicate things, Ivanov and his chums are booked in under false names. It's common practice for GRU operatives under cover on foreign soil.'

Monica sighed. 'I don't know how you keep up with it all, and I'm sorry for Ivanov, or whatever you call him, missing out on all the fun.'

In fact, it wasn't strictly true, for Ivanov had just had a most charming surprise. He'd gone upstairs with Kurbsky, who'd decided to retire to his suite early. Kurbsky unlocked the door of his suite and entered. Ivanov was going to follow him, when the door of his room, the interconnecting one, opened and a young woman, blonde and more than presentable, in the uniform of a chambermaid, appeared, carrying a few crumpled sheets.

One of the reasons he had been chosen for the assignment was that he spoke reasonable French. He said, 'Hello, is there a problem?'

She answered him in Russian. 'I'm Ukrainian. Call me Olga. I do night shifts only here, but it's the Ritz and the money's good and I get to meet interesting people, like you for instance. I know all about you and your boss, in from Moscow.'

There was a cheeky insolence to her and Ivanov said, 'What's the problem?'

'The day maid, a bitch from Warsaw called Anya, has made a disgusting mess of the bed, so I've got to change it fast, because if the supervisor finds out, I'll get sacked. Is it okay?'

'Of course it is.' He was excited, and then she looked beyond him, which made him turn and there was Kurbsky leaning in his doorway, arms folded, smiling slightly.

'You appear to be in control of the situation. I'll leave you to it.' He moved back and closed his door.

Ivanov went into his bedroom, which was incredibly elegant by the standards he was used to. There was a four-poster bed, a desk on one side of the room, a reasonable seating area on the other with two comfortable easy chairs and a wardrobe area beside the connecting door to Kurbsky's suite.

He was aroused, no question of that, and went and sat by the window, got himself a vodka miniature from the room bar and waited. She returned with fresh sheets and attacked the bed and Ivanov watched as she stretched and turned, her skirt rising over her thighs as she leaned to smooth the sheets.

He ran a hand up her right leg. She straightened. 'Now, that is naughty.'

He stood, his hands all over her, turning her, kissing her passionately. She responded, but when he started to make free with his hands, she said, 'No, not now, I've got things to do. Later, I'll see you later.'

He pulled away. 'Yes, I'm being silly. I've got to go next door for a while.'

'Is he a queer or something?'

'Don't be stupid. I'm supposed to guard him from a chair in the sitting room. It's orders. He's a very important man.'

'So you sit here all night?'

'Well, no. It's a shift system with the other two, but they've gone out on the town at the moment.'

'Well, you'd better hope they get back in good condition so they can do their shift. I'm on till eight in the morning. Who knows?'

She plumped the pillows, turned down a corner of the duvet, patted his face and walked out.

Ivanov took a deep breath, got up, knocked on the connecting door, opened it and walked into Kurbsky's sitting room. There was no sign of him, although the television was on. Kurbsky appeared in pyjamas, wearing a hotel bathrobe.

'I said the chambermaids at the Ritz would excite you.'

'She's a Ukrainian called Olga.'

Kurbsky was amused. 'For some reason, I find that very funny. You poor bastard, duty before a good shag. I admire you. Go, get a drink from my bar and watch television. I'm for bed.'

Ivanov did as he was told, had another vodka and then another, caught by an old movie about French paratroopers in the Algerian War. Finally, he fell asleep in the armchair and came awake to find it was half-past two. He went into the bathroom and splashed his face, then went and listened at the bedroom door. Everything was still, so he let himself out into the quiet corridor and tapped on Kokonin's door. There was no response and neither was there from Burlaka. He was bitterly angry, and then a staff door marked *Service* opened and Olga appeared.

'Looking for your friends? They arrived back an hour ago, drunken pigs both of them. They had to have a couple of porters bring them up and help them into their rooms. One was sick in his bathroom. The porters had to do a cleaning-up job. I've got a pass key if you want to take a look.'

'Yes, I would, if you don't mind.'

In spite of the porters' good work, there was a whiff of vomit in Kokonin's room. Ivanov got out quickly and she let him into the next room, where Burlaka sprawled on his bed half-naked, snoring hugely.

'Bastards,' Ivanov said. 'A disgrace to the uniform. I hope they've caught the pox.'

It was very quiet there in the corridor at that time in the morning. He felt awkward and helpless and it showed. She said, 'Poor old boy.' She kissed him briefly.

'Careful, we're probably on CCTV,' he told her.

'Not on this section of the corridor.' She took his hand. 'Let me show you something.'

She opened the door marked *Service* and he saw that it was a small room, shelved and stacked with bedding of every kind. 'It's nice in here, nice and warm, and cut off from every-thing, don't you agree?'

When she closed the door, the light faded to a red glow

and she was a creature of infinite mystery as she pushed him back on to a bolt of duvets, hoisted her uniform skirt and straddled him. Her hands opened things up expertly and it occurred to him that she had probably done this before and in the same place, but he didn't care, didn't care at all, and he simply lay there, allowing her to ride him.

And when it was over and she stood there adjusting her dress, he got up and tried to embrace her at the door and she pushed him away. 'Oh, no, you've had your ration. Anyway, you're not leaving till Thursday morning.'

'That's true.'

'I've got a split shift tomorrow, half in the afternoon, half at night. So I don't start till eleven. Sort your friends out over the guarding business and maybe I'll sneak into your room.'

He was thrilled and showed it. 'I'll fix it, I promise you, they'll have to do as they're told, especially after tonight.'

She opened the door, led the way out and he went back to the suite and let himself in. All was quiet and he tiptoed through to his room, leaving the door open, took off his jacket and shoes and lay on the bed, suddenly conscious that he'd never been so happy in his life, smiled and fell asleep.

Dillon spent the night with Monica at Dorset Street and they drove out to Farley Field together in his Mini. Ten o'clock was the departure time for the flight to Paris, and Ferguson had come to see them off, as Harry had with Billy. Lacey and Parry wore the kind of navy blue uniforms that pilots did the world over with a little gold braid to sharpen it up. It wasn't a good morning, bad March weather, and they stood under the golfing umbrellas that Lacey had produced, and chatted.

'What can I say?' Ferguson smiled. 'It should be an easy one. You'll be back before you know it. That's when the really important part of the job starts, the transformation of Alexander Kurbsky.'

Lacey led the way to the Chieftain, where Parry was already at the controls, and Ferguson and Harry walked with him. Monica went first, then Billy. Ferguson said to Dillon, 'Paul Bleriot is waiting at Charles de Gaulle. He'll put you up, provide everything you need. A good man. You can depend on him.'

Dillon ducked in and sat on the other side of the aisle from Monica opposite Billy, and Lacey closed the Airstair door and joined Parry in the cockpit.

'Who is Bleriot?' Monica asked.

'Very old chum of Ferguson's. He's his man in Paris when you need a helping hand.'

'Such as?'

'You'll see.' He grinned at Billy. 'Check that bar box, Billy, and see if they've slipped half a bottle of champagne in.'

Which they had and Billy opened it and poured it into plastic cups. 'So elegant,' Monica said.

'Just like a picnic.' Billy opened half a bottle of water.

'Well, let's hope it stays a picnic,' Dillon toasted them. 'To us.'

* * *

The flight was uneventful. The Chieftain landed and taxied to the private section of the airport, where they were offloaded. Parry stayed at the controls and Lacey saw them out.

'St Denis tomorrow,' he said and heaved up the airstair door.

They had light luggage only, but a porter insisted on earning his tip by carrying it on a trolley to security and then out to the pleasant-looking man in his sixties wearing a tweed cap and an old leather coat. His eyes were very blue and he smiled a lot.

'Lady Starling, a sincere pleasure. I've always been enchanted by beauty and brains.'

'Good heavens, you are a charmer.' He took her hand and kissed it.

'I feel as if I know you all, having had your pictures thoughtfully faxed to me by my friend Charles. You already seem like old friends. I have a suitable vehicle waiting.' He nodded to the porter and led the way out to a Renault station wagon in the car park. The porter loaded the luggage, took his tip and went off.

'Where to now?' Dillon asked.

'I have a club restaurant on the Seine. I thought you could spend the day with me. I've no idea why you're here and I don't want to know. Let's keep it that way.'

La Belle Aurore his place was called, quite charming and close to the Quai St Bernard, with a fine view of the Notre

Dame. There was a basin for moorings close at hand, quite a few motor cruisers with winter covers on them, and a row of barges in which people lived.

'The red one is mine,' Bleriot led the way along a narrow gangway and they boarded and followed him below. It looked like it had everything that was needed for a comfortable life, an enormous stateroom running into an open kitchen area at one end, a shower room and two bedrooms at the other.

'Yours for the day, my friends. Freshen up and then we'll have a lunch in the restaurant, but first, a present for you from Charles Ferguson.' He unlocked a cupboard, took out a Gladstone bag and put it down on the large coffee table in the centre of the stateroom and said to Dillon, 'Yours, I believe?'

Dillon opened it and discovered two Walthers with silencers and a Colt .25, also with silencer, which he handed to Monica. 'How thoughtful of Ferguson. No good-looking woman should be without one, that's what I always say. I hope it's not too heavy for your handbag.'

'If you're being a male chauvinist pig, Sean Dillon, it doesn't suit you. I would remind you that I've used a Colt .25, and quite effectively, as you well know.'

'Don't let him get to you, Monica,' Billy said, as he checked a Walther. 'I don't think we're into a shooting war this time.'

'Nothing, my friends, is ever certain in this life,' Paul Bleriot said. 'So let's go and have a drink at *La Belle Aurore*, and you can decide how you would like to fill your day.'

*   *   *

At the Ritz Hotel, Kurbsky was still having breakfast in the suite with Ivanov when he received a request for an audience from the duty manager.

'May I ask why?' Kurbsky said.

'I deeply regret to inform you, Monsieur Kurbsky, it concerns irregularities in the behaviour of your companions.'

'Indeed,' Kurbsky said. 'Well, we can't have that. Come on up.' He turned to Ivanov. 'Trouble with the management about my companions? What's been going on?'

'The two of them were so drunk they had to be put to bed by porters. One vomited in his bathroom.'

'How delightful,' Kurbsky said. 'I've always said, put a peasant in uniform and he's still a peasant. It hardly covers the Russian Federation with glory.' The doorbell rang. 'Answer it.'

The manager was so apologetic that it irritated Kurbsky immensely. 'Of course their behaviour doesn't meet the standards the Ritz expects. It doesn't meet the standards I expect. They will be dealt with appropriately when we return to Moscow. As I'm due at the Elysée Palace this evening, I must request your indulgence. We are leaving in the morning, as you know.'

'I apologize for having to bring this to your attention, Monsieur, as I know you are to receive the Legion of Honour from our President this evening.'

Kurbsky felt like saying, 'So what?' but contented himself with, 'Your consideration has been all that I would have expected from the Ritz.' The manager bowed himself out, and Kurbsky said to Ivanov, 'In here now, both of them, and don't bother to dress. Bathrobes will do.'

Walking dead men was an apt description. They both looked dreadful and were experiencing the most appalling hangovers. They stood there in their robes, obviously very ill indeed.

Kurbsky said, 'You are officers in the GRU, on assignment abroad, in one of the world's greatest cities. You are representing your country. You are supposed to be showing some pride in the Motherland, and what do you do? Disgrace yourselves, disgrace Russia. You might as well have stood there and urinated against a wall in the Champs Élysées and, frankly, you are not fit to accompany me to the Palace this evening.'

'Please, sir, I don't know what happened,' Burlaka croaked. 'I think there was something in my drink.'

'The oldest excuse in the world. Get out of my sight, get yourselves downstairs to the Sports Club. See what the sauna and steam room can achieve.'

They backed out. Ivanov said, 'What happens for the rest of the day?'

'Well, I've no intention of sitting here on my backside, and according to the rules, you've got to accompany me, which will probably bore you to death. I like art, great art, so the Louvre is a must. I might just allow you a cruise on the Seine or a trip up the Eiffel Tower, but that's it.'

*   *   *

'Four first-class tickets on the midnight train for Brest from the Gare du Nord. They're private compartments linked by a door. Each compartment takes two in the sense that you can pull two bunk beds down, but with the connecting door, it will suffice for a party of four. Here are the tickets.'

Bleriot put them on the table and Monica examined them. 'Excellent. We'll travel in style. There is a restaurant car, I presume?'

'Yes. I know the train well. It has a kind of faded splendour and the rolling stock is charming, but old. For example, there is a toilet at each end of the corridor, nothing private.'

'Hardly the end of the world,' Monica said. She turned to Dillon. 'So, what do we do now?'

'Go for a walk, see the sights. Does that suit you, Billy?'

'Absolutely.'

'Remember you may use my barge as much as you want. There's a lot of time to fill before your train leaves, and you'll need a couple of the restaurant umbrellas. It's not exactly the best time of the year to go walking by the Seine. I've things to do. I'll see you later.' Bleriot got up and went.

'There's always the Louvre, the Eiffel Tower, Notre Dame.'

'Been there, done that,' Monica said. 'What about you, Sean?'

'My dear girl, I used to live in this great city years ago, in the days of my wicked past. I even had a barge like Bleriot's.' He turned to Billy. 'What about you?'

'I've never been to Paris, the Louvre isn't my cup of tea, and I'm not into cathedrals. The Eiffel Tower, though, is something I always wondered about when I was a kid.'

'Right,' Dillon said. 'We'll get a cab and go. Afterwards, I'll take you somewhere special.'

They didn't know that they had missed Kurbsky and Ivanov by only forty minutes at the top of the Eiffel Tower. In any case, the visit was something of a non-event because of the rain mixed with mist which draped itself across the city.

'I enjoyed Blackpool Tower more,' Billy said, as they descended in the lift.

'Spoken like a true Englishman,' Dillon told him, approached a taxi rank and in rapid and fluent French told the driver to take them to Quai de Montebello opposite the Ile de la Cité.

'Now what?' Billy demanded.

'Wait and see.'

A short while later, they parked at the side of a cobbled quay. 'What's all this?' Monica asked, getting out and putting up an umbrella.

'*Bateaux Mouches*,' Dillon told her. 'Floating restaurants. Sail up the river and have a meal and a bottle of wine, see the sights. It's a regular thing. They follow a timetable.'

'In this bloody weather,' Billy said.

'If you notice, there are ample deck awnings, and you can sit inside if you prefer.'

'Don't be a grouch, Billy, it looks like fun,' Monica told him.

Two deck hands were about to pull up the gangway, but paused to let them on board. A waiter approached, smiling.

'Will you be dining?'

'If it's not too late for lunch,' Dillon answered in French.

'Of course, Monsieur, we never close. Not too many customers today. It's the time of the year and the weather. Choose where you would like to sit and I will start with a drink for you.'

They went up to the upper deck, but the sides were open and the rain was blowing in, so they went back down and found a nice table by the stern window so they could see all the sights as they passed. Dillon and Monica had champagne, grilled Dover sole and Lyonnaise potatoes, Billy a large bowl of bouillabaisse.

'I've got to give it to you, Dillon,' Billy said. 'This stew is the business. I'm really enjoying the whole thing. Notre Dame looks great up there, the barges. It's nearly as good as the Thames.'

Monica patted his hand. 'There's no answer to that. My fish was marvellous. All I'd like now would be coffee.'

The waiter, hovering, started to clear the plates. 'At once, madame.'

Dillon lit a cigarette, passed it to her and lit another. 'They're French,' he said. 'Nobody's going to throw us off the boat.'

'How do you think things are going?' Billy said. 'With Kurbsky?'

'Kurbsky seemed confident in his ability to handle the guard in his room tonight,' said Dillon. 'Considering his military experience, he should be.'

'I suppose I'm just nervous because we've got nothing to do except wait for him at the gate for that midnight train at the Gare du Nord,' Billy said.

The waiter brought coffee, Billy asked for English breakfast tea and Dillon a Bushmills whiskey. Monica said, 'I'm still fascinated by the whole venture, the future. I can't get my head round what's supposed to happen to Kurbsky.'

'Maybe he can't either,' Billy said. 'We'll just have to wait and see.'

Kurbsky had been slightly surprised to discover that the dress for the ceremony was not black tie. The new President had decided to open things up, and business suits were the order of the day. It was five-thirty when Kurbsky finished dressing and examined himself in the mirror in the bedroom wardrobe. Very much as he had done in New York, he wore black and had to confess it looked good. He went and kicked on the door of the connecting room, then went and found his jacket.

Ivanov came in. 'You wanted me?'

'How are they?'

'Obviously better than they were. A long hard day.'

'Bring them in.'

Ivanov departed, Kurbsky pulled his jacket on, fixed his cuffs, checking himself in the sitting room mirror. Burlaka and Kokonin were obviously revived by the day's regime, had tried hard with their appearance, and he knew from what Ivanov had told him, that they had put themselves in the hands of the hotel's barber.

'Have you had a good day?'

They looked hunted and didn't seem to know what to say. It was Ivanov who answered for them. 'They behaved stupidly, but they've learned their lesson. It won't happen again.'

Kokonin said, 'Never, I swear it.'

'In the circumstances, I've decided not to take any further action in this matter,' Kurbsky said, then to Ivanov, 'You will make no report of the affair when we return to Moscow.'

Their relief was immediate. 'Thank you, Comrade,' they chorused.

Kurbsky wondered how they'd feel when they discovered he'd done a runner. It'd be a blot on their records sufficient to ruin any prospects of advancement in their chosen careers. What would they think of Alexander Kurbsky then?

He said, 'Come down to the bar. I'll buy you a drink.' They were astonished. 'Come on, we haven't got time to waste.' He opened the door and went out.

They stood at the magnificent bar and he ordered four vodkas and said, 'You can't all come with me to the ceremony. Only one aide is allowed to accompany me inside, so two of you have to wait in the limousines. In the circumstances, you will understand that I'm choosing Ivanov.'

'Of course, Comrade,' Burlaka said gamely and glanced at Kokonin.

'And the fact that Ivanov spent the whole night obeying my orders and guarding me was, I believe, detrimental to his love life. It won't be the same tonight. You two must sort it out when we get back.'

They nodded almost eagerly, the four vodkas appeared before them. Kurbsky raised his in a toast and surprised them by not mentioning himself.

'To the Motherland, which bred me, and to Vladimir Putin, Prime Minister of the Russian Federation.'

He emptied his glass and turned it upside down on the bar and said to Ivanov, 'We'll go now. There is a Mercedes due from the Embassy. Speak to the concierge.' He led the way out.

At the Elysée Palace, they were checked at the main gate and passed through to the courtyard and parking area. Kurbsky and Ivanov left the others and joined a sizeable crowd of people pushing towards the main doors of the palace.

All life was there, a mixture of uniforms and civilian attire, and the palace guards in their gorgeous outfits. There was a great hubbub as they went in, chandeliers sparkling over the incredible opulence of it all. A colonel in the dress uniform of the Foreign Legion standing at the entrance to a cordoned-off section of the crowd saw Kurbsky and beckoned.

When Kurbsky approached, he said in English, 'Mr Kurbsky, this is an honour. We've been worried – your Embassy was supposed to be in touch an hour ago to confirm you were on the way. It's a good thing I saw you. Is this your aide?'

'Yes, Lieutenant Ivanov.'

'Right, he'll be seated in one of the three back rows. You'll be in the front row, of course.' He offered Kurbsky an embossed card. 'Give this to the usher up there.'

Ivanov said, 'Good luck, Comrade.'

Kurbsky went along the aisle and offered the card to some sort of major-domo who examined it and led him to his seat, which was at the very end of the front row on the right. It meant that Kurbsky only had the person on his left to make small talk with. The man was very old and wrinkled with a shock of white hair.

He smiled when the man looked sideways at him and spoke in German, which unfortunately was not one of Kurbsky's languages. He said something unintelligible, so Kurbsky said, 'Hello, how are you?' in Russian.

He seemed alarmed and Kurbsky tried English. The old man immediately looked wise and said, 'Who are you?' very slowly, as if taking his time over each word.

'Alexander Kurbsky.'

'Why are you here?'

'To receive the Legion of Honour.'

'What for, what do you do?'

'I write books. I'm a novelist.'

There was a nod of puzzlement. 'I have never heard of you.'

Kurbsky laughed out loud and people turned to look. 'What about you?' he asked. 'Why are you here?'

'For the Legion of Honour. My name is Hans Kruger.'

'And what do you do?'

'I'm a nuclear physicist.'

'Well, that's all right. I haven't heard of you either.'

And then, voices hushed, there was a fanfare of trumpets and the proceedings began.

It took a long time and there were speeches and more speeches that numbed the mind as well as the backside, as the whole thing dragged on. Recipients were called in turn, and it all began to be slightly reminiscent of a conveyor belt, and Kurbsky wasn't even aware of the magic moment. He certainly was there when the President pinned on the insignia of the Legion of Honour and words were said, but what they were he could never be sure.

And then it was all over. The President moved on and Kurbsky went with the flow, the crowd of people searching for the food. Ivanov was tugging his sleeve. 'Wonderful. Great stuff.'

'You know something, I'm not certain you and I have experienced the same affair. What's the time?' He glanced at his watch. 'Good God, it's half-past nine already. Where have I been?' He shook his head. 'Where's the buffet?'

Ivanov had it all worked out and led the way. At that point, Kurbsky realized he was clutching a box covered in Moroccan leather in his right hand and had been for some time. He looked at it, puzzled, then realized what it was and opened it, unpinned the Legion of Honour from his lapel and put it inside.

'You shouldn't take it off, you should wear it with pride,' Ivanov said, but Kurbsky put it in his pocket and they pushed through the crowds helping themselves at the buffet, got plates and took their turn. It was hardly worth it, for people, as people do in crowds, were tending to become difficult. He managed a few sausage rolls, then said to Ivanov, 'I've had enough. Let's have a drink.'

They found the champagne bar and had a glass and the Foreign Legion colonel found them. 'Where is it, you haven't lost it already?'

'No, it's in my pocket.'

The colonel took a glass of champagne himself. 'Mind you, I suppose it's just another gong to you. You must have earned plenty.'

'And you,' Kurbsky said politely.

'Do you ever wonder what it's all about?'

'Every day of my life.' Kurbsky emptied the second glass of champagne Ivanov had handed him and said, 'Goodnight, it's been a sincere sensation.' He patted the colonel on the shoulder and turned to Ivanov. 'Let's go.'

They found the Mercedes and the others and left, reaching the Ritz at ten thirty. He dismissed the driver and went inside. Ivanov said, 'A drink, perhaps?'

'No, I've had enough. To be frank, I want my bed. If two

of you lads want to have something, feel free, but I'm going to the suite. Who's coming with me?'

Ivanov helped things along, impatient for the joys of Olga to come. 'It's been a big night and one I'll always remember, but I'm ready for bed now, too.'

Kokonin said, 'Well, in the circumstances, I'll take the first half of the night. If that's all right with you?' he queried Kurbsky.

'Fine by me, we'll go up then.' They all got into the lift and went up together.

In the suite, Kurbsky went to his bedroom and left Kokonin to settle himself in the sitting room. He decided against locking the double door leading into Ivanov's room because if Ivanov wanted to see him for some reason, finding the door locked might give him pause for thought.

The television was on in the sitting room, he was aware of that, and opened the door of the bedroom a crack to listen. He was all worked up and impatient. He checked his watch and saw it was ten forty-five. If he was early at the station, what did it matter? It was a waste of time and opportunity to wait like this. He took his jacket off and put the bathrobe on and walked out into the sitting room. Kokonin had a movie on and glanced up in surprise.

He started to move and Kurbsky said, 'Don't get up, I just want something from the room bar.'

Kokonin eased down again, Kurbsky passed behind him, turned and delivered a rabbit punch to the neck with extended knuckles, then, as Kokonin moaned, held him with one hand

and squeezed his thumb into the carotid artery, until Kokonin slouched over the arm of the big easy chair.

Kurbsky darted into the bedroom, tearing off the bathrobe, revealing a silenced Walther in a belt clip at the small of his back. He pulled on his jacket, took his leather coat out of the wardrobe, went to the door of the suite and opened it. The corridor was quiet. He moved out, locked the door and was at the door opening to the stairway in seconds. Four flights down and he'd never descended stairs so quickly in his life. He emerged into the foyer and walked straight out of the hotel door. It was raining hard now, but there was the taxi rank.

At that moment, Olga, with thoughts of her split shift starting at eleven and Ivanov waiting, was hurrying to the staff door and, seeing Kurbsky paused in the shadows, felt puzzled. The doorman offered him his umbrella.

'Taxi, sir, where to?' They walked to the first cab.

'Gare du Nord,' Kurbsky said.

'And which gate, sir?'

'Midnight Express to Brest.'

'That would be gate three,' the porter told the driver, opening the door for Kurbsky and accepting the tip he gave him.

The taxi drove away and Olga, still puzzled, went in through the staff entrance and clocked in for her shift.

In the taxi, Kurbsky took out his mobile and called Monica. She was already on the train, sitting in one of the private compartments with Dillon and Billy.

'Alex, where are you? Are you okay?'

'I'm on my way in a taxi. Everything's worked like a charm. I know I'm early, but I couldn't wait.'

'I don't think that matters. We'll see you soon.'

She clicked off, smiling hugely at Dillon and Billy. 'He's on his way.'

'Well, that's great,' Dillon said. 'We'll go and meet him together. Let's get moving.'

THE MIDNIGHT

EXPRESS

7

At the Ritz, Olga clocked in, then went to the women's staff room, opened her locker, undressed and changed into staff uniform. She reported to the supervisor and then went up to her station on the fourth floor. It was just after eleven when she went into the linen room, still puzzled about Kurbsky. Then she wondered about Ivanov. Was he even there? There was one way to find out. She went and knocked on his door lightly, then used her pass key.

He was lying on the bed, jacket off, propped up against pillows, watching television, and sat up with a smile, swinging his feet to the floor.

'I've been waiting for you.' He took a quick step, enfolded her in his arms and kissed her passionately. She pulled away.

'When I saw your boss leave the hotel, I wondered what was going on. I wasn't even sure you'd be here.'

'What are you talking about?'

'Kurbsky. I saw him getting a taxi downstairs on my way in.'

He shook his head. 'But that's impossible.'

'It was him, all right. Ask the doorman. He got him the taxi. It was to the Gare du Nord. I heard quite clearly. The porter asked which gate, and your boss said he wanted the Midnight Express to Brest, and the porter said gate three.'

Ivanov turned, ran to the interconnecting door to the suite, opened it and rushed in. Kokonin was leaning over in the chair, holding his head in his hands and groaning. Ivanov pulled his hands away and shook him.

'What happened?'

'I was watching television. He came in, said he wanted a drink from the room bar and passed behind me. He must have punched me or something. I just blacked out. I only opened my eyes a minute or so ago. Where is he?'

'Gone. Cleared off. Olga here saw him leaving the hotel and getting a taxi.' He turned to Olga, who stood in the doorway. 'Get my friend from his room. If he's undressed, tell him to get his clothes on again and come and join us.'

'What is it?' she demanded. 'What in the hell has happened?'

'My boss has decided to defect, that's what's happened, and if he gets away with it, me and my friends might as well defect, too, because if we go back to Moscow without him, we'll end up in some gulag in Siberia. Go and get the other guy.'

She went, and Ivanov pushed Kokonin into the bathroom. 'Take your shirt off quickly. Come on, I'll give you one of my shirts. You haven't got time for a full shower, but a few minutes with your head under the cold spray will help.' He opened the shower door and turned it on ice cold. Kokonin did as he was told, leaning in and then withdrawing and towelling himself dry. Ivanov went and got a fresh shirt for him, and as he was pulling it on, Olga came back.

'Your other pal was in his pyjamas, but he's dressing as fast as he can. Is this bad for you?'

'Not if we can get him back.'

'Do you think that's possible?'

He glanced at his watch. 'Eleven fifteen and the train leaves at midnight. How long does it take to reach the Gare du Nord?'

'I think maybe fifteen or twenty minutes.'

'We could make it then.' There was a knock at the door and Burlaka appeared. 'Could someone explain what the hell is going on?'

Kokonin came out of the bathroom. 'I'm okay now.'

Ivanov said to Burlaka, 'Get your raincoats and meet me at the lift.' They went out obediently. He pulled Olga over. 'I suppose we'll always have the linen room to remember.' He kissed her, then went into his bedroom and found his coat and old slouch hat. She followed him and he said, 'We'll leave everything in our rooms. The Embassy will see to them, and if I were you, I'd keep your mouth shut.'

She followed him out into the corridor. 'You don't have to tell me. Do you really think you can get him back?'

'I'm not sure, but if we can get close enough to kill the bastard, that would be just as good.'

He turned and ran to the lift where Kokonin was holding the door, and it closed on him. Olga stood there, thinking about him. A nice boy and she'd liked him, but, so what? Life could be cruel sometimes, but the last thing she needed was any kind of trouble with Russian intelligence. She turned and went into the linen cupboard and got on with her work.

Kurbsky found them waiting outside the gate, the sight of Monica like an old friend. She came towards him, glowing, hands reaching out. 'Alex, this is wonderful.' She kissed him on both cheeks and hugged him fiercely. 'Are you all right?'

'Never better. Introduce me to your friends.'

Which she did. Dillon said, 'We have plenty of time, forty minutes. Let's have you straight on board and we'll get you a drink. I think you've earned it. Was it difficult?'

'Not at all. Astonishingly simple.'

They walked along the platform, station noises echoing, people's voices sounding strangely distorted, a whistle in the distance, a train across the platform starting up and moving forward.

'Everybody seems to be going somewhere,' Kurbsky said.

'Well, you certainly are. Just follow me.' She got into the coach and he went after her.

Billy paused as Dillon made a call on his mobile, which Roper received in Holland Park. 'Our package has arrived safely. Just under half an hour or so, and we'll be off.'

'Did he kill anybody?' Roper asked.

'Not that he mentioned.'

Ivanov had promised the taxi driver double fare, which worked in spite of the dark and the rain. They reached Gare du Nord with fifteen minutes to spare and Ivanov led the way to the nearest ticket window and slapped his credit card down.

'The train is quite full, gentlemen,' the young woman said. 'All first class has gone.'

'That's OK,' Ivanov told her. 'Anything will do.'

'I can manage three club car seats, so you can at least have refreshments, but you'll have to sit up for the night.'

Within five minutes, they were passing through the gate and starting along the platform. Ivanov pulled his black hat down over his eyes. 'You two keep to the other side of the platform, I'll scan the windows of the train. I'll join you further along.'

It was actually easier than he thought it would be. The three first class coaches were at the front behind the engine, with a fourth that was the bar and restaurant. Walking past, his head slightly averted, Ivanov found Kurbsky sitting opposite a good-looking woman, two men on the other side of them at a bar table. It was enough. He hurried back along the platform to Kokonin and Burlaka at the rear of the train.

'He's there, sitting with a woman and two men in the bar in first class. We'll board, find our seats and think this thing out.'

Over the champagne, Kurbsky went over the events of the evening with the others. He even found the Legion of Honour medal in its box and offered it to Monica for a look.

'A remarkable souvenir of today,' she said. 'What was it like, the award ceremony?'

'Crowded and noisy and bizarre. A very old white-haired nuclear physicist sitting next to me asked me what I did, and when I told him, he said he'd never heard of me, which brought me down to earth considerably. So much so that I found myself asking what in the hell I was doing there.'

'What about the Ritz?' Dillon asked. 'You said it was astonishingly simple.'

'Well, I didn't have to kill anyone. I had young Kokonin sitting on guard. I knocked him cold, an old unarmed combat trick, grabbed my coat and quite simply ran for it. I was being handed into a taxi by the doorman about four minutes later.' He smiled. 'The rest you know.'

The train was moving, gliding along, picking up a little speed as it left the station, a melancholy whistle echoing into the gloom.

'I love trains, especially at night,' Kurbsky said. 'I once did the Trans-Siberian all the way to Vladivostok. An amazing experience. I got some interesting poetry out of it.'

'I didn't know you wrote poetry,' Monica said.

'Bad poetry, I think, so I don't advertise it.' As if to prevent any further discussion on the matter, he said, 'I'd like to freshen up. Can we return to the compartment?'

'Of course,' Monica said. 'It has a pull-down basin to wash your face or shave, but no toilet. Those are at each end of the corridor.'

'I'm sure we'll get by.'

Dillon and Billy went first, Monica next and Kurbsky followed, and Ivanov and his friends watched through the glass door at the other end. 'Back to our seats now,' Ivanov said, and led the way to the club car at the rear of the train.

They had the end table, four chairs grouped around it, but the fourth was vacant. When the steward came with a drinks cart, they ordered half a bottle of vodka and ice. Ivanov heavily overtipped the man.

'We prefer privacy, my friends and I.'

'I take your point, Monsieur.' The steward produced a reserved notice, smiled and moved on with his cart.

'What are we going to do?' Kokonin demanded.

'Let's assess the situation. We've no idea who these three people with Kurbsky are,' Ivanov said. 'But they don't know who we are. Only Kurbsky does.'

Kokonin said, 'I don't see how we could do anything much on the train anyway. As long as Kurbsky stays up there in first class and we stay down here, we'll get by. We're armed, all three of us. That's in our favour. We can wait until they get off.'

Ivanov held up a timetable. 'I've found this in the seat pocket. The train doesn't go non-stop to Brest, it drops off at several places. Rennes, for example. They could get off anywhere.'

'Exactly, and maybe we wait for that,' Ivanov said. 'But I'm going to speak to Colonel Luhzkov and discuss it with him. He gave me his mobile number. I'll go into the toilet so no one can hear.'

Which he did, going to the one at the end of the coach and locking himself in.

In London, Luhzkov was in his quarters in Kensington Palace Gardens, preparing for bed, when he received the call. He listened intently as Ivanov explained the situation.

'It pains me to say this,' Ivanov said, 'but Kurbsky seems to have defected. He knocked Kokonin unconscious and fled the hotel. It was only by chance that the chambermaid servicing our rooms saw him getting into a taxi as she came on shift, and heard his destination. That led us to the Midnight Express to Brest. We're on the train now, and Kurbsky's in first class drinking with a woman and two men. He doesn't look like a prisoner.' Which Luhzkov could have confirmed, since he knew who the woman and the two men were.

There was no way he could pull Ivanov's coals out of the fire. He and his friends should have been left high and dry at the Ritz while Kurbsky disappeared into the night. The

British, of course, would expect Russian security to try to recover him, and they would take appropriate action. Knowing Dillon and Billy Salter as he did, Luhzkov knew the reckoning would be harsh.

He remembered Putin's words in Moscow. 'His defection must appear genuine at all times. His GRU minders in Paris should not be informed of the real facts. If they fall by the wayside, so be it.'

He took a deep breath and said to Ivanov, 'When they get off, follow them. That is all I can suggest. See where it leads you, then contact Major Gregorovich at the GRU safe house outside Moscow. Take care.'

He sat there, thinking about it. Starling, Salter and Dillon did not know Ivanov and the boys by sight, only Kurbsky did, so only he could alert the others to their presence on the train. But if Ivanov and the other two sat at the other end of the train for the entire journey, keeping out of the way, they'd be able to follow Kurbsky at leisure when their quarry left the train.

He had to alert Kurbsky, had no choice.

Kurbsky had his phone in his right trouser pocket on vibrate. Monica was reading a book. Dillon was reading *Paris Soir* at the other side of the table, and Billy was dozing, his head back against a pillow by the open door to the connecting apartment.

Kurbsky smiled at Monica, excused himself, got up and went to the lavatory at the end of the corridor, entered and locked the door. He answered the phone and Luhzkov said, 'Thank God you answered.'

'What is this? I told you I didn't want to speak to you every five minutes.'

'Shut up and listen.' Luhzkov explained quickly what had happened. 'So you see, my friend, Ivanov and his two chums are on the train with you, and they now think you a defector and a traitor to the Motherland.'

'Holy Mother of God,' Kurbsky said.

'What are you going to do?'

'I don't know. If I tell the others, they'd need an explanation as to how I knew.'

'You could say you'd taken a walk along the train and seen them.'

'And they hadn't seen me? Come on, get real, Boris.'

'Well, you'd better think of something, because if this screws up the whole operation, you'll not only be in deep shit, but your sister will be condemned to live out the rest of her days in the far north of Siberia.'

Kurbsky fought hard to control himself and kept his voice low. 'Damn you, don't threaten me.'

'Alex, I'm not. He's got me by the balls, too, our glorious Prime Minister. There's no either-or here. The great man hates being disappointed. He always gets his way. So what's it to be?'

'I don't seem to have much choice,' Kurbsky said. 'I'll speak to you again. Don't call me, I'll call you.'

He left the lavatory, moved along the corridor through the dining room and the coaches behind where most passengers were curled up in sleep. He was careful, paused at each connecting door and scanned the passengers inside, looking for his quarry, and finally reached the club car, and there they were at the far end. He withdrew and was approached by the head waiter as he went back through the restaurant car. There were only about a dozen people eating.

'Would you and your friends like a table, Monsieur?'

'I'm not sure. When is the next stop?'

'Belleville, Monsieur, about an hour and a quarter.'

'I'll see what my friends think.'

He returned to the compartment and found Monica asleep on one of the pull-down bunks, and Dillon and Billy with their heads down in the second compartment, so he picked up Monica's book, something to do with the Roman army in Britain which she'd written herself, went back to the restaurant car and took a table.

He had a sort of Russian breakfast, vodka, caviar, smoked salmon and herrings and strong black bread, more vodka and then black bitter tea. All this was provided with impeccable service. Monica's book was fascinating and made the meal a true experience.

The time had passed so quickly that when they started to slow, he was quite caught out, and then they were gradually stopping, and the head waiter said, 'Belleville, Monsieur.'

Kurbsky peered out. He saw only a small station building and platform and a few decaying warehouses. Some people had got off to walk around, stretching their legs, ambling between stacks of railway sleepers. And then Kokonin and Burlaka walked past, hands in pockets, chatting to each other.

There was a kind of inevitability to it and Kurbsky moved along, found an open door and went down the steps. They were over by a coppice of crowded trees and then they seemed to disappear. He hurried, half-running, went round a corner and found them standing at the edge of a deep ditch, half filled with water.

He was upon them before they realized he was there, pulled his Walther from the belt clip at the small of his back. Kokonin said, 'You!' and put a hand in his inside pocket. Kurbsky shot him between the eyes, the silenced Walther making a dull thud. He was blasted backwards and fell half over the edge of the ditch. Burlaka actually got his gun out, but too late, as Kurbsky did exactly the same to him as he had to Kokonin. He rolled first one, then the other, into the water, turned and walked away round the coppice, joining the few people getting back onto the train.

He returned to the restaurant car, and found the book where he had left it. The head waiter approached with the bill. Kurbsky paid him in Euros and tipped well. 'I'm obliged to you. It was excellent. When is the next stop?'

'Another hour, perhaps more, Monsieur – Rennes.'

Instead of returning to the compartment, he worked his way back to the club car and peered in. Ivanov was standing, talking to the car steward, upset. The steward was shrugging, obviously unable to satisfy him. So Kokonin and Burlaka had missed the train. Not his fault. They'd have to get the next one. That seemed to be the official attitude.

Kurbsky turned and went back. From the first day you put on a uniform, you had to accept you could die wearing it. He was fighting in a war of sorts, he seemed to have done so all his life. He should have had a little pity for the two dead men perhaps, but he'd used that all up in Afghanistan and Chechnya.

He didn't go in when he got back to the compartment, simply checked to see that his three companions were still resting, turned and started to make his way towards the rear of the train. It was time to finish the thing, whatever it took. The entire train seemed to be asleep, but for a passenger here or there with a magazine or a book.

After midnight, when anything is possible and death is in the air. It wasn't Shakespeare, he knew that, some minor writer from times past, not that it mattered. He had reached the club car. The car steward in his cramped booth was asleep and the passengers in their seats seemed well away, too. He walked along between the seats to where Ivanov sat by himself, eyes closed, head back, arms folded. Kurbsky slid into the opposite seat and Ivanov opened his eyes and nearly jumped out of his skin.

Kurbsky said softly, 'Don't say a word. You've been caught up in a matter of the highest secrecy, concerning the security of the State, we both have. Now keep your voice down.'

'What about Kokonin and Burlaka?' Ivanov whispered.

'Back at Belleville. I disarmed them and told them to run for it or else.'

'But why did you do this?'

'I am under orders, from Putin himself.' He stood up. 'We can't talk freely here. Come out on the viewing platform.'

He went and opened the door that gave on to the platform

with the ironwork rail: it was a spot very popular with smokers in these anti-cigarette times. Although there was a canopy, the rain blew in.

Ivanov said, 'We're going to get soaked. What the hell is going on?'

Kurbsky produced the silenced Walther, jammed the muzzle into him at close quarters and shot him in the heart. He lurched back, half-turning and fell head down over the rail. Kurbsky toppled him the rest of the way over, and the body was swept away in the darkness and rain. He replaced the Walther in his belt clip, his iron composure clicking in, and calmly worked his way up the aisle to the end, where the car steward still dozed in his booth.

After midnight, when anything is possible and death is in the air. It wouldn't go away, went round and round in his brain. He had killed three men without a hint of pity, but he'd have to put that behind him, as he had with so many others over the years. He was clear now to follow the future mapped out for him, however uncertain.

Back in first class, he went into the lavatory and called Luhzkov, who had not been able to sleep, waiting for news.

'It's done, Boris. I've killed all three.'

'Will there be repercussions?'

'I shouldn't imagine they'll be found for a while. Their bodies aren't on the train, if that's what you mean. By the time anybody finds them, we should be flying out from St Denis.'

'Did it give you any problem, Alex?'

'Boris, people like you, acting on behalf of the State, have sent people out to do your killing for years. When did you ever ask if it gave them a problem?'

He rang off, paused, and then called Roper.

Roper answered immediately. 'How are you? Dillon called just before the train left, saying you were in good hands. How's the trip so far?'

'It turned out to be rather lively.' Kurbsky started the lying now. The others were having a sleep and I went into the restaurant car for a bite to eat. We stopped at Belleville for fifteen minutes, a few people got off, and to my astonishment I saw Kokonin and Burlaka, two of my GRU minders, having a stroll.'

'How the hell did that happen?'

'Pure bad luck. I found out later some chambermaid saw me get into the taxi, heard where I was going, and told them. They got their act together and followed me to the station. They must have just caught the train.'

'So what did you do?'

'At Belleville? I slipped off the train, followed them to a suitable spot and braced them.'

'Which means what, exactly?'

'I shot them both, left them in a ditch and got back on board.'

'What about the third man?'

'Ivanov. When we got going again, I searched the train and found him in the club car. I think he thought they'd simply missed the train. I told him we were all victims of a complicated plot direct from Putin himself.' He lied again. 'When I asked him how he'd got on my tracks so quickly, he told me about the chambermaid.'

'And where did this confrontation take place?'

'On the viewing platform at the end of the train. It's a smokers' paradise these days, but not so much for him.'

'You killed him, too.'

'Of course, and put him over the rail. I had to, Roper, you can see that. Those GRU idiots would have cocked things up big-time. By the way, speaking of the GRU, has Boris Luhzkov turned up at the London Embassy yet?'

'So I hear,' Roper said. 'What were Dillon and Billy doing while all this was going on?'

'Sleeping the sleep of the righteous.'

'And it didn't occur to you that they might have appreciated the chance to join in?'

'You have a point, but there was Monica to consider, and frankly I thought it'd be more efficient if I took care of it myself. I'll leave you to break the news to Dillon.'

He left the lavatory and paused to look in at the compartment, where Monica was sitting up now and swinging her legs to the ground.

'Have you had a good trip?'

'At least I slept.' Sean and Billy were stirring next door. 'What about you?' she said.

'Trains and planes, I can never sleep on them,' he said. 'I had a great meal in the restaurant car and read your book on the Roman army in Britain.'

'And what was the verdict?'

'Wonderful. Action and passion, that's what I like. I'll go down and get a table for breakfast. I'll see you there.'

Billy was at the washbasin and Dillon had his mobile to his ear and looked serious, so Kurbsky got out fast.

Five o'clock and still dark outside, rain driving against the window. The head waiter provided the black bitter tea. 'Would you care for vodka with it, Monsieur?'

'Why not?' Dinner, breakfast – his time-sense was seriously out of joint. He swallowed some tea, knocked the vodka back, and examined the passport and papers Dillon had given him when he'd first boarded the train. Dillon arrived, still looking serious. Billy, on the other hand, was full of excitement.

'Three at one blow, Kurbsky! I always thought that was for flies on a slice of bread and jam.'

Dillon said, 'Damn it, Billy, this is serious.' He turned to Kurbsky, 'I understand discovering Kokonin and Burlaka was a shock, but you should have called us in. That's what we're here for.'

'Well, I didn't,' Kurbsky told him. 'I needed to act fast.'

'And Ivanov?'

'Look, I knew him, so I knew how to handle him. It's done now. How's Monica?'

'Upset,' Dillon said.

'She'll get over it,' Billy put in. 'She shot an IRA bastard dead in the Drumore affair, and she didn't have any trouble getting over that. Let's order breakfast.'

'I'll go and get her,' said Kurbsky. 'Would that be all right with you?'

'I don't own the lady,' Dillon told him.

'Tell the head waiter I'll have the same as I did before.'

She was standing at the washbasin in the compartment, looking in the mirror and applying her lipstick. 'Well, here I am,' he said. 'Are you angry with me?'

'Not any more. Let me just ask you: was it necessary?'

'They'd have tried to take me back by force, and it could have been very messy.'

She nodded. 'That makes sense. This venture you've embarked on, that we're all involved in, it was bound to bring demands and consequences we didn't perhaps anticipate.'

'You're right.'

'I know I am, Alex, and this may not be the last of them. But that's in the future. Right now, let's join the others for breakfast.' She brushed past him and led the way down the corridor.

They passed through Rennes and, twenty miles later, pulled up at St Denis, a small station in a pleasant market town. It was six-thirty, still that bad March weather, daylight now, a slate grey sky and the eternal rain. There was quite a press of people waiting to board, obviously going to Brest, the nearest big city.

Parry was waiting with an umbrella and approached them at once. 'I've got a car waiting with a driver. The airfield is eight miles from here, and we've had an order from General

Ferguson only an hour ago to bring our departure forward. I don't know what's up, but he wants you out of here as soon as possible.'

They piled into the car and Billy said as they drove away, 'You think Roper's had words with Ferguson?'

'Of course he has,' Dillon said. 'And wants us clear of French soil.'

They were at the airfield very quickly, and the driver, obviously obeying instructions, drove straight to the end of the runway where the Chieftain waited.

Parry said, 'Straight on board. We have friends here. It's taken care of.'

So five minutes later, he was heaving up the Airstair door and passing along the aisle to join Lacey in the cockpit. They were at ten thousand feet before they knew it, still bad weather, the Chieftain rocking in the turbulence but making steady progress out over the Channel Islands and pushing on towards the Isle of Wight and England.

Parry came back after a while. 'Coffee's back there, a bottle of champagne, Cokes, the usual things.'

'You certainly got us out of there fast,' Billy said. 'Good thinking.'

'Billy, I don't know what you've been up to and I don't want to know, but we had an order from Ferguson to get you out with the fastest extraction since we saved your hides in Iraq.'

He moved away and Dillon opened the bar box and found the bottle of champagne. As he opened it, he said, 'Ferguson was just being careful. He wanted to get us out of the war zone quickly, as it were. It should be a day or so before those bodies are found. Then it'll take a while to identify them as Russian GRU and sort out what the hell they have been doing operating in a friendly nation. The lies will start, the deceit, the demands for the bodies, and the story will fade because the public won't be particularly interested anyway.'

He poured and passed the first plastic glass to Monica, and Billy said to Kurbsky, 'There's a lesson for all of us. We said it would be smooth as silk, dead simple, and it would have been if that bird, the chambermaid, hadn't happened to be clocking on shift by the taxi rank and seen you.'

'Saw me and heard me, because the doorman asked for my destination to tell the taxi driver.'

'That's what doormen in top hotels do.' Dillon handed him a glass. 'It's called service.'

He raised his glass. 'Anyway, we've been there and done that. Here's to what comes next.' He smiled at Kurbsky. 'Who knows? You might grow to like it.'

Kurbsky said sharply, 'You obviously know what is intended for me. What does come next?'

'That's for General Charles Ferguson to tell you, he's the boss.'

'That was never clear to me. The boss of what, exactly?'

'The Prime Minister's personal security unit.'

'And you've obviously dealt with this kind of thing before.'

'Too bleeding right,' Billy told him. 'Our rules are there are no rules, not these days, not with all the terrorists and murderers emerging free from court, thanks to stupid laws and clever lawyers.'

'And how did you get involved with him?' Kurbsky asked.

'I used to be a gangster, but it got boring. So did my Uncle Harry. Dillon here was a top enforcer with the Provisional IRA, the two guys flying this plane are decorated RAF officers. The point is, we can be worse than the bad guys.'

Kurbsky turned to Monica. 'And you? Are you worse than the bad guys?'

She hesitated. 'Now and then, I can be useful.'

Dillon topped his glass up. 'Who knows what you could end up doing?'

At Farley, Ferguson's Daimler drove straight up to the Chieftain when it rolled to a halt, Parry dropped the Airstair door and Kurbsky went down and got in the rear seat beside Ferguson. It sped away at once, and the General said, 'Charles Ferguson,' and shook hands. 'Heard about the spot of bother on the train.'

'Yes, rather unfortunate,' Kurbsky said.

'You're here now and that's the main thing. We're going to the Holland Park safe house. Most of my work emanates from there and Major Roper is based there. It has the fullest facilities, extreme security, and it's very high tech, which saves on staff. I need only a couple of Military Police sergeants to keep things smooth. One of them, Doyle, is driving the car now, and Sergeant Henderson is back at the house.'

'And what about me?'

'We've put together some ideas, which we'll explain to you shortly. I think you'll find them rather interesting.'

'Excellent,' Kurbsky said. 'I can't wait to see what you have in store.'

Back at Farley, Harry drove across the tarmac to the Chieftain in his Bentley, put the window down and leaned out, grinning.

'Let's be having you. Ferguson wants us all down at Holland Park.' They climbed in and he drove away. 'So it worked okay, he's here. Bleeding marvellous. He must be a right villain, knocking off three like that.'

'Ferguson told you?' Billy demanded.

'He certainly did. We're like a club, Billy, the six of us. We're the ones who know everything. He won't tell Svetlana about this. Kurbsky being her nephew and everything, she mightn't like to think of him running around and knocking off people. Let's face it, though, he's obviously got a talent for it. I tell you, he'd have done well in the East End in the old days when the Krays were running things. He'll be giving you a run for your money, Dillon.'

Monica leaned forward and said, 'Harry, you're one of a kind.'

At Holland Park, they found Ferguson and Kurbsky with Roper in the computer room. Harry needed an introduction and shook hands warmly.

'You certainly don't take prisoners, my old son.'

'Only if there is a choice and there wasn't.' Kurbsky turned to Ferguson. 'What about my aunt? She must be anxious to see me.'

'Of course. I've put her and Katya in one of our staff apartments.' He turned to Monica. 'Perhaps you could do the honours? You know where it is.'

'Of course.' Monica led the way. 'It's on the ground floor and not far.' A couple of minutes later, she paused at a door. 'It's a big moment, Alex, for both of you.'

'For her especially, I think, because of her age. I must get it right, for her sake.'

'For both your sakes.' She reached up and kissed him on the cheek and held his hand for a moment.

'You are a remarkable woman.' He raised her hand and kissed it. 'Sean Dillon is a very lucky man, I think.'

He opened the door and Monica glimpsed Svetlana on a sofa by the window, Katya beside her. Svetlana got to her feet and Kurbsky stood there for a moment. Then Svetlana held out her hands and said, 'Alexander, can it be you? I can't believe it after all these years.'

'Like the bad penny, I've turned up again, *Babushka*.'

There was a flood of tears, he closed the door. A short while only and it opened again, and Katya emerged and closed it. 'He introduced me, but it's very emotional for Svetlana in there.'

'Let's leave them to it and go and join the others,' Monica said.

Ferguson was in the corner of the bar area talking to Dillon and Harry. Billy was sitting with Roper, and the two women joined them.

'How did it go?' Roper asked.

'Floods of tears from Svetlana. Her precious boy back after all these years. He even called her *babushka*.'

'I thought that meant grandmother in Russian?' Roper said.

'It seems it was his pet name for her when he was very little. She is so relieved to see him. Just can't believe he's got here safely.'

Monica glanced at Roper, who nodded. 'Tell her what happened. After all, you were there.'

When she was finished listening, Katya looked grave, but not particularly shocked. 'It's a bloody nose for the GRU, but Alex is what he is.'

'God knows, he saw enough during the years of war,' Monica said.

'I think there's more to it than that.' Katya moved to Roper's side table with the bottles, opened the vodka and poured one. 'Something else, something deep in his soul, perhaps, blossomed during the wars and won't go away again.'

'Perhaps.' Monica was uncertain.

Roper reached for his whisky, the pain in his left shoulder and back suddenly intense. 'She's got a point, Monica. Take you. A class act. An academic at a famous and ancient university, with doctorates galore, and yet when push came to shove, you shot that IRA bastard dead last year. I mean, where did that come from?' He swallowed his whisky. 'I know, I'm the pot calling the kettle black, but one thing's certain. It would be difficult for Svetlana to take on board the fact that her beloved nephew has just stiffed three people.'

'I think we're all agreed on that,' Katya said. 'I'll go and see how they are getting on.'

She went out, and Billy said, 'One smart lady, Katya.'

'Well, I wouldn't disagree with you.' Roper pushed his glass over and Monica poured another Scotch. 'Is it a bad day?' Monica asked him.

'Monica, it's always a bad day, but I'm alive, if not exactly kicking, when I should have been in bits and pieces, like a lot of the poor sods coming back from Afghanistan and Iraq these days. It occurs to me that in the great scheme of things, there might have been a meaning to my survival.'

'I didn't know you were religious,' Billy told him.

'I'm not, Billy, but I believe in reason and purpose.'

The conversation was cut off by the appearance of Katya with Kurbsky, and Svetlana on his arm. Katya said, 'Svetlana wants Alex to watch my show now, so that he knows what we have in mind. I've spoken to Ferguson, and he and Dillon and Harry have gone ahead to the viewing theatre.'

'I wouldn't miss it for the world,' Roper said.

Katya had tweaked the film a certain amount, but it was pretty much the same as when she had first shown it to Svetlana, Dillon and Monica at Chamber Court. She talked it through, and when she was finished, said, 'Let's show it once more, I think, so that Alex really gets the idea.'

There was silence when she finally froze on the final image of what he had become, standing there in hospital scrubs.

'Very impressive,' Kurbsky said. 'An audacious plan.' He turned to Svetlana, 'What do you think?'

'It would be wonderful if it gave you the chance to stay at the house, at least for a while, so that I could get close again, get to know you.'

'Let's analyse the situation. If the GRU thinks I'm in London, they'll try and seek me out. On the other hand, the last thing they'd want to do is advertise the fact of my presence here. They'd prefer to kidnap me or kill me, in some unobtrusive way.'

'All that makes sense,' Ferguson said.

'So, I don't think they'll bring in the heavy artillery. They'll wait and watch. If I become wretched Henri Duval, the walking ghoul, dying of lung cancer, racked by the effects of chemotherapy, the odd job man living over the garage at the house, it'll be so different from what they expected to find that eventually they'll just move on. Of course, if it doesn't work and they sniff me out, I can always do a runner.'

'So you're up for it?' Dillon said.

'The sooner the better. To make such a fundamental change in me so quickly will vastly increase our chances of success.'

Ferguson was excited. 'That's it then, people.' He turned to Katya. 'When do you want to start?'

'As soon as possible. I've brought my make-up box in the car, my hairdressing essentials, certain drugs I want him to take. I understand you keep a wardrobe of assorted clothing and footwear here as a backup for your operations.'

'We certainly do, and anything extra that you need, we can get.'

'Excellent.' She kissed Svetlana on the cheeks. 'Go now, love, back to the apartment. Billy will take you. He'll make sure you get anything you need.'

'Gold room service,' Billy said, gave her his arm and took her to the door. She stopped him and turned, looking at Kurbsky. 'I'm afraid, Alexander, that in finding you again, I will lose you.'

He blew her a kiss. 'You will never lose me again, *Babushka*, I swear it.'

They left. Katya said, 'Right, the stuff from my car, and you, Monica.' She nodded. 'Yes, you can assist me. It will be good to have you there.' She turned to Ferguson, 'But no one else. This must be understood.'

She turned and walked out, with Kurbsky and Monica following.

LONDON

8

The wardrobe area at Holland Park was rather theatrical, when you considered it, walk-in wardrobes filled with a wide selection of clothes, even uniforms. There was a screen high up in the corner, and when Katya switched it on, it showed the final image she had frozen on the viewing theatre set, the lost-looking hopeless creature in hospital scrubs.

She made Kurbsky undress and put on cotton pyjama trousers and he sat, facing the mirrors, the hair wild, the beard tangled. 'You look like Sir Francis Drake getting ready to sail against the Spanish Armada, doesn't he, Monica?'

'Is that so?' Kurbsky said. 'Romantic tosh!'

'Shut up and take these.' She opened a box and shook out two large pills. He examined them. 'What are they?'

'You don't need to know.' She poured a glass of tap water. 'You will take two each day. You will notice a darkening under the eyes, which will look like bruising. This will help in the illusion that you are on chemotherapy. They work very quickly.'

'How do you know this?'

'I'm in theatre. It's my business to know.'

He shrugged and washed the pills down. 'Now what?'

'A sheet about his shoulders, Monica.' She turned to a selection of scissors. 'So, now I shall be Delilah and you Samson, I think. The beard first.'

She was very expert, and quickly reduced the beard to the point where she was able to go to work with an electric razor. The clear chin and mouth really made a difference to the appearance. Then she started hacking the long hair off in handfuls. He made no complaint, even when she obviously hurt him, and finally it was reduced to a stubble. Now she spread foam over the skull, massaging it into the face also, and went to work with the electric razor again.

Finally, she produced a cutthroat razor. 'Good God, not that as well?'

'It's necessary, believe me.'

And she was right. It had changed his appearance totally. The skull, the cheekbones well-pronounced and hollow. She applied some sort of cream, massaging it under the eyes and into the scalp. 'It's making things darker already. In a little while, it will be even darker, but the drug is more permanent in that way. It helps with the haunted look.' She turned to Monica. 'What do you think?'

'I wouldn't have believed it if I hadn't seen it myself. It's just not the same person.'

'And we haven't even started on dress. Let's see what we've got.'

The wardrobes were as big as small rooms, and the three of them explored. 'What am I supposed to look like?'

'A street person, someone on welfare, a struggling student. In all these personas, there is a constant. You're on chemotherapy and you have lung cancer. Roper has inserted you into the Royal Marsden Hospital's cancer records. If anyone checks, you're there. He did the same at London University where you took an English degree. You've worked for the *Daily Express* and the *Mail*. It says so in their records. Born in Torquay in Devon to a French doctor and an English mother. You lived in Paris for ten years, then your father was killed in a car accident – again, that's all a matter of record – and your mother and you returned to England. You understandably have a tendency to speak with a French accent.'

'What's happened to her?'

'Breast cancer four years ago.'

'I feel as if I should take it personally.' He started working his way through clothing. He finally settled on a drab olive green T-shirt and pulled it on. Next he discovered some baggy olive-green trousers with big patch pockets.

'Ah, the military look,' Monica said.

Katya said, 'Not really. The kind of people I'm talking about wear stuff like this all the time. It's extremely cheap. The sort of thing you can pick up in surplus shops.'

He found a pair of French paratrooper boots next, which fitted well, and a large three-quarter-length combat jacket of some sort, once again with capacious pockets.

'I may not have much, but even on the street I'll need a bag of some sort.' Katya, rummaging on a high shelf, had the answer. Again olive green, it was a good size and had grabhandles or a cross-body strap if preferred. She passed it to him and he examined it. The interior base had an inside zip, providing, in effect, a secret compartment.

'This will do me.'

'Change of underwear, extra T-shirt, socks?' Katya said.

'Now you're spoiling me.' He slung the bag by the body strap across his chest and worked his way along the shelves. He found a black woollen hat and pulled it over his skull. 'Will I do?' he asked Monica.

'I suppose so, if you want a job on a building site.'

He continued to search, found a reasonable pair of leather gloves and put them in the bag. His back was turned, and as he rummaged further, he found a couple of black knitted ski masks staring up at him with empty eyes and wide mouths. He hesitated, then stuffed them in the bag, too, along with a couple of British Army Field Service wound packs from a stack he found on the shelf.

Katya said, 'Is that it?'

'I think so.' He walked out into the bathroom and looked at the stranger in the mirror, standing there in drab olive green, the bag hanging at his left side. 'You were right about the haunted look.' He took the woollen hat from the bag and pulled it on. 'God in heaven, I look worse.'

'Walk slowly, take your time. Speak in a low sort of measured way. You don't smile because you can't smile.'

'I get the point. I'm permanently weary.'

'You've got it exactly,' Monica said. 'I must say you don't look like you at all. You've done a fabulous job, Katya. Let's go and show the others.'

Katya and Monica found Svetlana in the safe house apartment where they had left her. 'What's happening, my dear?' Svetlana asked.

'General Ferguson and the others are meeting. He'd like us to join them.'

'And what about Alexander?'

'He'll be there,' Katya said.

She gave Svetlana her arm and they went out, Monica following. When they went down the corridor, the doors of the viewing theatre were open and Kurbsky was standing there in all his glory. He stared at them, then pulled off his woollen hat and scratched his head.

Svetlana barely looked at him and said, 'Where are we going? Where is Alexander?'

'The computer room,' Katya said. They carried on, and Kurbsky called, 'No, he isn't, you made your point. I'm here, *Babushka*.' They paused and turned. Svetlana gazed at him, puzzled.

'I'm here,' he said again and opened his arms.

She screamed and cowered against Katya. 'What is he saying? Where is Alexander?'

She really was terribly upset and the others came running from the computer room, Ferguson calling, 'What the hell is going on?'

They stopped dead, all staring, and then Roper arrived in his wheelchair. 'My God, I'd never have believed it.'

'And neither can she.' Katya hugged her tight. 'It is Alexander, my darling. It's just that I've changed him.'

'It's me, *Babushka*.' He reached to kiss her on the forehead. 'It really is me.'

'Can you change back?'

'Not for the moment.'

She shuddered. 'Such a fright. I need a drink. I've never been so shocked in my life.'

Ferguson gave her his arm. 'Coming right up. We'll all go to the bar and celebrate.'

'Celebrate what?'

'Well, if you can't recognize him, it's doubtful anyone else will.'

Sitting there in the corner all together, Katya said, 'I've got another idea. Could be rather clever. Not far from us in Belsize Park is an old-fashioned corner shop. We buy many things there. When Marek worked for us, he often shopped there.'

'What are you getting at?' Kurbsky asked.

'I think you should turn up there in the morning. You're trying to find our house, but you're not sure where it is. You'll have a letter with you – which I'll write before we leave. It will be an offer of employment to you saying that Marek recommended you to us. It'll also say that we are aware of your medical condition and will allow you to come and go according to the requirements of your treatment.'

'I get the point,' Dillon said. 'If anyone makes inquiries at the local shop about Duval, they'll get an acceptable answer.'

'I'll go and type the letter now, if I may use your office, General?'

Monica said, 'So you'll stay here tonight?'

'Move into Chamber Court tomorrow, that's the general idea.'

Dillon said, 'Take it easy, take time to settle in.'

'I intend to. Look, Sean, I was a paratrooper, then special forces, and a final year with GRU.'

'Military intelligence?' Monica said.

'A licence to murder and, just like you, the rules were no rules.'

'I read *Moscow Nights*,' Dillon put in. 'And it occurred to me it wasn't art imitating life, but probably the other way round.'

'Very astute of you.' Katya returned with an envelope. 'Thanks,' he said. 'I'll see you tomorrow.'

He gave Svetlana a hug. 'Let Katya take you home, *Babushka*. You'll get too tired.'

She kissed him and patted his cheek. 'Be a good boy.'

They went, and Dillon said to Monica, 'I'll run you home. You haven't had a chance to freshen up. We'll see you again, Alex.'

Monica kissed him on the cheek. 'Stay cool,' she said, and went out with Dillon.

The Salters followed, pausing on the way, and Harry said, 'Listen, if you want to look in at our pub, the Dark Man, just give us a bell. We're at Wapping, Cable Wharf.'

Billy cut in, 'It would be like testing the water.'

'That's a thought. I'll see.'

They went, and he looked in at the computer room, where Ferguson and Roper were talking. Ferguson said, 'I've got to go, I've got a meeting at the Ministry of Defence. Roper's in charge now. He's your control officer. Anything you need, he'll supply. Take tomorrow as it comes and we'll talk again.'

Suddenly, it was quiet, just he and Roper, a quiet buzz to things. Roper poured a whisky. 'I drink a lot. The bomb that didn't succeed in killing me left a great many of its fragments in my system. They hurt, sometimes intolerably. The cigarettes help and so does whisky in large quantities. No wild, wild women, though.'

'That's a shame.'

'Do you have any special requirements?'

'Money, weapons. All I have is a knife. I had a Walther, but after I dealt with Ivanov, I tossed it away as the train was passing a convenient river. It seemed the smart thing to do.' A lie, of course, for the Walther was already in the secret compartment in his bag.

'No problem. I've got a credit card for Henri Duval here

in this drawer. You can draw cash from any bank's hole-in-the-wall for as much as one thousand pounds a day.'

'That's very generous of you.'

'Weapons for our people are standard. A silenced Walther, and a Colt .25 for ankle use. Anticipating your request, I had Sergeant Doyle draw them for you. There's also a bullet-proof vest. Everything is in the drawer here, together with five hundred pounds to get you started. Help yourself.'

Kurbsky did, unzipped the false bottom of his bag and placed the items inside, putting forty pounds into one of his pockets. He said, 'Don't you get bored just sitting there and watching computer screens all the time?'

'You couldn't be more wrong. I roam the world to steal people's secrets. There's always something. For instance, see this, a report from French railway police in Brittany to head-quarters in Paris – it appears that a badly damaged body has been discovered at the side of a track on the direct line to Brest. His papers indicate he was a Russian named Turgin. That would be Ivanov, I assume.'

'Yes. The GRU directs that all operatives operating on foreign soil use false papers.'

'Which will make any investigation by the French police difficult,' Roper said. 'As I say, it's amazing what these screens can disgorge.' His fingers danced over the keys. 'Alexander Kurbsky, for example.' The screen filled before their eyes. A current photo, the wild one that went on the back of books, and early, small photos – his mother, his father in KGB uniform, and Tania, her seventeen-year-old face frozen in time, with a line that read: deceased, March 15, 1989.

Kurbsky felt a kind of surge in his chest and banged his fist on the counter. 'No, not that, if you don't mind.'

Roper switched it off at once. 'I'm damn sorry. It must be hard for you, remembering the circumstances.'

'That my father used her death as a weapon to get me back? An old story.' Kurbsky got up. 'Look, I didn't sleep at all last night. Can I go and find a bed?'

'Use the apartment your aunt was in. I'll see you this evening.'

At the Embassy, Colonel Boris Luhzkov looked up at the knock on the door, and it opened as Bounine looked in.

'Come and sit down,' Luhzkov said. 'Here's something you should know. French police have discovered a body in Brittany, bearing false papers in the name of Turgin.'

'And so?'

'It was by the rail track. Turgin is Ivanov.'

'So Kurbsky killed Ivanov? What's Moscow doing about it?'

'Putting out a story of rogue elements in the military, deserters. It will be embellished when the other two bodies turn up, as they surely will. False papers, of course. A chambermaid who serviced their rooms, a Ukrainian named Olga Soran, has already been visited by our people in Paris and sent home on the first plane available.'

'So what happens now? Are you going to try and speak to Kurbsky?'

'I think we'll leave him to settle in. They've undoubtedly

taken him to Ferguson's headquarters in Holland Park. That's
where they will debrief him.'

'And then what?'

'Who knows? They could keep him there in complete
comfort and privacy for as long as they like.'

'But he won't want that, a man like Kurbsky. He'll get too
restless.'

'I agree. We must wait for Kurbsky to contact us. Charles
Ferguson is an extremely clever man, Bounine. Kurbsky is a
problem to which a solution *must* be found. There won't be
a quick one, so we wait, but this doesn't mean a holiday for
you, my friend. This is your first posting here, so use your
time wisely. Take Oleg as your driver, he knows the city. He's
been here two years. Get him to show you the sights, as it
were. You're Major Bounine now. Use your authority.'

'Thank you, Colonel, I'll do that.' Bounine turned and
withdrew.

It was just after six when Kurbsky returned to the computer
room. Roper sat there alone, music playing softly. 'Cole
Porter?' Kurbsky said. 'You like that kind of music?'

'It's a comfort,' Roper told him. 'How do you feel?'

'The sleep did me good.'

Roper reached for the whisky. 'A drink?'

'Not at the moment. The Salters invited me to call in at
their pub, this Dark Man on Cable Wharf.'

'The first joint Harry owned. He's got millions in property now. So you fancy spreading your wings?'

'Billy said it would be like testing the water.'

'He could be right. Past the Tower of London, Wapping High Street, down to the river.'

'I remember Wapping well. Those two years I spent with Svetlana at the university, I got to know the city backwards. Seventeen to nineteen is exactly the right age for that, and already I'm remembering it all. Tell me about this place we're in now.'

'Local people think we're some sort of sanatorium. Of course, people in the business, like Boris Luhzkov, know very well who we are, but we're protected by all sorts of security, double blinds, secret exits and entrances, the works.'

'So I could simply walk out?'

'If you want to. Two hundred yards past Holland Park to the main road, plenty of cabs cruising, and the world's your oyster.'

'And it would be all right?'

'Not for Alexander Kurbsky, but okay for Henri Duval. If you want to test the water, my friend, do it.' He lit a cigarette. 'What is it you want? You've jumped over the wall, you're free.'

'Am I really?' Kurbsky shook his head. 'In personal terms, I look on myself as the invisible man, because no one sees the real me. I could write about that and what it's like.'

'That's certainly an interesting thought. I would think it would make an extraordinary book.'

'But first, I must experience it.' Kurbsky stood, picked up his bag and slipped the carrying strap over his head so that the bag was on his right thigh.

'I'll tell you later.'

'You surely will. I'm part of the furniture. The Judas gate opens automatically when you approach because I've punched you into the system.'

Which it did. He stepped through and found himself on a quiet street, most of the properties Victorian, some walled, others in sizeable open gardens. It was dark now, street lamps glowing, lots of parked cars, everything perfectly normal. The main road was extremely busy. He stood at the edge of the pavement and flagged down a black cab and told the driver to take him to Wapping High Street.

He sat there, looking out at the busy streets, the evening traffic, the buzz of what was still the greatest city in the world, remembering so much from his youth. He was aware of the driver glancing at him in the mirror occasionally and decided to say something, trying for just a hint of a French accent.

'You know the Dark Man on Cable Wharf at Wapping?'

'I certainly do.' The driver was obviously a cockney.

'Just drop me off at the High Street end. I want to go to a shop there.'

'Fine by me. Watch it walking down to the Dark Man. It's a great pub, but some of the streets leading down there are a problem. Bloody kids and their knives. The world's gone mad. It's all the drugs, I reckon.'

'I wouldn't argue with that.'

The cabby's eyes flickered over him again. 'Are you okay, mate? You don't look too well.'

Kurbsky decided to go all the way. 'Chemotherapy. It takes its toll.'

'Cancer? Christ, mate, I'm sorry. It must be bloody rough.'

He obviously felt subdued and said nothing more, all the way to the Tower of London and further into Wapping High Street. He finally pulled in at the pavement under a street lamp and Kurbsky alighted and leaned down to pay him.

The driver gave him his change. 'Take care, mate.'

He drove away hurriedly and Kurbsky turned and discovered a dress shop, mannequins in the window. There was also his reflection in a mirror, looking like a ghoul.

'My God, Alex, where did you go?' he said softly, walked a few yards and came to a lane with the sign Cable Wharf above it. It was dark and somehow sinister, the streetlamps of the old London gaslight pattern, some broken. He didn't feel the slightest fear, though. For one thing, he had the bone-handled gutting knife inside his right boot. He started to walk down towards the water.

It had obviously been an area of thriving warehouses in its day, but most of them were decaying now and boarded up, waiting for the developers. He walked along the centre of the street carefully, aware of voices up ahead, and some sort of fire. As he got closer, he saw what it was, an old trash can with rubbish of some kind burning away in a courtyard behind a broken wall.

Two youths drinking from bottles were standing beside the fire, taking turns to kick an old ragged tramp who lay whimpering on the ground. There was an old woman in a beret and layers of coats, a bag on the ground, its contents spilled. She was very drunk and crying.

'Stop it, you'll kill him.'

The youths were laughing and the taller one shoved her away. 'Piss off, you old cow.' He turned and kicked the man in the head again.

Kurbsky stood and watched. The youth said, 'What the fuck are you looking at?'

'She's got a point,' Kurbsky said, and unzipped the false bottom of his bag. There were two Walthers in there and the one which had killed the GRU men on the train had some surgical tape he'd found in the bathroom around the butt.

The youth reached in his anorak, produced a flick knife and sprang the blade. 'My friend's got one, too,' he said, as his companion produced a similar weapon. 'Let's see what you've got in the bag.'

'My pleasure.' Kurbsky took out the Walther from the train and hit him across the side of the head. The youth dropped his weapon with a cry of pain and fell on one knee, his friend backed away, and Kurbsky picked up the knife, closed the blade and put it in his pocket. 'This is a Walther PPK, the real thing, not an imitation. It has fantastic stopping power.' He fired at a tin can amongst the rubbish, there was a dull thud, it jumped in the air. 'Imagine what that could do your knee. Now go away very fast.'

The undamaged one said, 'Come on, for Christ's sake, he means it.' He darted away up towards the High Street while the woman was piling her belongings into her bag and the old man was getting to his feet. The youth Kurbsky had injured had fallen to his knee again and the old couple moved past him surprisingly fast. He came up slowly, a brick in his hand.

'You bastard, I'll smash your skull.'

Kurbsky's hand swung up, he fired, and the lower half of the youth's left ear disintegrated. He screamed, and plucked at his ear, blood oozing between his fingers. He fell back against the wall.

Kurbsky said, 'You never learn, people like you. Now clear off and find a hospital.'

He walked away, swallowed by darkness. The youth cried, 'You fucking bastard,' then turned and stumbled away.

Kurbsky came out of the darkness and walked along Cable Wharf. On his left was the panorama of London on the other side of the river, lights gleaming everywhere, the sound of distant traffic, a pleasure boat sailing by, all lit up. He came to a multi-storey development of what looked like exclusive apartments, but the Dark Man standing beside it was a typical river pub that obviously dated from Victorian times. There was a car park and, beyond, several boats moored at the jetty. He went to the entrance, paused, then went inside.

It wasn't particularly crowded. The bar was very Victorian:

mirrors, lots of mahogany and marble. The beer pumps were porcelain. The Salters were sitting in a corner booth, with two hard-looking men leaning against the wall behind, listening to the conversation. As he discovered later, they were Joe Baxter and Sam Hall, Harry Salter's minders. Nobody noticed him, he hesitated and turned to the bar, where an attractive blonde was serving. She looked at him curiously, as did two or three customers standing enjoying a drink together.

'What's your pleasure, love?' she asked.

'Vodka, if you please, madame.'

'Tonic?'

'No, as it comes.'

She put the glass before him and he took off his woollen hat. She winced perceptibly. 'Are you all right, love?'

'Absolutely.' He took the vodka straight down.

Billy appeared. 'Henri, my old friend, we'd just about given you up. You've met our Ruby, Mrs Moon? She's captain of the ship; keeps us all in order. Henri Duval, Ruby.'

She seemed uncertain and Kurbsky said, 'You have been very kind, madame.'

Billy whisked him away, and she watched as Harry greeted him, and Baxter and Hall were introduced, and then Billy returned. 'Another large vodka for him and a Scotch for Harry.'

'Is he all right?' she said. 'Or does he have what I think he has?'

'Answering your first question, he gets by, and yes, he has lung cancer. He's on chemotherapy at the Marsden.'

'So he's French?'

Billy proceeded to give her Henri Duval's background, which included his lack of relatives. 'He normally lives in Torquay, but he needed to be in London for the treatment. His mother was a cousin of Harry's.'

'I see. I feel so sorry for him.'

'Well, you've got a good heart, Ruby, we all know that.'

She took the drinks across and said to Kurbsky, 'I'm so pleased to meet you. Billy's been telling me all about you. When you feel like something to eat, let me know. Steak and ale pie tonight.'

'Sounds marvellous,' Kurbsky told her.

'We'll all have a go at that,' Harry said.

Ruby nodded and went away, and Baxter and Hall drifted to the other end of the bar and joined two men drinking there.

Harry nodded at the vodka. 'Should you be drinking that in your condition?'

'I've checked it out. It varies with people.' He took it down, Russian-style. 'I suppose it reminds me that there's still a real me lurking around inside.'

'I take your point,' Billy said. 'How's it going?'

'So far so good. I walked down from the safe house, hailed a cab. Dropped off in Wapping High Street.'

'And walked down here?' Harry asked. 'You've got to watch that,' Harry told him. 'What with all those streets empty and waiting for the developers, you get some funny people hanging around.'

'Not that I noticed,' Kurbsky said.

'Anyway, it does seem to be working?' Billy asked.

'So it seems. Take Ruby, she was troubled. I had a cab driver who asked me if I was OK. He said I didn't look too well.'

'Yes, well, he was sorry for you.'

Kurbsky didn't even smile. 'I'm not used to that, but Katya Sorin would be pleased. It's all working out exactly as she had hoped.'

'And where's it all going to end, that's what I'd like to know?' Billy said.

Kurbsky shrugged. 'Don't ask me, I'm just passing through.'

Ruby waved from behind the bar, and Harry said, 'That's enough for now. Let's have you in the back parlour for a big slice of Ruby's steak and ale pie. You'll love it, believe me.'

Around ten, Kurbsky decided he'd had enough and said he'd order a taxi back to Holland Park, but Billy wouldn't hear of it and insisted on taking him in his scarlet Alfa Romeo.

'It's no hardship, I like driving by night, particularly after midnight. I find it calming, locked in tight in your very own world.'

'And rain,' Kurbsky said. 'There's something special about that, the windscreen wipers clicking back and forth. It's hypnotic.'

Billy said suddenly, 'When I finished *On the Death of*

Men, I felt such a sense of loss, I started again at the beginning straight away.'

'I'm flattered.'

'It's the truth. I may be a gangster, but one day years ago, I was in some waiting room when I found a paperback about famous philosophers. It bowled me over. I loved that stuff, then Dillon came into our lives spouting the same ideas.'

'Dillon was that important to you?'

'Harry, me and the boys were handling a hot package from Amsterdam on one of my uncle's river boats. Diamonds from Amsterdam. There was a police sting. We'd have gone down the steps for ten years, only Dillon diverted the package.'

'What happened then?'

'He worked for Ferguson and drew us in. We've never looked back. To be honest, Harry's made millions out of development.'

'So who needs to rob banks?'

'Something like that.' They drew up at Holland Park. 'Are you coming in?' Kurbsky asked.

'Just give Roper my love, and good luck tomorrow.'

Kurbsky got out, watched the Alfa Romeo drive away. It was quiet and he turned and walked to the Judas in the main gate, was about to speak into the voice box when the Judas swung open. He stepped inside, walked forward, and it closed behind him.

Roper was seated in his usual spot, gazing at the screens. He turned. 'Did you have a good night? Tell me about it.'

Which Kurbsky did, sitting down and helping himself to

another vodka. 'There is one thing,' he said. 'People do look at me, because I'm unusual . . .'

'Or because they recognize you for what you are, an out-patient on chemotherapy, which means cancer. Most people know that, if only because it's a staple of medical soaps on television. They feel sorry for you.'

'Or uncomfortable. There were fifty or sixty customers in the bar just before I left, and I've got the feeling a number of them were happy to see me go.'

'I know what you mean. It's like people not wanting some soldier who's lost a leg in Afghanistan swimming in the local pool.'

'Human nature,' Kurbsky said glancing up. 'Just a moment, what's that?'

'A late night news program.'

'It said something about Shadid Basayev, or maybe I was wrong.'

'You weren't. General Shadid Basayev, a Chechen general. He's applied for and been granted asylum. It was on about an hour ago. I recorded the programme because there was an end piece I needed on Al-Qaeda. Hold on, I'll rewind. Here we go.'

There was some footage from the first Chechen War, the general in a tank, then inspecting men at some hill station, a burly man with a brutal hard face and the cheekbones of some Mongol warrior. His uniform was understated, the cap crumpled, the military blouse of a common soldier, a worn leather coat, boots. As he walked along the front rank, men turned their faces towards him.

'That's a nice touch,' Roper said.

'Yes, Nazi style. He introduced it to his men.'

'Did you know him?'

And Alexander Kurbsky, who had known him very well indeed, said, 'Everybody in the Russian Army in Chechnya knew the bastard.'

The television program said Basayev had applied for and been granted political asylum after fleeing the Russian Federation and living for a while in Monaco. Political pressure aimed at his extraction had forced him to move to London, where similar pressure from Russia had proved futile, judges of the High Court having accepted that to return him would most certainly put his life in danger.

'So, asylum granted,' Kurbsky said.

'It seems that while he was in charge of certain affairs in Chechnya, oil revenues or something like that, he succeeded in transferring millions into the City of London.' Roper shook his head. 'He has it all. It's been crawling through a court for nine months, but he's finally made it.'

'What happened to the war crimes charges?' Kurbsky asked, although he knew very well what had happened.

'Witnesses disappeared, intimidation. Nothing came of it. I like this bit.' They were interviewing Basayev in his house in Mayfair, and he was speaking of going to evening mass every Sunday. They even showed the church. It was Roman Catholic – St Mary and All the Angels. Basayev was a Christian, not a Muslim. Kurbsky remembered that, remembered it well. He had a memorial to his wife in the churchyard and visited it on a daily basis in the morning.

'Many Chechens are Christian,' Roper said. 'But surely they'd have been Russian Orthodox or something like that? Let's look at his details.' Roper tapped the keys and the facts came up. 'What do you know? He was a Muslim, did a law degree in Rome in his early twenties and changed religion to marry a Rosa Rossi, a fellow student. That explains the Roman Catholicism. Involved in politics for years in Chechnya. No children. There was a bomb attack on his car in Grozny in 1989. Unfortunately, he'd been delayed and it was his wife who was travelling. He blamed the KGB very publicly.'

'He would, but then it probably was them,' Kurbsky said.

The show switched back to the Church of St Mary and All the Angels. It was of late Victorian vintage because that was when Roman Catholics had been allowed to build again in England. It wasn't very pretty and there was a clock tower. A limousine drew up, and Basayev got out and his driver gave him flowers. The camera showed the time on the clock tower as ten. Then it cut to the cemetery. Basayev appeared and paused at a memorial stone with a photo inset, which he kissed before changing the flowers.

'You'd think he'd paid to be able to look that good,' said Kurbsky.

'Oh, the BBC let him have his interview, but their documentary on his activities in Chechnya totally condemns him.'

'Which won't bother him in the slightest. The truly wicked do seem to survive rather well in this life, but I suppose that's the way of the world. I'm going to bed. I'll see you in the morning, and then it's off to Chamber Court and the ladies.'

He lay on the bed thinking about it, the hell of Grozny, the Chechen capital, of General Shadid Basayev and what had happened a long, long time ago.

CHECHNYA

1994

9

Grozny, the Chechen capital, resembled hell on earth, and in spite of constant rain, there were fires everywhere. Heavy tanks had thrown everything they had at the place and the aerial bombardment had been constant, and yet the Chechens stubbornly resisted, street by street, house by house, urban guerrilla warfare at its most intense.

Alexander Kurbsky, a lieutenant by rank, was the only officer left in what had, two weeks earlier, been the 5th Paratroop Company, a special forces unit consisting of fifty men. Now they had been reduced to twenty men, having spearheaded their way into the heart of the city, using on occasion the sewage system, and in those filthy and foul smelling tunnels, they had found an enemy that fought like rats.

They finally emerged via manholes in the central square, a wilderness of half-standing buildings and fires smoking in the heavy rain, and found themselves facing what was left of the Astoria Hotel.

Yuri Bounine sprawled close to Kurbsky. Bounine was an unlikely-looking paratrooper, with his chubby face and steel army-issue spectacles fastened together with tape. His bulky combat uniform was filthy, but then so was everyone else's. His rank of sergeant was temporary, because Kurbsky and he had become friends, and Kurbsky trusted him for his brains as much as for anything else.

'Are we going, then?' a man named Nebit called, someone who didn't take kindly to discipline and resented Kurbsky anyway because of his youth. 'We might get a cup of coffee in there.'

'Keep your head down,' Kurbsky told him but Nebit was already standing up, and two men next to him followed. A burst of fire blew away his combat beret, fragmented the back of his skull, and hurled him over a pile of bricks. A machine pistol had obviously caused the damage, knocking down the other two also. Instant death, for there wasn't a sound from them.

'So now we are seventeen,' Kurbsky said.

Bounine nodded, 'So what do we do?'

Kurbsky raised his voice. 'Follow me back to the sewer. We'll see where it comes out a little closer to the hotel, slowly and with care and covering each other. Nebit was stupid, so he paid the price.'

He led, disappearing down into the tunnel and proceeding,

half bent over, checking the outfalls to left and right. There was water running a couple of feet deep, a mixture of brown sludge in it which didn't bear thinking about. He came to a kind of concrete chamber, a notice saying Astoria Hotel and paused, and the others closed up.

'I'll go, you cover me, Yuri.' He went up cautiously, found a steel door, depressed the handle and pushed, finding himself in a room containing the central heating system. He went to the end door, opened it cautiously, and found what must have been the kitchen staff's changing quarters, white chef's uniforms hanging from pegs, toilets and a row of open showers. There was a door marked *Kitchen*.

The others cried excitedly, 'Great, there must be food,' and Kurbsky turned, saying, 'No, wait.'

He was too late. Four crowded through, and as he got to the door there was heavy firing, a cry of agony, two of the men blown back, shot several times. He scrambled over them to the shelter of a steel food bench, keeping low as sustained firing continued, found a grenade at his belt, pulled the pin and tossed it over to the other side of the kitchen. There was a cry that was more like a scream, and he jumped up and fired a burst from his AK47 at the wide doorway opposite.

He moved forward cautiously over the bodies of his men and found what he was looking for, a Chechen soldier, uniform soaked in blood, trying to breathe, and nothing but a death rattle there. A steel helmet had come off and, very slowly, the head turned, hair cropped, eyes staring at him mutely.

Bounine came up behind him. 'Christ, a girl. I hate that. Are you going to finish her off?'

Kurbsky took her hand and spoke to her gently. She smiled, then her eyes closed and her head lolled to one side.

'What did you say to her?'

'I said "Go in Peace" in case she was a Muslim.' He turned to the others. 'Fourteen of us now. So just follow me.'

He went straight out into a large restaurant, walked through the tables into the foyer of the hotel leading to the main doors. All was still, and on one side was the entrance to what had once been one of the most luxurious bars in Grozny.

Someone said, 'My God, look at all that booze.'

There was a surge, Kurbsky fired a short burst into the ceiling. Everyone turned. He said, 'Not yet. You bastards stink, and I stink, because we've been in the shit for weeks. So follow me right now.'

He led the way through the kitchens to the staff quarters, stepped into the first walk-in shower exactly as he was, in combat uniform and clutching an AK47. He switched it on full. 'Come on in, the water's fine.'

They stared at him in astonishment and Bounine was next. 'A bloody marvellous idea.' He stepped under the next one.

The rest of the men followed boisterously, like schoolboys after football, the filth and the stench of the sewers washed away in dark brown rivulets.

Later in the bar lounge they rested, eating a whole range of canned foods from the kitchens, discovering that the electricity worked in parts of the hotel and that there were lights in the bar. 'Not that we could use those,' Bounine said. 'It would attract everyone in the city.'

Kurbsky had informed Command of their whereabouts and had been promised fresh orders, which hadn't come. He and Bounine had been working their way through a bottle of champagne and he was just refilling their glasses when there was a sound of vehicles outside.

Kirov, who'd been left on guard duty at the door, ran in. 'They're ours, Lieutenant, somebody important, I think.'

Which it was. About a dozen men appeared, flooding into the foyer, excited at the riches the bar disclosed, started forward and came to a halt, reacting at once to shouted commands. A moment later, General Chelek, the area commander, walked through the crowd. There was little to distinguish him from his men, he was just as unshaven, his uniform just as filthy.

Kurbsky and his men stood up. He came forward and took the bottle of champagne from Kurbsky's hand and looked at the label. 'Very nice, you lads are doing all right. Who are you?' He took the glass from Kurbsky's hand and it was filled.

'Fifth Paratroop Assault Platoon.'

'The Black Tigers, isn't that what they call you? I thought there were fifty in your unit.'

'What you see is what you get, General, thirteen.'

'Unlucky for some, they say.'

'Which means you need us for something rotten?'

Chelek went behind the bar and grabbed a bottle of vodka. He glanced at his men, who stood waiting. 'Okay, pitch in.'

Which they did. He sat at the end of the bar with Kurbsky. 'Who are you?'

'Alexander Kurbsky, Comrade, I'm the only officer left.'

'Your name is not unknown to me. Yes, I've got something pretty heavy for you. One of our most implacable foes in the Grozny area has been General Shadid Basayev. You've heard of him?'

'Of course.'

Bounine, who had been standing close, said, 'He went to Rome to university, General, studied law. He's a Muslim who married an Italian woman and became a Catholic.'

Chelek shrugged. 'Men will do strange things where a woman is concerned, even a man like Shadid Basayev. You seem well informed, Sergeant.'

'He was once a lawyer,' Kurbsky explained. 'At Rome University.'

Bounine said, 'The KGB put a bomb in Basayev's car before the war here in Grozny. His wife was using the car, not him, and he has never forgiven us. That's why he kills Russians with such venom.'

'I'm aware of that. Basayev has withdrawn into the mountains for a while. My intelligence sources say he is at the Monastery of Kuba. That's about sixty miles from here. It's at the head of a valley, there's a plateau perhaps five miles away. Our informant is a Father Ramsan, a priest. He contacts us by radio, says Basayev has only twenty men with him.'

'So what are you suggesting, Comrade?' Kurbsky asked. 'That we put together a hunting party and go after him? We

wouldn't last an hour out there. Every peasant, every shepherd on a crag, are his eyes and ears.'

'You're absolutely right, but I'm not suggesting you go
out by road. By chance, at the Grozny military supply airstrip,
there is a Dakota transport plane. Very old, but very reliable, or so I'm informed. It could have you over the Kuban
Plateau in no more than an hour one way or the other.'

There was a heavy silence. Bounine said, 'You mean the
Dakota would land on the plateau?'

'Of course not. I mean you would jump, you idiot. You
are paratroopers, are you not? You have jumped into action?'

'Yes, I have, Comrade,' Bounine told him. 'And five of my
comrades.'

'But I haven't,' Kurbsky said. 'And neither have six of my
men. The demands of the war in the last year in Afghanistan
meant that a lot of paratroopers didn't get jump training.'

'Well, that's just too bad,' Chelek said calmly. 'My experts
on staff say a pass over that plateau at four hundred feet will
have you on the ground in a matter of seconds. The chutes
are available, they rig an anchor line in the plane, you clip
your static line on it and you jump out. It's all automatic. You
are the Black Tigers, are you not, and an elite unit?'

'Of course, Comrade,' Kurbsky said. 'When would we go?'

'Tomorrow some time. I'll arrange for a truck to pick you
up from here during the next couple of hours or so. I'll see
you at the airfield tomorrow.'

He called to his men and walked out and they followed.
The Tigers were muttering amongst themselves and young
Kirov came forward.

'Is it true, this business, Comrade, something about parachuting out of a plane? We couldn't hear it all. I've never had parachute training, neither have others here.'

'And neither have I,' Kurbsky told him. 'But in case you hadn't noticed, this is the Russian Army, so if General Chelek tells you to jump out of a plane, you do it, even if you don't have a parachute. Sergeant Bounine's the expert. You take over, Yuri?'

He sat in the corner, thinking about it, fiddled in his right paratrooper's boot and found his favourite knife in a secret pocket. It was very old, carved like a Madonna in some kind of bone, and at the press of a button, a blade jumped out, razor sharp. A gutting knife, used by some Caspian fisherman way back in the past. He checked that it was working to perfection, aware of the talk among the men, the anger, then closed the knife and sheathed it again in its secret place.

Bounine came, went behind the bar, got a bottle of vodka and came back with two glasses. 'You might as well get drunk while we're waiting for the truck,' he announced. 'It'll help when you have to think that tomorrow at some time or other, you're going to be jumping from that Dakota.'

He gave Kurbsky a glass. 'Vodka, Lieutenant?'

'What would I do without you?' Kurbsky said.

The airstrip was on a section of highway just outside the city, normal road traffic diverted elsewhere. A tented town had sprung up, mixed in with prefabricated buildings on what had originally been farmland. Planes were coming in and out all the time, mainly transport. Everything was makeshift, even what passed as air traffic control.

The pilot was an old hand named Bashir, a contract man brought in for the war. He'd flown in Afghanistan, old Dakotas bought from various Asian sources, workhorses that could fly anywhere. He'd dropped paratroopers during his time in Afghanistan, before helicopters became such an important part of that ill-fated campaign. However, he knew his stuff and had an anchor line rigged before Kurbsky and his men arrived.

He was squat and ageing and badly in need of a shave. 'There's nothing to it. You strap on the parachute, clip your static line to the anchor cable and jump one after the other. You're on the ground before you know it.'

'Have you ever jumped?' Kirov demanded.

'That isn't the point.'

Bounine intervened. 'This is a waste of time. You wear a helmet and your usual uniform, and help each other to strap on the parachutes. You'll pack a canvas bag containing weapons and explosives, with a hanging strap clipped to your belt. It lands below you and thumps the ground, letting you know you're about to land. Very useful in the dark.'

'Only you won't be going in the dark, there will be some light, just a little,' Kirov said.

'And when does this happen?' Kurbsky asked.

'Well, according to my orders, about four thirty in the morning. You'll certainly be there by five thirty.'

'Tomorrow morning?' Bounine asked.

'Those are my orders. Now I suggest we rig one of the

men in all his gear, equipment bag, the lot and have a demon-stration.' He turned to Kurbsky. 'Is that okay, Lieutenant?'

Everybody had heard. Bounine turned to Kurbsky and said, 'To those of you who have never jumped before, I would say this: In the last war, all flyers in the air force carried a parachute in case their plane was shot down, but they didn't practise beforehand, they were just thankful it was there.'

'Why doesn't that comfort me in the slightest?' Kurbsky asked.

But they went through everything several times to make sure everyone got the idea. Each grab bag contained a Stechkin pistol, an AK47 with folding stock, fragmentation grenades, plastic explosive and pencil timers and a field service medical kit including morphine ampoules. They rested ner-vously in one of the tents and it rained and the tent leaked, but outside the war went on, planes of various types landing and taking off, and away in the distance there was the thump of artillery and fires in the city.

'It's Biblical.' Bounine had brought a bottle of vodka from the hotel in his knapsack and sat drinking from the bottle occasionally and gazing out through the darkness to the flames of the city. 'Death on a Pale Horse, destruction everywhere.'

'What in the hell are you talking about?' Kurbsky demanded.

'Oh, humankind,' Bounine said glumly. 'Thousands of years of civilization and we only succeed in butchering each other.'

'Yes, well, that's the way it is, nothing changes, so I'm going to go and get my orders from Chelek and you'd better come with me, so put the bottle back in your knapsack.'

They found him in one of the prefabricated buildings which housed the command post that seemed full of radio equipment and staff. A request to see him produced a suggestion that they take a seat. They were still there an hour later. Kurbsky approached the desk again. The young aide looked up inquiringly, but at that moment General Chelek emerged from his office and dropped a file on the desk.

'So there you are,' he said to Kurbsky. 'I've been waiting. I want to get this show on the road.'

'I've brought my sergeant, Comrade General.'

'I've no objection.' They went in and he sat behind his desk. 'You've sorted the parachuting out?'

'Yes, Comrade.'

'Excellent. This is a very simple operation and that's the way I like things. The monastery at Kuba has been taken over by Basayev, the monks all kicked out. He's there now with twenty men. I want you to wipe them out.'

'You're absolutely sure they are there?' Kurbsky asked.

'Father Ramsan has always proved reliable in the past. He was allowed to move into a farm about a mile from the monastery when Basayev took over. He tells me of an old tunnel, long disused, which gives access to the monastery. He will act as your guide.' He put a knapsack on his desk. 'There's a radio in there, and all the instructions you need to contact Ramsan.'

Kurbsky glanced at Bounine. 'Sergeant.'

Bounine took the radio. Chelek said, 'I've had a look at your record, Kurbsky, it's remarkable for one so young. Decorated twice in Afghanistan.' He smiled. 'I envy you your inevitable success.'

'We'll try not to disappoint you, Comrade.'

They went, pausing only at the entrance as the rain increased heavily. 'I've often thought about this war and asked myself why any sane person would want this place,' Bounine said.

'It's a game, my friend,' Kurbsky told him. 'People like Chelek move the pieces to suit themselves, it's their particular vanity.'

'And the pieces are the people like us who do their bidding,' Bounine said. 'I told you – it's Biblical.'

'Idiot,' Kurbsky said. 'But let's get on with it. Maybe there could be a medal in it for you.'

'But I've got a medal,' Bounine said plaintively, and followed him, as Kurbsky ran out through the rain and back towards the tent and the others.

So, in the darkness at four thirty, they sat in a line on a bench seat in the Dakota, the anchor cable above them, each man fully kitted out, Bounine, as the most experienced, seated close to the door. Kurbsky, at the other end of the line, had his radio at the ready and the engines were already throbbing.

Bashir said, 'Right, Lieutenant, here we go.'

The Dakota started to move, the roaring of the engines

filled the plane, and then they were lifting and speeding away at low level to get away from Grozny as quickly as possible.

The rain continued, hammering the aircraft, the wind howled, but Bashir held her steady, flying at four thousand feet, the mountains shrouded in cloud below. When he finally started his descent, they went into a kind of mist and then burst out of it and there was visibility, a grey pre-dawn light infused with a kind of luminosity that covered the mountains. He was very low now, drifting through a wide canyon at a thousand feet, and spoke to Bounine over the radio.

'Door open, Sergeant.' A red light blinked on and off. Bounine called, 'Clip on and stand.' They all did as they were told. The Dakota was at five hundred and there was much more light now in the flat expanse of the Kuban Plateau. Bashir made his pass at three hundred and fifty feet, the red light turning to green, and Bounine tapped Kirov, the first in line, on the shoulder and yelled 'go,' which the boy did, followed by the others, tumbling out one after the other, Kurbsky last. Bounine yelled on his radio, 'All gone!', clipped on to the anchor cable and dived out.

Bashir started to climb up to four thousand, levelled out and switched to automatic pilot, got up, went back and closed the door. He returned, took control again to ten thousand, levelled out and turned back to Grozny. 'Well, I'll never see any of that lot again,' he murmured. 'Madness. Bloody crazy.'

* * *

Kurbsky, looking down, could see the rough moorland of the plateau below, outcrops of rock here and there, and it was all over in what seemed a flash, his supply bag thumping into the ground, followed by himself. He seemed to bounce and fell sideways and a stiff wind billowed his canopy. He started to drag, grabbed at his quick-release buckle, and it opened and the wind in the parachute pulled it off him and blew it across the moor.

He unclipped his jump bag, got it open and armed himself quickly. The Stechkin stuffed in his blouse, the bag slung from his back. With the AK still folded he started searching for the others, which was easy enough, for he could see them dotted around, struggling with their canopies in the wind. He dumped his helmet and put on his beret.

Bounine was free and helping those who were having difficulties, working his way from chute to chute. He reached one on the far left and leaned down. He turned and beckoned. Kurbsky hurried towards him, others following, and found him standing over Petrovsky.

'Dead already. Broken neck.' Bounine shook his head. 'Ridiculous. He jumped in Afghanistan a number of times with the Storm Guards. Now he has to get it in a shitty place like this.' He looked around the bleak moorland, the rain hammering down.

Kurbsky said, 'Put him behind those rocks over there, collect those parachutes, and hide them as best you can behind the outcrop. Fifteen minutes and get your ponchos out.' He looked up at the turbulent sky as thunder rumbled. 'It's really going to storm, my friends.'

He got the radio from his pack, crouched down and tried to contact Father Ramsan.

'Black Tiger calling, Black Tiger calling. Are you receiving me?'

It was rather dramatic, but that's what Chelek had given as a codeword for the enterprise, and it received an instant response. 'Receiving you loud and clear.'

'Ramsan? This is Lieutenant Kurbsky. We've arrived in the jump zone safely, one man dead. Harsh weather up here, but we should see you in a couple of hours.'

'I look forward to it.'

'Over and out.' He turned to the men. 'Let's get on with it.'

And rain it did and he really pushed them, leading at the half trot, the twelve of them in their ponchos with the hoods up over their berets. Five miles and two hours later they came to moorland farm territory, extensive rough granite walls, wild-looking sheep that scattered before them. They reached a shepherd's stone hut and crouched behind the wall beside it.

Bounine produced a bottle of vodka from his pack, unscrewed it and took a swallow, offered it to Kurbsky, who did the same, then passed it along so that everybody could have a pull. Perhaps a mile or more across the valley was the monastery, half-concealed by the gloom and rain. At that distance, it was not possible to see any signs of activity. In any case, what concerned him was the farm below.

It was single-storey, but reasonably extensive, with what

looked like a large barn at one end, and the only sign of life was chickens looking miserable in the rain, pecking their way in and out of the half-open barn door. There was a low wall around the property, a wisp of smoke coming out of the chimney. A track stretched down the valley, and no sign of life there either.

'We split, two groups of six, you go in from the left,' he said to Bounine. 'I'll take the right.'

They moved fast, Kurbsky leading his men crouching behind a granite wall and curving round to an orchard cramped in a small space at the side of the house. There was what looked like a back door. It opened on the turn of the handle and he led the way in to an extensive, if primitive, kitchen, with stone floor, very basic wooden furniture, an old iron stove with a wood fire burning inside; a great pot on the stove.

Kirov took the lid off. 'Smells good. Some sort of stew and enough to feed an army. Maybe it's meant for us?'

'That could well be.' Kurbsky turned to the others, who'd been searching elsewhere. 'Anything?'

'A couple of bedrooms, a pantry with a lot of canned food and wine.'

He went and opened the front door and saw the others through the half-open door of the barn. Bounine appeared. 'Come and have a look.'

There was an old battered truck with a canvas hood and a stack of military jerry cans. 'A hell of a lot of petrol here,' Bounine said. 'What about the house?'

The Tigers clustered around, passing cigarettes. 'Food

cooking, fire in the stove. No sign of Father Ramsan. I'll try the radio again,' and at that moment there was the sound of an approaching engine.

They waited, weapons cocked, and a bearded priest in his black robes drove in from the track on a motorcycle, crossed the yard and entered the barn. He showed no surprise at all and on closer inspection wore black trousers, his cassock hitched up as he sat astride the bike. He switched off the engine, dismounted and pulled it up on its stand.

'So you are the Black Tigers?'

'Yes, Father, I'm Lieutenant Kurbsky in command.'

Kirov was examining the bike with admiration. 'Where did you get this? My uncle has one back home on his sheep ranch near Kursk. A Montessa dirt bike.'

'What's so special about them?' Bounine asked.

It was Father Ramsan who answered. 'They were specially developed for shepherds in the Pyrenees in the Spanish high country. You can ride them at five miles an hour, or more if you want, negotiating very rough country, or much faster. They are perfect for the plateau country here. General Basayev obtained it for me.'

'That would seem very generous of him,' Kurbsky said.

'Of course, but then I'm on his payroll and he trusts me.'

'And so does General Chelek,' Bounine pointed out.

'We live in a complicated world, my friend.' Ramsan turned to Kurbsky. 'Bring your men into the house. I have food waiting.'

*   *   *

They ate well of the stew and he provided jugs of rough red wine. 'So no one lives here with you?' Kurbsky asked.

'A peasant family farmed the land, but they've been driven off. Basayev doesn't like people around when he's in residence at the monastery. He chased the monks away from there, but he tolerates the peasants when he's off to the war. Since he's back, they have to clear out to a village about five miles on the other side of Kuba.'

'So no staff in the monastery?'

'He's a soldier's soldier and expects his men to be able to look after themselves. Sometimes they go and procure women for obvious purposes.'

'Are there any women at the moment?'

'Definitely not. When he comes on these occasions, his time seems to be spent on planning strategy. He has a sophisticated radio room and keeps in touch daily with his forces in the field. I have heard them on occasion when I've been there.'

'So why does he keep you around?' Bounine asked.

'As some sort of link with the locals. I am, after all, their priest. I am also a visible presence at the monastery when he's not here to remind people who the boss is.'

'Where have you just been?' Kurbsky asked.

'The monastery. He likes the chapel kept up to scratch. He's a religious man who likes everything to be just so. Candles, incense, the holy water, flowers.'

'Well, he sounds like a raving lunatic to me,' Bounine put in. 'So what do we do about him?'

'You may be right,' Father Ramsan said. 'But as to a plan

of action.' He looked at his watch. 'It's nine thirty. They're military, they follow a fixed routine. Two of the men are appointed cooks. I keep them supplied with plenty of fresh food, driving to the village in the truck every two or three days. Their mid-day break is in the old monastery dining room next to the kitchens, starting at noon. They drink quite heavily. The monastery was known for its wine. Basayev joins them only sometimes. I couldn't guarantee he would be in the dining room. Often he prefers to eat in his own quarters.'

'You're sure of all this information?' Kurbsky asked.

'Based on what I have seen when I'm there.'

'And his men,' Bounine put in. 'What do they do all day? What are their duties?'

'To guard the monastery and protect him, it's that simple.'

'So what are you suggesting?'

'To surprise them during their mid-day meal. As I've said, they drink heavily and you would have total surprise on your side.'

Gorky nodded. 'What's this secret way inside that Chelek mentioned?'

'Outside the walls is a decaying vineyard, decaying because with the monks not there, nobody has the expertise to look after it. It's overgrown badly and in the thickets there is the entrance to what was an escape tunnel during the bad times three centuries ago.'

There was a groan from the men, and Bounine said, 'Not the damned sewers again. We've had enough of those in Grozny.'

'No, there are steps down and headroom to six feet. I have been through it many times over the years. You emerge through a false wall on a pivot into a series of cellars leading to an underground hall, used for storage years ago during sieges, but quite empty when I last looked in, and that was a year ago. From there, wide stone steps lead where you want to go.'

'Fascinating,' Kurbsky said. 'You could always show us the way.'

'That wasn't in the bargain, I think,' Ramsan said calmly.

'I appreciate your survival instincts,' Kurbsky told him. 'So, what's the plan?'

'Simple enough. I'll drive you down in the supply truck and deliver you to the vineyard. The rest would be up to you. I would suggest leaving here at eleven thirty. They should be in full swing in the dining room by the time you get there.'

Kurbsky turned to his men. 'Go over your weapons: pistol, AK, check your grenades, then do it again. After that, rest. It's been quite a day already, and a lot more to it before it's over.'

It was just after noon when the truck turned in at the gate of the old vineyard, moved along the track under a spread of tree branches and came to a halt. They all climbed down and followed Ramsan as he led the way through decaying vines, a battery lantern in his left hand, and came to an old stone outhouse. He opened the door and stood on the step. It was very black wood.

He leaned down and felt on the inside of the step. 'There's an iron ring. That's it.' He pulled and raised a section of the floor which folded back to disclose stone steps about six feet wide dropping into darkness. He turned and offered the lantern to Kurbsky, who shook his head.

'You take it. After all, you know the way. I'd feel safer.'

'That wasn't the deal.'

'Well, it is now.' Ramsan looked as if he was about to speak, then he took a deep breath, switched on the lantern and went down.

It was perfectly dry, quite airy, and as Ramsan had said, a good six feet in diameter. He played the light out well in front of them so they could see the false wall up ahead. He paused on getting to it, reached into a corner and pulled some sort of lever, and the wall pivoted. There was a cellar on the other side with an archway.

Ramsan turned and said, 'The door can only be locked from the other side. Leave it ajar.' He carried on, leading the way through one archway after another, walked through the last one, and suddenly switched off the lantern and ran.

Panic ensued. 'Where the hell is he?' Kirov cried, just as floodlights were turned on to reveal the underground hall Ramsan had mentioned. On a stone shelf about four feet high, two light machine guns on tripods were mounted, with two men behind each one. Other men were ranged at the sides, AK47s at the ready.

Ramsan, still on the run, was making for the broad steps

he had mentioned, soldiers waiting there, and Shadid Basayev walked through.

One of the Tigers called, 'You lying bastard,' raised his AK to fire at Ramsan and was cut down by a burst from one of the machine guns.

'Is this what the rest of you want?' the General asked. 'I am Shadid Basayev. If I say slaughter the lot of you now, my men will be happy to oblige. It's all one to me. Who is Kurbsky?'

'That would be me.' Kurbsky stepped forward.

'And these are the Black Tigers?' Basayev nodded. 'A sad-looking bunch, if you don't mind me saying so, and only eleven?'

'We used to be fifty.'

'That's good, we must be winning the war.' He stood there, hands on hips. 'Come on, Lieutenant, what's it to be?' He stepped very close. 'Of course, you could shoot me now in a mad moment, but my men wouldn't like that.' Kurbsky stared into his eyes, trying to work him out, and Basayev smiled. 'One soldier to another. Articles of war strictly observed at all times.'

It wasn't that Kurbsky believed him. It was just that if there was even the smallest of chances that he was telling the truth, it was better than all of them being reduced to bloody pulp on the spot here.

'All right, lads, stand down.'

He started to remove his packs, and placed his weapons on the ground and, reluctantly, his men followed his example. Chechens moved in and started stripping the Tigers of anything worth having. Father Ramsan stood on the steps, watching impassively.

'So, our man of God is still with us,' Kurbsky said.

Bounine did a strange thing. 'Bastards.' He bit the end of his thumb. '*Infamita*. May you rot in hell.'

'Hey, what is this? Is your sergeant an Italian or something?' Basayev demanded.

'No, he's Russian, but he studied law at the university in Rome.'

Basayev was confounded. 'So did I.'

'I was some years after you,' Bounine said.

'Did they remember me?'

'They spoke of the Italian girl who became your wife as a most wonderful person and much loved.'

'She was – she was. We must talk.' He turned to Kurbsky. 'Now, what am I to do with you? Like me, I suspect you are a true soldier. I've been reading this German philosopher lately. He says that for authentic living, what is necessary is the resolute confrontation of death. Would you agree?'

'Heidegger,' Kurbsky said. 'His writing was Heinrich Himmler's bible.'

'You've read Heidegger? We must talk some more.' He turned to one of his officers. 'Take these two to the cell on floor one. No need to tie them. Lock them up with a bottle of wine. I'll send for them later.'

Kurbsky said, 'What about my men?'

'They'll be dealt with.'

'You gave me your word. One soldier to another.'

'So I did. Do you doubt my word? That would make me very angry. Take them away – now.' His voice lifted, and the young officer nodded to four men who herded Kurbsky and Bounine up the steps into an echoing hall, then up a second flight. There was an iron-banded door at the top with a key in the lock, and they were pushed into a room with two narrow beds and a barred window.

The officer said, 'One of my men will be back with the wine, but may I offer some advice? Do not annoy the General in any way. The results could be disastrous.' He went out.

Kurbsky said, 'I get the feeling I may have handled this whole affair terribly badly.'

'Don't be stupid,' Bounine told him. 'We were sold out by the man of God before we even got here. So much for General Chelek's reliable source.'

The door opened, they turned, and a soldier tossed a bottle of wine at them, which Bounine just caught. The door closed, the key turned.

'Not wine, some sort of brandy with a screw top. Must be good.' Bounine got it off, tried it and shrugged. 'Not bad, really. A kind of plum brandy.' He handed the bottle to Kurbsky, who tried it and at that moment, elsewhere in the monastery, someone screamed.

'Mother of God, not that,' Bounine said in a kind of prayer. He put out his hand for the bottle and held it against him. After a while, the screaming stopped. 'Thank God.'

'I'm afraid not.' Kurbsky stood at the barred window, looking down into the courtyard. Bounine joined him.

A long pole was stretched between two tripods about seven

feet above the ground. Three men manhandled a body with a noose around its neck and a hook on the end, which they slipped over the pole, and the corpse simply hung there.

'Could you tell who it was?' Bounine asked in a low voice.

'Too much blood on his face.' Kurbsky held out his hand. 'Give me the bottle.'

He took a long drink and someone else screamed. 'The bastards,' Bounine said. 'They're going to finish all nine.'

'All eleven when he remembers he's got us waiting.' Kurbsky handed the bottle over.

An hour and a half later, there were seven out there hanging shoulder to shoulder. 'Like washing on a line to that bastard,' Bounine said.

There was more thunder, a rumble, and the skies opened in a deluge again. They watched body number eight hung up.

'Not long now.' Bounine put the bottle to his lips. 'Christ, it's finally empty.'

He looked as if he was going to toss it away, but Kurbsky took it from him and smashed it against the wall. He handed it back, ignoring new screams, and the broken and splintered end looked incredibly dangerous.

'Hold it carefully. It's a hell of a weapon.'

'What for?' Bounine asked in despair.

'To fight with. I've got a weapon, too.' His hand went down to his right boot, he found the gutting knife, pulled it out, and held it up, springing the blade. 'My little secret.'

He closed the blade. Whoever it was had stopped screaming. He went to the window and watched as they hooked him up. Shadid Basayev and Father Ramsan walked down steps from the main door. Laughter drifted up, and Basayev said something to Ramsan, who turned and went back inside.

'What are we going to do?' Bounine asked.

'Kill whoever enters this room, if possible, and then run like hell back down to the cellars. Remember, Ramsan left the secret door ajar. If we can get out to that truck, we could be driving away before they realize what's happening.'

'But where to? They'll be after us with every vehicle they've got.'

'I could have an answer to that back at the farm.' There were steps in the corridor, voices, the key turned in the lock.

Ramsan himself had come or, more probably, had been sent. He entered hesitantly, and a burly Chechen with a Muslim-style beard moved in behind him, holding an Uzi machine pistol at the ready.

'The General has sent me to bring you. I'm sorry.'

The Chechen moved to one side and gestured with the Uzi. Bounine said to Ramsan, 'Sorry, are you, you bastard?'

Kurbsky half-turned to the Chechen, he pressed the button of the gutting knife and thrust the razor-sharp blade under the chin, penetrating the roof of the mouth and sticking it into the brain. At the same moment, Bounine's hand swung from behind his back, where he had been concealing the bottle. He stabbed Ramsan in the side of the neck, severing the carotid artery. He pushed his falling body on to the bed. Kurbsky pulled out his knife, picked up the Uzi dropped by the Chechen, opened one of his belt pouches and found three clips of ammunition, which he stuffed into the pockets of his combat jacket. He was through the door and, a moment later, Bounine was on his heels and rushing down the stairs.

Strangely, the only thing on his mind as he ran through the cellars was if Ramsan had left the key in the truck, but he had, and Kurbsky scrambled up behind the wheel, Bounine joining him, reversed out of the vineyard, turned and drove as fast as possible back to the farm.

Bounine said, 'What was it you had in mind? They'll be after us soon.'

'I'll show you,' Kurbsky said, as they turned into the barn.

He jumped down and went to the Montessa. 'This will go where they can't. It was specially built for riding in rough high country. I'll drive, there's a pillion for you and the rear side panniers could take a jerry can of petrol on each side. I'll strap them on while you go into the house and fill a bag with food and find a couple of overcoats. There's bound to be something in there. Cross-country to Grozny over the mountains will be rough, but we could do it in a couple of days.'

Bounine was back in minutes. 'This is the best I could do.' There were a couple of old army greatcoats and they pulled them on and he managed to stuff the food somewhere along with the jerry cans.

'I've been thinking, Chelek isn't going to be pleased.'

Kurbsky, astride, started the engine. 'Screw Chelek, but

the Army's the Army and there are rules. You always report to your commanding officer.'

Bounine sat astride the pillion. 'So let's go.'

Which they did, climbing up rough tracks. Bounine looked back and saw a couple of trucks in the far distance, but then the rain started again and they simply vanished.

They reached Grozny in four days, not two, and reported to Chelek's headquarters, to discover that the previous day he'd insisted on making an inspection of his sector of Grozny standing in the turret of a tank and a Chechen sniper had shot him in the head.

The desk colonel controlling things while waiting for a new general to arrive told Kurbsky and Bounine to put their report in writing, which they did. He actually read it, shaking his head.

'Nine guys, just like that. These Chechens are animals. As for Shadid Basayev, we'll put him on the most wanted list as a war criminal.'

'And us?' Kurbsky asked.

'There's a shortage of good people in intelligence these days, and it seems you've got a law degree, Bounine, which interests the GRU. You're going to leave all this shit behind. It's Moscow for you, and there's a commission waiting.'

'But I don't want a commission, Comrade.'

'What you want isn't the point, Bounine, it's what your country wants.'

'And me, Comrade?' Kurbsky asked.

'You stay, Lieutenant – or should I say, Captain? You're promoted. You stay here in the killing ground of Grozny. I'd say it suits your particular talents to perfection.'

And to that, of course, there was no answer.

Holland Park

Mayfair

Belsize Park

10

Bad memories led to an extremely disturbed night for Kurbsky, who didn't fall asleep until the early hours. He came awake suddenly, surprised to discover it was eight o'clock. He tried to shake himself awake with a good shower, but it didn't have much effect, and when he examined himself in the mirror, the circles around the eyes really did look much darker. He dressed and went in search of life and discovered Roper, in the computer room as usual, who looked him over.

'You look satisfactorily ill,' he said. 'That's the only way to describe it. Bad night?'

'You could say that.'

'It's not surprising. You've been through it in a big way

in the last day or two. I'd get yourself to the dining room. There you'll find a lady named Mrs Maggie Hall, the pride of Jamaica, whose speciality is the great English breakfast. If that doesn't revive you, nothing will.'

'Sound advice, and I'll take it.'

He came back dressed for the street, his bag slung from his shoulder, his gutting knife stuffed down his right boot. The knife he'd taken from the youth at Wapping the previous night, he took from his pocket and placed on Roper's desk.

'Present for you.'

Roper pressed the button and the blade jumped. 'Nasty,' he said. 'Where did you get that?'

'Unlooked-for gift. I thought you might find it useful as a letter opener. I'll be on my way.'

'Give the ladies my regards and take your time, Alex. I'm here for you day or night in this damn chair. It's the one constant in an uncertain world.'

'My anchor?' Kurbsky said.

'If you like.'

'I'll try and remember that.' He turned and went out.

He walked down past Holland Park, thinking about it. Svetlana and Katya would be expecting him at Chamber Court and he needed to visit the local shop to establish his credentials, but that could wait. He glanced at his watch. It was just before nine and he knew where he wanted to be, had to be, if you like, and he emerged on to the main road, flagged a black cab and told the driver to take him to Marble Arch.

He'd already taken the first step on a journey from which there was no going back. In the apartment at Holland Park he'd found a paperback A to Z of London, with maps, lists, everything you needed to know. He'd already checked on church listings and discovered St Mary and All the Angels in Hive Street, Mayfair. He'd chosen to alight at Marble Arch so as to be inconspicuous, and a brisk fifteen-minute walk brought him to St Mary's. Rain started to fall and it occurred to him that it might possibly put Basayev off, but if so, there would be other days. He pulled up the hood of his combat jacket.

The church looked familiar to him from the television report. He didn't go in by the main doors, which had a pseudo-medieval look about them, oak banded by iron, but followed the side path which brought him round to the cemetery at the rear.

There were cypress trees, rhododendron bushes, pine trees. Not much in the way of flowers, but that was the season of the year. On the other hand, this was Mayfair and the paths and grass verges were scrupulously kept.

Kurbsky had always rather liked cemeteries and their melancholic atmosphere, and St Mary's was a superb example: Victorian-Gothic tombs, winged angels, poignant effigies of the children of the rich, and symbols of death on every hand.

The television footage helped him find Basayev's wife's grave quickly, too. It was neat enough, a curve of speckled marble rising in the centre to a portrait of a handsome dark-haired woman in a circle of glass. *In Memoriam. Rosa Rossi Basayev. Never Forgotten*, that was the inscription in gold lettering followed by a date.

Kurbsky stepped back to the other side of the path, where there was a marble doorway, a bench across it, a standing cross behind. He sat down, opened his bag and found the silenced Walther. He cocked it and held it by his side, remembering Kuba, the monastery, and what Basayev had done so long ago. He felt calm, quite detached, and it was quiet, just the rain rushing down. Maybe Basayev wouldn't come after all, but that was all right. He could come back.

The Mercedes pulled up in front of the church. The chauffeur had served under Basayev in Chechnya, had been his driver for years. He had an umbrella on the floor beside him, which he took with him as he went to assist his master. He opened it and handed it to Basayev as he got out.

A few yards from the church, on the corner of a side street, a young woman sat under a canopy with flowers for sale. 'The usual, Josef, bring them to me,' Basayev told his driver.

He turned into the side path to the cemetery, and Josef got another umbrella from the back of the car and approached the girl.

Basayev was quite close to his wife's memorial before he noticed Kurbsky, and he slowed. 'What are you doing here?' He spoke in English. 'What do you want?'

'You,' Kurbsky told him in Russian. 'It's been a long time since Kuba. Remember the monastery, the courtyard, the nine Black Tigers who weren't dancing on air because you'd butchered them before you hung them up? It was raining then, too.'

'What in the hell are you talking about? Who are you?'

'Alexander Kurbsky, and don't tell me that name hasn't meant something to you over the years. Remember the cellar in the monastery where you persuaded me to surrender? You gave me your word, one soldier to another, that the articles of war would be strictly observed at all times, then you butchered nine of my men.'

At that moment, Josef came round the corner with the bunch of flowers in one hand, the umbrella in the other. 'Here I am, boss,' he said in Russian.

Basayev turned and shouted, 'Help me, Josef, he's going to kill me.'

Josef dropped both the flowers and the umbrella and drew a pistol. Kurbsky, with no option, shot him in the heart and turned to find Basayev already scrambling away through the gravestones. He shot him in the back of the head, fragments of bone and brain spraying out as he fell on his face. He walked back up the path to Josef, still dying, and finished him off with a head shot.

He stood listening for a moment, but everything was still, no evidence of any disturbance, thanks to the silenced Walther. It was now that his examination of the street maps paid off. He walked quickly to the other end of the cemetery and found what he was looking for, another gate leading out to a quiet back street, and he started to walk through Mayfair, one street after another.

He felt no elation, no satisfaction. It was not needed. Shadid

Basayev had been responsible for carnage and butchery and the ethnic cleansing of several thousand people. Thanks to the stupidity of society, he had been rewarded with many millions and the right to live in luxury in the best part of London. Now, his account was closed.

An hour later, he stopped in a small square with a garden and benches. There was no need to tell Roper and company about what he'd done. On the other hand, Moscow would be delighted to hear of Basayev's assassination, and he had Tania to think about, after all. It would be to his credit.

He used his encrypted mobile to reach not Luhzkov but Bounine and got him straight away. 'Yuri, it's me, Alex. Where are you? Can you talk?'

'In my office.' Bounine was surprised. 'Yes, of course I can talk.'

'Did you see Shadid Basayev on BBC television last night?'

'I sure did. The scum.'

'Tell me, does he have a chauffeur named Josef?'

'Yes, Josef Limov. He served under him in Chechnya. He's been his personal hit man for years.'

'Ah, that's good, I don't need to feel bad about killing him.'

Bounine said, 'Killing him? Are you crazy?'

'I hope not. I've just shot him dead in the cemetery at St Mary and All the Angels, along with Basayev, of course. He was my primary target. You know he said he liked to look in on his wife's memorial every morning? I thought I'd say hello.'

'Alex, there hasn't been a word of this on radio or television.'

'Because they haven't found the bodies yet.'

'But how could this happen? Is this something to do with Ferguson's people?'

'They don't know a thing about it and that's how it stays.' He lied now. 'I'm very happy living in the safe house at Holland Park. I have an arrangement where I'm allowed out for a break on my own. They trust me completely.'

'So you're going back in there?'

'Why wouldn't I? Tell Luhzkov I'll be in touch again when I feel like it, I don't want him trying to call me. This should make him look good in Moscow, don't you think?'

'What about your aunt?'

'What do you mean? The whole idea was to guarantee my anonymity so that no one except Ferguson's people know I'm here. Svetlana is the last person I'd want to involve. I don't want her bothered, Yuri, you understand me?'

He clicked off and at the other end Bounine shook his head and smiled slightly. 'Christ Almighty, Basayev. I hope he rots in hell.' He got up and went off to find Luhzkov.

Kurbsky walked further until he finally came to Oxford Street. He was thinking of Svetlana and Katya now. It was time he made his way to Belsize Park, and then he came to a large book store, the windows full of displays and deals, and there was *On the Death of Man*. It was a new edition from his London publisher. On impulse he went into the store, took off his woollen hat and put it in his pocket, then wandered around a little before approaching the counter.

The assistant he chose was a long-haired young man of studious and intense appearance. 'Can I help you?'

Kurbsky put on his French accent. 'There is this novel *On the Death of Men* by Alexander Kurbsky. I've read it in French, but I see you have a new edition in English? I would enjoy comparing the two.'

The young man turned away and was back in a moment with a copy. 'An excellent idea. I suppose it could be argued that to really get the essence of it, one should read it in Russian.'

'I see your point,' Kurbsky said. 'Have you read it?'

'Good heavens, yes, who hasn't? A remarkable man.'

He had the book in his hand and Kurbsky said, 'The French edition I read had no photo.'

'This one has, a most excellent one.' He showed it to him.

Kurbsky nodded. 'He looks like quite a character.'

The young man smiled with real enthusiasm. 'I only wish we could get him in here for a book signing. They'd be queuing round the block. Will you take it, sir?'

'Certainly.' Kurbsky paid cash and, playing his role to the hilt, said, 'I'm going in for more therapy. Reading it will help pass the time.'

The young man's face clouded. 'I hope things go well for you.'

'So do I.'

He went out, dropped the book in his bag and pulled his woollen hat back on. It was the ultimate test and he had passed it. Time to report in at Chamber Court. He decided to go on the underground and made for the nearest station.

It was around that time that Father Patrick Meehan, after an hour of hearing confession in St Mary's, went into the vestry, found an umbrella and went out through the side door to have a smoke. He had managed to get his consumption down to five a day. A desperate struggle, but he was trying hard. He lit up, turned into the cemetery and almost fell over Josef.

As someone who had served as a parish priest in Belfast during the Troubles, death was something he was extremely familiar with. Josef, with blood all over his face, was clearly gone, so he rushed to Basayev and saw immediately he was a lost cause, too.

He took out his mobile and called for an ambulance and then informed the police. He returned to Josef and felt for a pulse, just to be sure. There was none, but in the circumstances, his duty as a priest was clear. He began to recite the prayers for the dying. *Go, Christian soul, from this world in the Name of God the Father Almighty who created thee.*

Soon sirens sounded, and not one, but two ambulances braked hard outside the church and the paramedics came on the run.

The general store that Katya had mentioned to Kurbsky carried a sign: *Patel & Son.* It was what the English were fond of calling the Corner Shop, a place that was always open and sold everything. It was quiet, no customers, the radio was playing softly in the background and the young man sitting behind the counter was Indian, wearing jeans and a black bomber jacket, and he was reading a book, which he put down when Kurbsky appeared.

'Can I help you?'

'I hope so,' Kurbsky said. 'A friend of mine, a Polish guy named Marek, had a job at a house near here with two ladies? He worked in the garden, did odd jobs and they let him live over the garage.'

'That's right. I knew Marek well. I'm Hitesh Patel.' He offered his hand.

Kurbsky shook it. 'I've had a letter from them offering me the job, now that he's gone back to Poland. Marek recommended me.'

He produced it. Hitesh read it and nodded. 'I see. What's the problem?'

'I'm not sure if I've got the right house. I'm new to London, and I seem to have gotten all mixed up.'

Hitesh came round the counter, took him to the door and pointed. 'It's right there, with the high walls. They're big on security. Front gate or side gate, there's a voice box, so you speak to let them know you're there. They're really nice ladies. You'll do well there.'

'That's good to hear.'

Hitesh was concerned. 'So you need regular chemotherapy?'

'That's right. Lung cancer.'

'I'm sorry. You've really got to take it easy. Can I offer you a cup of coffee? We've got the machine there.'

'I'd rather have tea.'

'I'll join you.'

They sat on either side of the counter, and Kurbsky said, 'You're not very busy.'

'Not during the lunch hour, it's all local trade.'

'There's just you then?'

Hitesh laughed. 'My father and mother have gone home to Bombay for three months, and I'm sitting in for them. A couple of local ladies come in part time.'

'What do you usually do?'

'I'm a medical student, just starting my fourth year.'

'Where did you go to university?'

'Here in London.' He laughed. 'A great disappointment to my father, because I'm not a businessman. I'm too English for them. I was born here.'

'I know the feeling. I have a French father and I was born in Devon. I read English at London University, then I worked as a journalist, before . . .' He gave an excellent performance. 'Well, you know what I mean. Look, thanks a lot. I'll see you again.'

'Take care,' Hitesh told him, and Kurbsky left.

He approached the house from the mews. Katya answered, opened the gate, and he walked through the garden and found her waiting on the terrace. She took his hands and kissed him on both cheeks.

'We were getting worried. We expected you earlier.'

'I've just been having a cup of tea with Hitesh Patel and showed him your letter. He's a nice guy.'

'Svetlana's waiting.'

They went into the conservatory and found her in her usual wicker chair. She reached up to kiss him. 'We were worried for you.'

'No need, *Babushka*. Last night I went down to the Salters' pub at Wapping and had supper. I got a taxi and then walked the streets. This morning, I did the same. Actually, I had a funny experience in Oxford Street.'

'What was that?' Katya asked.

He told them about the episode in the book store. 'Isn't it wonderful?' he said. 'Even with my photo on the book he was holding, he still didn't recognize me.'

Katya said, 'There was a call for you.'

'There couldn't have been,' he said.

'Sorry, I mean the call was through me. Major Roper gave me one of those encrypted Codex mobiles. He said he'd been trying to get you, but couldn't get a response.'

'I've had mine on vibrate. I'll speak to him.'

'I've got chilli con carne for lunch. I'll show you the room over the garage afterwards.'

'But first, there's champagne,' Svetlana told him. 'A celebration of your return after all these years.'

'Just give me a moment,' he said. 'I must call Major Roper.'

'You were trying to get me,' he said, when Roper answered.

'Yes, there was no response, so I got worried.'

'I put my Codex on vibrate and it's easy to miss that faint

tremble, especially when you're walking in the crowds of Oxford Street. What did you want?'

'There's a breaking story on all the news shows. Shadid Basayev and his driver, a man named Josef Limov, were stiffed at that church in Mayfair where he has a memorial to his wife.'

'And when was this?'

'The priest, a Father Meehan, came across the bodies in the church cemetery not much more than an hour ago.'

'So information will be thin on the ground at the moment. What do you think, a Russian connection? SVR perhaps,' he said, naming the Foreign Intelligence Service that was in many ways a successor to the KGB.

'I'm not so sure. In the old days, they often hired the IRA to do their dirty work. These days, Muslims are popular.'

'Mind you, he was a bad one, Basayev,' Kurbsky said. 'He won't be missed.'

'I'll give it some thought. We'll speak again.'

'I might drop in to see you.'

'You know where I am.'

Luhzkov heard what Bounine had to say, was shocked and delighted. There was no point in holding back on the story, and as it started to break, he contacted the Prime Minister's suite at the Kremlin and spoke to Putin.

'I am obviously pleased that Basayev has finally met his end, but the manner of it gives me pause for thought.'

'I can see that, Comrade Prime Minister. He treads a

dangerous path. You don't want to make fools of Ferguson and his people.'

'On the other hand, it's a brilliant stroke if he gets away with it,' Putin laughed. 'I like it. Let it ride, Colonel, and we'll see where it leads.'

Bounine, sitting opposite him, said, 'How was he?'

'Delighted. I think the idea of Kurbsky making fools of Ferguson's company actually pleases him. I won't try to speak to Kurbsky. I'll leave it to you, Yuri, you're the man he trusts.'

The living quarters over the garage were not quite as he remembered them. The bathroom had been improved, but the big room where Kelly had taught Kurbsky judo had been developed into another apartment, a kitchen area in one corner, a living room in another and a wide window looking out over the garden. It was nicely furnished and in good order.

'I had cleaners in after Marek left, and a plumber to improve the bathroom and kitchen. It's linked to the central heating system in the main house,' Katya said. 'Svetlana wants this to work, Alex, and so do I.'

'Sit down for a minute.' She faced him across the table and he took her hand. 'You've been great to me, your input in this affair has been fabulous, and I know you're a true friend to my aunt. It seems to be working, my new identity. As I've told you, I've been out and about, and I feel that Alexander Kurbsky is the invisible man. I can come and go at Holland Park as Henri Duval. Let's take it a day at a time.'

'Good,' she said. 'Regarding your new identity, I hesitate to bring this up, but –'

'But you think I'd better actually do some gardening now and then, to fit my cover story, right?'

'Right,' she said with relief. 'I'll just show you the garage and the equipment and we'll go back to Svetlana.'

Downstairs she pressed a button, and the garage door lifted. There was a riding mower, garden tools of every description, and a small Ford van in dark green. 'It doesn't look much, but I use it as a general runaround. It's been in here for years. Just use it as you see fit. The right documents are in the glove compartment, and they include Henri Duval's name. The key's in there also, and a hand control to let you in or out at the front gate.'

'Excellent.' He smiled. 'Let's go back to the conservatory and help Svetlana finish that bottle of champagne.'

Shortly after the news came out of the bloodbath at St Mary and All the Angels, Ferguson had spoken to Roper. 'It's like Belfast on a bad Saturday night in the old days. The Prime Minister and the Cabinet Office are not pleased.'

'People like Basayev shouldn't be allowed in our country just because they've got a few hundred million or a billion or so and it suits the City of London and the Treasury.'

'That's as may be, but it doesn't look good in the papers.'

'Oh, dear, I'm heartbroken, I really am.'

'So who's responsible? Have you spoken to Lord Arthur Tilsey?'

'As a matter of fact, I have, and the Security Services are just as mystified as the rest of us.'

'It's the Russians. It's got to be. They tried to collar Basayev in Moscow. That's why he fled here in the first place. Have you had words with Special Branch at Scotland Yard?'

'Yes, and the word under the counter is the killings are definitely the work of a professional hit man who knew what he was doing. Basayev really asked for it, advertising to the world that he liked to visit his wife's memorial at that church every morning.'

'It's got to be the Russians. Putin will be over the moon.'

'That's what Kurbsky said.'

'What's he got to do with it?'

'We watched Basayev in that television appearance last night. After all, Kurbsky was on the other side in Chechnya. When I spoke to him today at Belsize, he suggested the SVR as a possibility.'

'Do you think that?' Ferguson asked.

'Too direct. As we know better than anyone, they used to give their dirty work on contract to the IRA, or some Muslim faction or other like Al-Qaeda. They like to be able to blame someone else.'

'True enough. And due to Britain's kindness in operating an open-door policy these days, there are an awful lot of real asylum-seekers here, real victims, any one of whom might have relished the thought of shooting that animal.'

'And perhaps did,' Roper said.

'Well, to other matters. It won't have escaped your attention that the American Vice-President, Grant Hardy, is in Paris at the NATO meeting.'

'Yes, I've seen it on the news, and seen Blake Johnson with him. He said in an interview that Blake would be coming to London to discuss NATO matters with the Ministry of Defence. Does that involve you, Charles?'

'Amongst others. But it raises the question again of when we can tell Blake and President Cazalet about Kurbsky.'

'You gave your word, Charles, to preserve his anonymity. Therefore the choice is his, not yours.'

'Is he coming in?'

'I wouldn't be surprised.'

'Do me a favour and raise the matter with him, that's all I ask.'

'Consider it done.'

'Where's Dillon?'

'He's gone to stay with Monica for a few days in Cambridge.'

'How the mighty are fallen.'

Roper poured a Scotch and tapped into the news of the Basayev investigation. The fact that he and his chauffeur had both been armed had leaked and was being made much of. The Russian Ambassador had denied any involvement in the matter, and so had Moscow.

So, with no more story, television had to fall back on fill-in stuff, clips from the war coverage in Chechnya, Basayev in the thick of it, dirty and unkempt and thoroughly ruthless. What was bad wasn't just the carnage of war, but the bodies tumbling into open graves, filmed for real as machine guns did their deadly work, actual footage of Basayev standing there gloating like some Nazi. It was to be expected that he was a hate figure to the Russian Army. And yet Kurbsky had seemed curiously indifferent.

On impulse, Roper tapped into Kurbsky's details again, particularly his war record with the Black Tigers. There were his decorations, and God knows, there were enough of them. Six in all, and a short citation with each one.

On the 5th of February, 1995, this officer, with no previous parachute training, jumped with his men over the Kuba Plateau in an attempt to apprehend General Shadid Basayev. The mission failed, but Lieutenant Kurbsky and Sergeant Yuri Bounine succeeded in rejoining the army, the only survivors of the unit.

Roper sat there looking at it and Sergeant Doyle came in with a mug of tea and a bacon sandwich. 'There you go, sir.'

'Tony, what if I told you I had a man who dropped into action by parachute without any parachute training? What kind of man would do that?'

'A bleeding loony, sir, or a bloody hero. I remember one example I read about: the biggest paratroop drop in history, Arnhem in 1944. One of the outfits lost their doctor with a broken ankle just before boarding, and another young doctor who had no training took his place. They strapped on his chute in the plane and he did the business.' He paused at the door. 'Some people will do anything for a laugh.'

He went out and Roper sat there, and then tapped in Sergeant Yuri Bounine. Decorated twice, once for the same operation as Kurbsky. Transferred to GRU. Present rank Major. Commercial attaché at the Dublin Embassy.

He phoned Kurbsky. 'Where are you?'

'Sorting a few things out in my new quarters over the garage. I spoke to that guy at the local shop up the road. He's Indian – Hitesh Patel. An interesting guy, actually – a fourth-year medical student minding the store while his parents are in Mumbai.'

'What are you up to this evening?'

'I thought I might come and see you. Is that okay?'

'I'm certainly not planning on going anywhere else. The television's been full of the Basayev shooting. Some of the old footage from the Chechen War shows him in a less than flattering light. Was that your opinion, too?'

Roper knew something, it was obvious from his tone. The finest way of handling that was to tell the truth. Kurbsky said, 'He was a vile, sadistic monster, evil in every way. Even the Devil would reject him from Hell, and am I happy that somebody shot the bastard? I couldn't be more delighted.'

'Well, that's plain enough.'

'By the way, Katya's given me a Ford van of the kind gardeners use, to help with my cover. It's green and I'll give you the number.'

Roper took it: 'I'll see you later then.'

They rang off. Kurbsky sat there, then called Bounine and found him in his quarters. 'It's Alex, Yuri. How did Luhzkov take it?'

'He was terribly put out at first, but phoned Putin on his special number. The Prime Minister was delighted and apparently approves of you making fools of Ferguson's people. Luhzkov says he's going to leave contact with you to me, because I'm the only person you trust.'

'That's good, but I have Roper to contend with; a difficult man to fool. Tell me, Yuri, if you bring up your career details on computer does it show the London posting?'

'No, that's classified information because of the peculiarities of the job. It's word of mouth only. As far as my records are concerned, I'm still commercial attaché at Dublin.'

'Excellent. I'll speak to you whenever.'

'Just a minute. Something's come up and it affects someone who's a friend of Ferguson and his people.'

'Go on.'

'His name is Blake Johnson, and he's head of personal security for President Cazalet, so he's big stuff and, according to Luhzkov, very close to Ferguson's group. When he was in London the other year, Luhzkov hired somebody to assassinate him, but it was foiled by this man Dillon and somebody else. Luhzkov's still got a bee in his bonnet about him, don't know why. Anyway, Johnson is apparently coming to London tomorrow on NATO business – and Luhzkov's thinking of kidnapping him.'

'Are you sure about this?'

'I'm not involved, but I sat in. He's using Petrovich and Oleg to do it, you remember them from the safe house outside Moscow?'

'I do indeed. They'd shoot a dog, those two. But anything that touches on Ferguson and his friends touches me, too, so I'm concerned about this. This seems like madness, Yuri!'

'I agree, but Luhzkov's intent on it. You should have seen his face. Must be some old bad blood.'

'Well, keep me informed. Don't let Luhzkov know I know. Keep this to yourself.'

'Of course, Alex, you come first.'

He went through the garden to the house and entered the conservatory, where Svetlana sat playing patience with a background of Rachmaninov's *Fourth Piano Concerto*. Katya stood at her easel, doing a pastel drawing of Monica.

'That's excellent,' he said.

'Not at all. I've got the face, but where's the soul?'

'I've no answer to that. I'm going out for a while down to Holland Park. I was going to drive, but I've been drinking, so I'll find a cab.'

'Are you sure?'

'No problem.' He gave Svetlana a kiss on the forehead and smiled at Katya. 'Don't wait up for me.'

'I've no intention.' She went to the sideboard, opened a drawer and returned with the control device for the gate. 'Now you can go and come as you please.'

'What a woman.' He kissed her lightly on the mouth and went out.

It was pleasant walking down through Belsize Park along Abbey Road, which made him think of the Beatles, and then he came to Swiss Cottage, where there were dozens of cabs swirling by. He hailed one and sat in the back, thinking about what Bounine had just said. Luhzkov was feeling the sap rising because Putin had approved of what Kurbsky had done. So Luhzkov had failed in some previous attempt to deal with Johnson and now the idea of kidnapping him appealed to him, which seemed utterly ludicrous to Kurbsky. If Luhzkov succeeded, what on earth was he going to do with Johnson? He shook his head.

He told the driver to stop at the end of the street, paid him off and walked to the entrance of the safe house. He announced his arrival, the Judas gate opened, he stepped through, and it closed behind him.

11

Doyle nodded to him at the door as he went through to the computer room, where he found Roper watching the news from Moscow.

He turned and smiled. 'There you are, old stick. I must say that cream she's used under your eyes is really doing the trick. You're beginning to look like someone out of an old Hammer horror movie. You didn't drive down, then?'

'Svetlana got the champagne out. A kind of celebration that I'm back in the house.'

'It must be strange for you after sixteen years.'

'And amazing to be with her again. So much of that time has already returned to me with extraordinary clarity. London when I was a teenager, sharp and fresh and full of zip.'

'The age when anything's possible.'

'Or you believe it is.' Kurbsky nodded to the news programme from Moscow showing old war footage of Basayev. 'See, they've even got him for home consumption, black and white and grainy, just like the bastard was in real life.'

'The Kremlin is rejecting the scurrilous charges that they had anything to do with it – while making it clear that the large numbers of people who suffered at the hands of this brutal war criminal, as they describe him, no doubt feel that they have finally seen justice done.'

'I'll drink to that.' Kurbsky went to the sideboard and poured a large vodka. 'Here's to nine good friends of mine who suffered appallingly at his hands. I wasn't quite honest with you when you asked me if I'd known him and I said everyone in the Russian Army did. The truth is I was involved with a unit in Chechnya called the Black Tigers, a special ops paratroop outfit. A reliable source discovered Basayev was at a monastery in the mountains. We were dropped in to try to assassinate him, only the reliable source turned out to be not so reliable.'

'Oh, dear, it was ever thus,' Roper said.

'There were only eleven of us left. He had nine tortured and strung up, and my sergeant and I managed to escape and got back to Grozny.'

'Pass me the whisky.' Kurbsky did and Roper said, 'The sergeant would be Bounine? He must have been a useful chap.'

'Good God, you know all this?' Kurbsky managed to look amazed. 'But how?'

'Your army career on the internet. There's a brief citation next to each decoration explaining the reason for the award. In this case, it also said you jumped without training.'

'Several of us did.' He became very open now. 'Bounine had jumped a time or two in Afghanistan. The most unlikely-looking paratrooper you ever saw. He had a law degree he kept secret from the Army, too.'

'What happened to him?'

'Somebody found out about the law degree and he was transferred to the GRU. There was some talk of a commission, but I was promoted to captain and back in deep shit. I never heard from him again.' He looked at Roper. 'But something tells me you know more than I do.'

Roper grinned. 'Well, cyberspace can reveal all. He's done well for himself. A major and still in the GRU, posing as a senior commercial attaché at the Dublin Embassy.'

'He always had a brain, that was the lawyer in him. That would make him stand out in any crowd.' He sat back. 'So tell me, what's not being reported? You must know the right people at Scotland Yard.'

'Oh, I do, and it's almost funny. Josef Limov, the chauffeur, had been Basayev's hit man for years, and he had a Walther, drawn but not discharged. Basayev also had a Walther, only his was still in his pocket. The post mortems have not been completed, but rounds already recovered from the bodies indicate the weapon used to kill them was also a Walther.'

'It isn't almost funny, it *is* funny.' Kurbsky went to his bag, opened the secret compartment and produced the

Walther he'd been issued. 'So this one makes four. A very popular weapon, thanks to James Bond, easy to use and a hell of a stopping power. The preferred weapon of many hit men in Moscow . . . So you think it was a professional hit?'

'Hard to say. Here you have a thoroughly nasty bit of work full of himself on London television, rich beyond most people's wildest dreams, and amongst the two or three million Londoners watching the programme, there are bound to have been refugees and asylum-seekers who suffered at Basayev's hands.'

'In other words, who would have loved the chance to bump him off? You could say his appearance at the church was an open invitation. There's only one thing wrong with that. From what you say, both men were armed and Josef got as far as drawing his weapon, and yet the killer got both of them. That's the mark of a professional.'

'So that means the Kremlin, either directly or through a contract killer. Since the fall of Communism and the advent of capitalism the battle for money has led to an incredible rise in contract killings in Moscow. Journalists, politicians, businessmen. In this case, I'd say the only questions are who paid and whether the killer was imported or local.'

Roper poured another Scotch. 'And if it's local, there are plenty of possibilities. The criminal scene has changed a lot since the old days of the East End gangsters. The Moscow Mafia has made its mark, and powerful Albanian and Rumanian groups have moved into London.'

'Not to mention the Irish Troubles,' said Kurbsky. 'Wars in Bosnia, Serbia, and Kosovo, the first Gulf War, Iraq and Afghanistan. That adds up to thousands of men not only trained, but used to war. I'm sure many of them would be perfectly capable of doing something like the Basayev killing, especially for money. There used to be a man in Moscow known as Superkiller, who charged fifty thousand dollars for a hit and was seldom unemployed.'

Roper nodded. 'What you're really saying here is that we might never get anyone for these killings, because there are just too many possible suspects? The general public sees a perfectly vile man sitting on his money and laughing at the world, and when he unexpectedly gets what's coming to him, the truth is, they're rather pleased. I guess that's why I can't get particularly worked up about the bastard myself. Anyway, there's something else I want to discuss, Ferguson asked me to raise it with you.'

'And what's that?'

'We've always had a close working relationship with President Cazalet, who has an outfit very similar to ours operating in Washington. It's called the Basement, and it's run by a very good friend of ours named Blake Johnson. He's coming to London tomorrow for a NATO conference with the Ministry of Defence.'

'And?' Kurbsky asked.

'And we do a great many things in tandem with them. Ferguson wonders if you'd agree to him passing on your story to Blake, and through him to the President. It'd be under the strictest secrecy.'

'No way. I made it plain that I would embark on this venture only if I was guaranteed anonymity. General Charles Ferguson gave me his word on the matter. He has a moral obligation to keep it.'

'He totally accepts that.'

'Then let that be the end of the matter.'

'I'll see that it is.'

Kurbsky left at ten o'clock, refused a lift by Sergeant Doyle and walked slowly down through Holland Park towards the main road. He paused at the end of one lonely street and phoned Bounine.

'Have you heard anything else regarding this Blake Johnson business?'

'A certain amount. Luhzkov invited me to have a drink and was very excited. Apparently, we've just reached a deal with a private airfield at Berkley Down that specializes in jets for millionaires. The place is about twenty miles out of London in Kent. Luhzkov talked about being able to book a Falcon to go wherever he wanted.'

'And the point of this is?'

'I'm getting there. He got quite worked up about all this. Told me more about the previous attempt on Johnson's life the other year. The mistake, he said, was to trust a low-life gangster and pay him well for the contract. Luhzkov got quite drunk while he was telling me this. Apparently, the gangster farmed the work out on the cheap to two second-rate specimens who were foiled by this man Dillon, an ex-IRA enforcer who now works for Ferguson, and someone called Salter, who also works for Ferguson.'

'Did this business involve anyone being killed?'

'I understand there was some damage done to those concerned. He said Dillon had a bad habit of shooting ears.'

'I wonder if Oleg and Petrovich are aware of the opposition they are up against?'

'I suppose if the affair proceeded in the right way, they wouldn't expect any opposition. We live in a world where anything is possible. You don't need to hunt for a public telephone, you have a mobile phone in your pocket that can handle a call to the other side of the world. And you can bang a man on the head in a London street and bundle him off in a car twenty miles into the Kent countryside, where a Falcon jet will have him in Moscow in five hours, instead of eating breakfast in the American Embassy guest house in Peel Mews.'

'I get it now. And this is your idea of fun, Yuri, for this poor bastard?'

'The American version is called extraordinary rendition. You fly some unlucky bastard from one country too civilized to harm him, to another where you can get someone to torture him for you.'

'No honour in that.'

'No honour, either, in refuelling the Falcon in Moscow for an onward flight to Siberia and Station Gorky, the last place God made.'

Kurbsky said, 'Okay, you've made your point. If I ever need a defence lawyer, it will be you, Yuri.'

Yuri said, 'Are you okay, Alex? You sound tense.'

'What would I have to be tense about? I'll speak to you tomorrow. Look for me round about noon.'

He thought about it as he walked to the main road and flagged a black cab, and instead of asking for Holland Park, he told the driver to take him to Grosvenor Square, because he knew that's where the American Embassy was. In the back of the black cab he put the light on and examined his A to Z London guide, found Peel Mews off South Audley Street running down from Grosvenor Square.

He put the guide away, turned off the light and sat there. Thinking. Boris Luhzkov, feeling his oats, was considering this mad idea of kidnapping the personal security adviser for President Jake Cazalet. It was a crazy escapade, but yet, as Bounine had said, in this modern world of today, when so much could be achieved in so few hours, it was eminently possible.

But it was a nasty business. In the shadowy world of spies and assassins, that sort of thing was to be expected, and the interrogations that went with it. A man like Johnson, so close to the President, would be subject to the most horrendous torture to extract the incredible amount of information he must have. But what would be the consequences?

He told the cab driver to drop him on the other side of

the square by the statue of General Eisenhower. As the cab drove away, he turned, aware of the great ugly slabs of concrete designed to protect the building against a terrorist attack, and walked back across the square and entered South Audley Street. Peel Mews was to the left some little way along. He paused for a quick moment.

It started to rain lightly, and he looked around him, taking everything in. Fine buildings, Georgian, Victorian, some superb shops. Mayfair night in the rain, cars swishing by, not too many people walking. It was dreamlike in a way, or was that just him? He continued steadily to the end, where he turned towards Park Lane and discovered the Dorchester Hotel, which was reasonably busy, night porters on duty, umbrellas at the ready, cars in and out and on the other side, the darkness of Hyde Park, the traffic cutting between in long streams.

What a great city this was, still the wonderland to which he had come when he was seventeen, all the way from Communist Moscow. It was still probably the best city in the world, and he knew quite suddenly, standing there, that he didn't like what Boris Luhzkov wanted to happen to Blake Johnson, and he knew why. It was Bounine mentioning an onward flight to Station Gorky that stuck in his craw. Yes, there was the cursed business with his sister and the sixteen years she had rotted there. Sure, he would have to continue to follow the path he was on in the hope of earning her freedom. But to consign someone else to the degradation and despair of such a place was something he was not prepared to do. In a way, it was his own private declaration of war and that was all that mattered, and he turned and walked to the cab rank in the side street.

Just before he went to bed at eleven, Ferguson called in to Roper. 'How did you get on with Kurbsky about the Blake Johnson matter?'

'He was absolutely firm. He said you'd promised him anonymity, given him your word, and that was the end of the matter.'

'All right, I give in.'

'Something interesting happened, though. When I asked Kurbsky earlier if he'd known Basayev, he said everyone in the Russian Army did. But when he came round tonight, he told me there was a bit more to it than that.'

'Did he indeed?'

'Mind you, I already suspected there was, because of my research online.'

'Go on, tell me.'

So Roper did.

When he was finished, Ferguson said, 'A hell of a story. God, if that swine Basayev had done that to any unit I commanded, I'd have hounded him in every way possible, shot him like the dog he was.'

Roper said, 'When you think of it, Kurbsky had an incredible motive to kill Basayev himself.'

'Himself? With his history? For God's sake, Giles, this anonymity Kurbsky so prizes would be right out of the window if he got involved with something like that.'

'All right, I take your point.'

'Try and get a good night's sleep for a change.'

He was gone and Roper, riven with pain, poured a large whisky and drank it. 'Sleep?' he said. 'Who needs that?'

At Chamber Court, Kurbsky spoke into the voice box and let himself in with the control, walking through the garden. The lights were on in the conservatory, Katya standing at the open door and Svetlana on her wicker throne inside.

'So there you are,' Katya said. 'Come and join us for a dish of tea.'

Which he did, taking off his coat and shaking rain from it. He kissed Svetlana's forehead and took Katya's hand for a moment.

'How are you my dear?' Svetlana asked. 'You look so ill.'

He laughed and said to Katya, 'Can't you persuade her that I'm supposed to look ill?'

He was handed a glass of tea, and Katya said, 'What have you been up to, then? Did you visit the safe house? How was Roper?'

'Oh, the world of spooks is very worked up about the shooting of the Chechen general, Shadid Basayev, and his driver.'

'It's been a staple diet on all the news programmes today.'

'A dreadful man,' Svetlana commented. 'Some of his deeds were unspeakable.'

'Did you know him?' Katya asked.

'He was one of the best-known Chechen generals and

universally reviled. Yes, I knew him,' Kurbsky said. 'A vile man who escaped retribution for many years, and as far as I'm concerned, he's finally met a just end.' He got up. 'I'm tired. I think I'll go to bed. God bless you both.'

After he had gone, Svetlana said, 'I worry about him. Something weighs heavily on his spirit. I know these things.'

'He has a lot on his mind, a lot to contend with,' Katya told her, and kissed her on both cheeks. 'Go to bed now and sleep well.'

'The things in his past, the years of war. Such terrible things must hang heavily on him. Some of the old film they showed today of the war in Chechnya, that dreadful man Basayev. Alexander was part of that.' She picked up her stick and got up. 'I'll see you in the morning.'

She went out, and Katya sat there, thinking about it, then went and found her laptop, sat with it on her knees and tapped in Alexander Kurbsky. There was nothing secret there, just the career of a great writer including an account of his military career and his medals and decorations. There were so many, and she felt a certain pride, aware that she was slightly in love with him. She started to read the citations, and the details leapt out at her of the officer who had jumped with his men over the Kuba Plateau in February, 1995, a failed mission with only two survivors. The target had been Shadid Basayev.

She switched off, her heart beating, went to the sideboard and poured a vodka and almost choked on it, her every instinct confirming what she did not wish to know.

*   *   *

Her night was restless, but she finally fell asleep and awoke suddenly at seven thirty to the sound of a motor outside. She got up, went to the window, opened it and looked out and saw Kurbsky seated on the mower, cutting the grass in long swathes.

'Hello,' she called and he stopped and looked up.

'Did I wake you? If so, I'm sorry.'

'I'm fine. So you're getting into the swing of things?'

'That's what I'm here for.'

'Have you had any breakfast?'

'An apple and a glass of milk.' He laughed. 'It's fine. I want to get this side lawn finished. I'll have a sandwich later.'

Svetlana often spent the morning in bed, soothing her arthritis and reading. Katya took her a tray of muesli, assorted fruit, toast and black Russian tea.

'He's started on the garden,' she said. 'Mowing the grass.' She went to the window and looked out. 'Bad March weather is not good for gardens. They lie still. Nothing happens.'

'Very Chekhovian, my dear, so it's a season of sadness, but perhaps the gardener will find the exercise beneficial.' Katya handed her *The Times*, and Svetlana made a face. 'More on that wretched Basayev.'

'There will be for a while, then something else will come along and replace it on the front page.'

'Another killing, a suicide bomb?' Svetlana shook her head. 'What a terrible world.'

'I suspect it always was,' said Katya and went downstairs.

*   *   *

At Holland Park, Roper sat at his desk, varying his screen images, turning from the autopsy report on Basayev, to the one on Josef, to the Scotland Yard forensic reports, taking it all in, tapping his desk with the flick knife Kurbsky had given him.

Doyle brought his tea and sandwich in. 'That's a nasty bit of work, Major. Where did you get that then?'

'Just a present to open my mail.'

'It'll open a bloody sight more than that if you ask me.'

He left, and Kurbsky came in. 'Did you have a good night?'

'I'm not sure if I know what that means any more. What are you up to?'

'Gardening. I'm establishing my position at Chamber Court so the neighbours get used to me. I sat in the saddle of the tractor and let the mower do all the work. The lawns are looking good. Any more on the Basayev business?'

'Not a thing. The autopsies, forensics and all the usual nasty details are available, but –'

'But it doesn't get us an inch further. To the media, it's Russian perfidy as usual.'

'Which means there's never a solution,' Roper told him. 'That's the trouble with you Russians, always getting away with things.'

There was an edge there that he hadn't been able to resist. Kurbsky was aware of it at once, but kept his response light. 'We are Social Democrats these days, Communism is dead, my friend.'

'Tell that to Vladimir Putin.'

'I doubt he would wish to speak to me now.'

'You never know,' said Roper.

Blake Johnson was a handsome man in his late fifties, hair greying a little, a shade under six feet tall. He was always received courteously at the American Embassy in Grosvenor Square, not only because of his position, but also because the Ambassador, Frank Mars, was a friend of many years and they'd served together in Vietnam.

A Marine captain escorted him upstairs and then went in search of the Ambassador. Johnson would have welcomed a Scotch after the flight, but with the NATO meeting coming up at the Ministry of Defence, he needed his wits about him. There was coffee on the sideboard, and he was savouring a cup when Mars walked in.

'Great to see you, Blake. I thought you'd be accompanying the Vice-President back to Washington. It's a pleasure to see you.'

'It's good to see you again, old friend.' Blake shook his hand. 'This meeting could be extremely important.'

'I presume this has to do with the future deployment of our troops in support of NATO forces.'

'Something like that, Frank. At this stage, you could say I'm just testing the water for the President.'

Mars said, 'Listen, about your accommodation tonight. We were going to put you up in the Embassy house, but I recall you had a slight problem there the other year.'

'Nothing worth mentioning,' Blake said. 'But there is a

hotel off South Audley Street called the Albany Regency. It's old-fashioned, but I stayed there some years ago and liked it. I asked the Paris Embassy to book it for me, and they tell me I have a suite on the top floor, a view over the rooftops to Hyde Park and everything.'

'Sounds lovely.'

'Good, I'll be on my way. I just wanted to drop in and say hello.'

'Any idea when you're flying back? Is there time to get together later?'

'Ah, well, possibly. I think you might have to put up with me a bit longer . . . but I can't discuss it now, Frank. I'll call you,' and Blake left, leaving a chagrined Frank Mars with the distinct impression that he wasn't getting the whole picture here.

There was nothing new about the Basayev affair, so Roper, bored, began trawling around on the computer. Thinking of Basayev naturally led him to thinking of Kurbsky, and that led him back to Kurbsky's history and the nightmare of his sister's death.

Moscow in upheaval, over fifty thousand body bags home from Afghanistan, riots in the streets, hundreds of dead and dying and among them, Tania Kurbsky. Her brother had been told that she was only wounded, and so he had rushed home, but it was a plot on his father's part to get him back to Moscow and he found her already dead and buried.

A thoroughgoing bastard, Ivan Kurbsky, but then he

needed to be to make colonel in the KGB. Also, a man with real influence to be able to get his daughter buried in Minsky Park Military Cemetery. Almost idly, he consulted the list of those buried at Minsky and there were over six thousand. He leaned forward, frowning, and tried again, but he had been right first time. There was no Tania Kurbsky buried at Minsky Park.

This was nonsense. Roper had seen a family photo of Colonel Kurbsky by grave #6007, the headstone engraved with Tania Kurbsky's name and dates. Very quickly, Roper explored the list of graves on his computer and there was number 6007 meticulously recorded by some clerk as . . . empty.

It took a lot to get Giles Roper excited these days, but he was now, a surge of energy spreading through him. January, 1989, Tania Kurbsky, apparently dead but not in her grave. So where are you? He poured himself another whisky and started to find out.

Kurbsky let it go until well into the afternoon before phoning Bounine. 'How are things at your end?' he demanded.

'Crazier than ever. We have an asset in Paris who works for the office that books embassy travel arrangements there. Before he left, Johnson made arrangements for a hotel called the Albany Regency in London. Our people have checked it out and he's definitely booked. It's a top floor suite.'

'So how are they going to proceed?'

'Apparently, they've got hold of a truck from the firm that

does laundry pickups and deliveries to hotels in the area. The idea is they grab him in his room and wheel him out under a pile of sheets or towels. They drive him to Berkley Down where the Falcon awaits, and the rest you know.'

'This is going too far,' Kurbsky said. 'When is it supposed to happen?'

'I don't know. Apparently, Oleg and Petrovich are going to park outside and wait for the right moment.'

'Why they think the result will be different than the last time Luhzkov tried to have Johnson assassinated, I don't know. Ferguson's people keep a close eye on Johnson at all times. Thank God you aren't involved, Yuri.' He hung up.

Thinking about it, it was reasonable to suppose that the most likely time to find Johnson at the hotel would be late afternoon or early evening. The stupidity of the whole idea was obvious, but on the other hand it was so absurdly simple that it might just succeed, and he couldn't have that.

He walked round the garden, checking his handiwork. He'd done well and it had needed it. Katya appeared and called to him and he joined her.

'Your aunt is so pleased. She loves her garden. Come and have a drink. You've earned it.'

So he went and she poured three vodkas and they toasted him. 'You look better, Alexander,' Svetlana said. 'Happier in yourself, I think. Full of energy and life under all that camouflage.'

He couldn't very well tell her why. 'To work with one's hands, plants, trees, the whole gardening thing – it's good for the soul, I think.'

'Will you eat with us tonight?' Katya asked.

'My thanks, but there are things I need to do at the safe house. But I won't be too late.'

He went out to the terrace and away. Svetlana said, 'You like him, my dear, don't you?'

'And I fear for him,' Katya said.

Kurbsky consulted his maps and discovered where the Albany Regency was. In the garage, he had found an old pair of black overalls and he changed clothes now, putting them on. There was a tweed cap, which he appropriated, and a khaki scarf, which he looped around his neck.

He had the gutting knife safe in his boot and now took the Walther from the secret compartment in his bag and slipped it in a patch pocket on the right leg of the overalls along with an extra clip. In the left patch pocket, he stuffed one of the black ski masks. Some cash, gloves and he was ready.

Down in the garage, he checked out the Ford van. Amongst the tools in the back was a 'Man at Work' sign, and three yellow cones, which could be useful. There was nothing else to do except get on with it, and he drove out a couple of moments later.

Katya, who had been watching from the trees, went back into the conservatory. 'He's gone,' she said. 'But to where?'

'All will be well,' Svetlana said. 'If necessary, he will be good in spite of himself, I am certain of it.'

* * *

Roper got his first breakthrough in his search for Tania by trawling the hospitals in central Moscow during the period covering the worst violence. There she was, a bullet in the left lung, another in the side, narrowly missing a kidney.

It was surprising they'd bothered to treat her, considering the attitude of the authorities in those troubled times, but somewhere there had been doctors and nurses who took their work seriously in spite of party officials, and Tania Kurbsky had lived. The next mention of her name was on a warrant for crimes against the State.

Roper got the feeling that it was then that things had changed. He suspected that her father hadn't at first been aware of what had happened to her. She had probably appeared to have disappeared in all the turmoil, but then she'd been arraigned for treason against the State, the penalty for which was death.

Yet Tania Kurbsky was not executed. More work produced a special court hearing, the testimony of Colonel Ivan Kurbsky and a new sentence: exile in perpetuity to Station Gorky. The numbered grave at Minsky Park was left in place, in consideration for Colonel Kurbsky's services to the State.

Roper switched the computer off, feeling so desperately sorry at what he had found. This was not what Alexander Kurbsky believed to be true for so many years. How could he possibly be told? And even more, told that his sister might still be a prisoner in one of the worst places in the world.

He switched back on, and tapped in Station Gorky.

12

It was one of the most unpleasant things Roper had ever done. There was something reminiscent of the Nazis about the details of those incarcerated at Station Gorky, of Heinrich Himmler's insistence on records of deaths, executions, gassing, so meticulously kept that eventually, those who had committed the deeds were condemned in open court by their own records.

It was the same now with Station Gorky. The archives, long buried, were available on the computer, lists written by hand or on cranky old-fashioned typewriters, thousands of names.

For a long time, he seemed to be getting nowhere and it was hard going, but in the end, sitting back, easing his pain with more whisky, the breakthrough came from a single phrase entered in the court documents referring to her sentence. *In perpetuity.* It was so simple in the end, like a codeword, and when he tapped in Station Gorky and followed it with the dread phrase, one list after another was revealed. There were hundreds of them, with dates of incarceration and, in most cases, dates of death over the years.

He tapped in one or two as a start and found sparse entries, usually no more than two or three lines and a photo of the convict, shaven-headed for both men and women, eyes lifeless, all hope gone.

And Tania Kurbsky, admitted 25 January, 1989, looked exactly the same, just like all the others, a creature beyond despair. To die of typhoid on 7 March, 2000, must have been a blessing.

Roper sat back, totally depressed. For sixteen years, Alexander Kurbsky had accepted that his sister was dead, buried in Minsky Park Military Cemetery. To be told now that she had lived for eight appalling years in the worst Gulag in Siberia would be a terrible thing to have to come to terms with, but then, did Kurbsky need to know? What purpose could there be in telling him? None that he could see, but that would mean keeping the whole rotten business from everyone, and that included Ferguson.

He buried his face in his hands and Doyle came in. 'You all right, Major? Have you been overdoing it again? We can't have that.'

Roper smiled. 'Here we go again, the old Jamaican charm offensive.'

'The old Jamaican *Cockney* charm offensive. How about I take you to the wet room and you have a bloody good shower?'

Roper poured a whisky and tossed it back. 'You know what, Tony, that's a good idea.'

Kurbsky reached the Albany Regency Hotel and discovered that the normal parking area had been temporarily extended. A substantial building had been demolished next door and there was room for more cars until construction began. Many vehicles had taken advantage of the situation.

Kurbsky took a spot in a corner, and noticed a manhole. He backed up against it, opened the rear door, found a crowbar amongst the tools, and levered up the manhole cover, then positioned the yellow cones around it and propped the *Man at Work* sign against the Ford's windshield. Now he was set for a while.

There was no sign of a laundry van. It was just after five, a certain gloom in the air as evening approached. He continued to search among the parked cars, and then he saw a notice on the wall. *Trade vehicles at rear entrance.* An arrow pointed to a narrow footway through an archway, and he hurried along.

Back from his meeting, Blake Johnson had been dropped at the front entrance of the hotel only fifteen minutes before Kurbsky arrived, and Igor Oleg saw it. He was wearing a green uniform, the name of a laundry company printed on the back. His companion, Petrovich, was waiting in the stolen truck in the courtyard at the rear of the building.

Oleg had gone round to the back using the very footway that Kurbsky was on now, and hurried down the steps to his companion, who already had a large four-wheeled cloth container waiting filled with towels.

'He's here,' Oleg told him.

'Let's get it done then.' They went in through the base-ment door, entered the service lift, and went up to the top floor.

Blake had taken off his jacket, loosened his tie and poured himself a whisky, and a large one. Not because of his exer-tions at the NATO meeting – the highly classified twenty minutes he had spent with his good friend Charles Ferguson afterwards had been much more demanding. The interesting thing about politics was that sometimes, though not often, you could help to make history just a little bit.

The door buzzed, he walked towards the door, drink in hand, opened it, and Oleg punched him very hard just under the breastbone. As Blake's legs buckled, Oleg caught him and dragged him backwards so that Petrovich could wheel in the laundry cart. His wrists were handcuffed together with plastic ties, his mouth was taped, a large plastic tie bound his ankles.

Towels were removed, they hoisted him between them and dropped him in the cart, then covered him with the towels again. Oleg opened the door, checked that the corridor was clear, and they walked to the end and discovered the service lift was on its way.

Oleg glanced nervously at Petrovich as they waited for the lift door to open. A Filipino cleaning woman in hotel uniform and carrying a mop and pail, emerged, nodded without a word, and walked off down the corridor. They got into the lift and descended, smiling at each other, emerging on the ground floor and pushing the cart out into the courtyard towards the truck.

Kurbsky, emerging from the walkway, saw everything. He remembered Oleg and Petrovich from the GRU safe house outside Moscow, and the fact that they were pushing the cart said it all. The top half of the back of the truck was stretched canvas, the bottom half metal. Opened, it provided a ramp to facilitate loading. They shoved the cart inside, closed the ramp and walked round to board.

Kurbsky was already rushing down the steps as the engine roared and the truck started to move. The bottom of the ramp protruded slightly and he got a foot on it and hung on by his left hand, clutching the twine that held the canvas tight. He reached in his boot, found the gutting knife, stabbed into the canvas and cut it from top to bottom. Then he sliced to one side, raised the flap he had created and pulled himself through.

Once inside, he replaced the knife in his boot, found the ski mask in his left leg pocket and pulled it on, stuffing his tweed cap into the pocket in its place. It was gloomy outside now and even gloomier in the truck. There was no sound from the cart, and there were several more all full of laundry, and he had to force his way through and listen from the back of the cab. He could hear voices, but not what they were saying.

He took out the gutting knife and sliced a hole in the canvas on the left side so that a flap hung down and he could see out to where they were going. Traffic, houses, but a busy road, obviously pushing out of the city. He turned to the cart and pulled out the towels, revealing Blake Johnson.

He had obviously recovered his senses and his eyes were wide open and staring. Kurbsky spoke to him in street Russian, heavily-accented working class. 'I hear you speak Russian? If I'm right, nod your head.' Blake did so, and Kurbsky carried on. 'You've been kidnapped by some pretty bad people. They're taking you to an airfield called Berkley Down in Kent, where there's a Falcon waiting to take you to Moscow or Siberia. I'll take the tape off now so you can talk, but keep your voice low.'

He yanked the tape off in one quick pull, and Blake winced. 'Christ, that hurt,' he said in English.

'Better we stick to Russian.'

Blake did. 'Who the hell are you?'

'You ask too many questions, my friend.' Kurbsky sliced the plastic ties at his wrists and ankles. 'There you go.'

His harsh uncultivated tones could have been the voice of some lowlife member of a Moscow Mafia gang, and Blake, pulling himself out of the laundry cart, had to grab hold of the nearest strut to stop himself from falling over.

'What's going on?'

'You Americans have a thing called extraordinary rendition, right?'

'I know that can happen and I'm not proud of it.'

'Well, this is the Russian version, and I'm saving you from it.'

'But why should you care?'

'Now you disappoint me, Mr Johnson.' Kurbsky pushed Blake so he fell on a pile of towels. 'Sit down and shut up.'

He peered out through the hole he had made in the left side of the canopy. They were moving out into country now, fields, woods, only the occasional house. He turned, went to the tailgate, and sliced the canvas till it was open from top to bottom, then undid the clamps on each side that held the ramp in place and nicked it open so that it trailed down, scraping on the road.

The truck swerved and he grabbed a stanchion and took out the Walther. Blake, rolling amongst the towels as the truck swerved again cried, 'What the hell are you doing?'

'Making them stop,' Kurbsky said.

They swerved again into a layby that stood empty for the moment, backed by trees and fields. There were voices raised, both of the cab doors banged open.

'Get ready,' Kurbsky said.

Petrovich and Oleg appeared from each side and stood there, amazement and shock on their faces. 'Good evening, Comrades,' Kurbsky said cheerfully.

'What is this?' Oleg demanded. 'Who are you?'

'Your worst nightmare. Mr Johnson doesn't fancy the holiday in Siberia. It's the wrong time of year.'

Petrovich suddenly pulled a Beretta out of his pocket and Kurbsky shot him in the hand. 'Really stupid, that. Now you've got to manage without knuckles.' He was out of the truck, followed by Blake, and said, 'Get their weapons.'

Which Blake did. 'Now what?' he asked, calmer and in control.

'Well, you won't want the police in on this, and neither will the pride of the GRU here, so we'll leave them and drive away. These days they're only a mobile call away from like-minded comrades who'll come running. Have you got one?'

Blake said, 'Luckily, I always carry it in my pants pocket.'

'Well, there you are. I'll drop you off at a service station.' He turned to Oleg. 'Raise the ramp and put the clip in place on the right-hand side. I'll do the left.'

Oleg was bitterly angry, his face said it all, but he did as he was told, until, seizing a moment as Kurbsky turned, pulled out a spring-blade knife and slashed. Kurbsky only just managed to ward it off. It sliced through the sleeve of the overall and into his left arm.

Kurbsky hit him across the face. 'That was very stupid, but you always were a moron.' He rammed the muzzle against Oleg's right ear and shot half of it off. Oleg howled, and Kurbsky shoved him into Petrovich, who was trying to stop the bleeding from his knuckles with a handkerchief and failing miserably.

'Are you OK?' Blake asked. 'You're bleeding.'

'I've bled before.' Kurbsky put the Walther in his pocket, took off his khaki scarf and bound it round his left arm as tightly as he could. He said to the two Russians, 'You bastards better call in for room service. You're lucky I didn't kill you. Come on, let's get out of here,' he said to Blake, went round and climbed up behind the wheel of the truck.

'Have you any idea what you look like?' Blake said.

'Yes, *Tovarich*,' Kurbsky laughed. 'A bank robber or international terrorist. Take your pick. See that big roundabout up ahead? That sends us back the other way, towards London. I drop you at the first service station and you call in your people and I'm away, like I've never been here.'

'But you have, my friend,' Blake said. 'And thank God for it.'

'No problem, *Tovarich*,' said Kurbsky, and he laughed harshly.

Ten minutes later, he pulled in on the edge of the approach road to a service station. 'There you go,' and Blake dismounted.

As Blake turned to say goodbye, the truck simply drove away, slowing only to enter the traffic stream, and Kurbsky pulled off the ski mask, and pulled on the tweed cap. His arm was hurting and he didn't know how bad it was, but that was all right. A good man had been saved from a bad end, that was the thing, and he settled down to drive back to London.

Darkness was beginning to fall as he reached Marble Arch. He left the truck on a building site and simply walked away from it, once more threading his way through Mayfair until he reached the Albany Regency, and went into the parking area and found everything as he had left it.

He cleared up the cones and his sign, his arm hurting, got behind the wheel of the Ford and drove away. He'd have a look at the arm when he got back to the house. One of those British Army wound packs that he had in his bag would take care of it.

His phone trembled as he was going up Abbey Road, and he pulled in to answer. Bounine said, 'Alex, you've been the greatest friend of my life. In fact, in the old days, you saved my life more than once. But something's happened here and I've got to ask you if you know anything about it?'

'Well, I can't answer until I know what it is.'

'We got a mobile call from Oleg out in the country requesting a pick-up for him and Petrovich. They tell an incredible story.'

'I'm listening.'

Bounine covered the facts pretty exactly, and when he was finished said, 'Forgive me for asking you this, but considering what has happened, our conversations, your interest in the operation, could it in any way have had anything to do with you?'

'Are you asking for yourself or for Luhzkov?'

'Luhzkov is convinced this masked man must have been Sean Dillon, because he shot off half of Oleg's right ear. He said it's Dillon's trademark.'

'Well, there you are then. All the same, it's a good man saved from a lousy fate.'

'So it was nothing to do with you?'

'My dear Yuri, I'm the man who's had a sister rotting in Station Gorky for nearly twenty years, and who might, repeat might, have a chance to bring her back to life if he's a good boy and does as he's told.'

Bounine's voice changed. He said hoarsely, 'Of course, old friend, forgive me. To do such a thing would be like a sentence of death for her. How could I have been so stupid?'

'Yuri, don't worry about it.'

'But I do. It's Luhzkov and his wild talk, always me he confides in. How he has strong contacts with Islamists, how he could bring terror to the streets of London if he wanted to.'

'Fantasyland, Yuri, dreams of power. It's gone to his head since he found himself face to face with Putin. Put it out of your mind, get a decent night's sleep. We'll talk again.'

He drove into the garage, switched off and got out of the van. He went out and saw Katya watching him through the trees, arms folded against the cold. He walked towards her.

'Have you had a good afternoon?'

'I went to the safe house.'

It was a lie, and she knew it because Roper had phoned a little earlier asking after him. She said calmly, 'Have you eaten? We haven't yet.'

'I need a shower. I'm not fit for human consumption,' he joked.

She said, 'What's wrong with your arm? Isn't that blood soaking through the scarf? What happened?'

'Nothing, it's nothing,' he said. 'I'll go and get changed, have a shower. I'll let you know how I feel.'

He went away quickly and she watched him go, waited until the lights turned on above the garage. She went in, troubled, and said to Svetlana, 'He lied to me. He said he'd been to the safe house, but Roper phoned me looking for him, and he's hurt himself in some way. I'm worried.'

'Then go and see him. Tell him you're worried.'

In the kitchen, Kurbsky stood at the sink, the top half of his overalls hanging down. The wound could have been worse, the tip of the knife doing the damage, not too deep but it was five or six inches long. He had one of the British Army wound packs unopened at the side of the sink when the door opened, and Katya entered. She came close and was shocked.

'My God, you need the hospital.'

'Absolutely not. I've got everything I need here. I'm an old soldier, remember. I've had far worse than this.'

She examined it and shook her head. 'I think you should go. It's a knife wound, isn't it? What happened?'

'A couple of young punks tried to mug me. One of them had a knife, there was a struggle. I gave them a good hiding. End of story, except that in hospitals the world over, if you tell how it went, the police get involved. So I'll see to it myself.'

'You really are very stupid. Just sit there and wait while I go and get Hitesh Patel.'

'No, I don't want him involved.'

'Well, I do.' She got a bottle of vodka from a cupboard and a glass and filled it. 'Drink that, shut up and wait.'

She was back in just under fifteen minutes with Hitesh, who was wearing a blue polo shirt and blazer and carried a black bag.

'What have you got there, the tools of the trade?' Kurbsky asked. He had tied the scarf around his arm again.

'I have my own instruments, it's part of the game,' said Hitesh. He picked up the army wound pack. 'My goodness, Henri, you are well prepared.' He removed his jacket and hung it on a chair, opened the bag and found some surgical gloves. 'Now let's have a look.' He nodded. 'Nasty. May I inquire if you have killed anybody?'

'I was attacked by two teenage muggers. One of them cut me, I knocked them about, and they cleared off. I'm a judo expert. I just don't want to get involved with the police. On the other hand, you're a young guy just into his career, and I wouldn't want to get you in trouble.'

'Well, you won't.' Hitesh said to Katya, 'Find me a big bath towel to cover the table with, some hand towels. I note that the central heating is on, so that means plenty of hot water is available. When you go for those, bring pyjamas and a robe and I'll get him out of his filthy overalls.'

*   *   *

The wound pack had everything, including morphine ampoules, and he snapped the glass tip off one and jabbed it in. 'Is that all right?'

'Sure, it's kicking in.'

'You know what a cicatrix is?'

'Of course, a scar.'

'From an old wound. You have several.' Hitesh smiled. 'Whatever else you are, you are an interesting man, Henri Duval. Anyway, the kit supplies needles and thread and surgical tape butterflies. I shall try four spaced stitches and fill them in with the butterflies. I would suggest a sleeping pill, which I shall give you, and a good night's sleep.'

'Then do it.' Kurbsky turned to Katya, who had been listening without a word. 'I think another large vodka is definitely indicated here.' She gave it to him and he tossed it down. 'Okay, let's get on with it.'

Not much more than half an hour later, Hitesh finished his careful and neat bandaging, tightly held together with surgical tape.

Katya had left them to go and speak to Svetlana, and she now returned. 'She is quite concerned. Would you care to eat something with us?' she asked.

'If you don't mind, I think I'll take the advice of my excellent doctor and go to bed.'

'I think you're wise,' Hitesh said. 'Here's your sleeping pill, swallow it now. I'll also leave you some pills, strong painkillers that will help you for the next three or four days. Just read the instructions. I'll leave you to it.'

'You're a star, Hitesh.' Katya kissed him.

He walked to the door, opened it and smiled. 'Of course, I haven't been here. No one saw me, right? But I'll check on him tomorrow,' he said, and left.

'He's a lovely young man,' Katya said.

'I'm indebted to him.' Kurbsky put his hands on her shoulders. 'And you.' He kissed her gently on the mouth. 'I am a great worry to you, I know this, and I'm sorry it has to be this way. However, I'm going to bed and to hell with everything for a while.'

She waited for him to climb the stairs safely and called, 'Night bless, Alex.'

But he was already gone, the only sound his bedroom door closing softly, so she was not aware of him going to his bathroom and spitting out the sleeping pill.

She went across to the conservatory and joined Svetlana. 'He's gone to bed, Hitesh gave him something to make him sleep.' She handed Svetlana a vodka and joined her.

'You're still worried about him?'

'He lied to me about having been at the safe house. I'm sure he's not telling the truth about how he came to be cut with a knife.'

'Then do as I say. Go and see Roper and tell him you're worried.'

'You know, I think I will.'

'Only send for a cab. You've been drinking.'

'Yes, you're right, of course.'

She phoned for a cab, got her coat on and called Roper, getting him at once. 'Hello,' he said. 'Did our wandering boy turn up?'

'I'd like to see you.'

'What, now?'

'Don't say no, Roper. I need to talk. I'm worried about him.'

'Why is that?'

'Because when he got back tonight and I asked where he'd been, he told me the safe house. And he had a knife wound in his arm.'

'Oh dear.'

'I sent for a cab. I think it's here now.'

'I'll be waiting.'

She looked in on Svetlana. 'My cab's here.'

'Take your time. I'll wait up for you.'

The cab dropped her at Holland Park twenty minutes later, the Judas gate admitted her, and Doyle met her at the entrance. 'Nobody else here but me and the major, Miss. How about a cup of tea? It might persuade him to have one.'

'That would be nice, Sergeant.'

She went and kissed Roper on the forehead and said, 'Good of you to see me so late.'

'We never close. How's Kurbsky?'

'I worry about him – too much, I think.'

'No, that's me.'

'Why would you?'

He almost came straight out with it. His discoveries about
Tania Kurbsky had preyed on his mind and would not go
away. Was there any point in revealing this most painful of
truths to Kurbsky after so many years? But that would mean
keeping the facts to himself and, in a way, that was a burden
and not to be shared with anyone.

Doyle brought in the tea, a mug each. 'Military style,
miss.' He withdrew.

'Tell me,' Roper said.

'I think I've rather fallen for him, silly me. I mean I'm
hardly in the first bloom of youth.'

'A woman to die for, most men would think.'

'Anyway, because I think of him slightly like that, I feel
I've an instinct about him, and it tells me things are not
right. Something's going on in that head, and Svetlana agrees.
He lies to me about where he's been, and when I know he's
lied, that makes me doubt everything.'

'You said he lied to you this evening?'

'He'd been out for some hours, drove away in the old
Ford van wearing black overalls and a tweed cap. When he
got back, I asked him where he'd been and he said the safe
house, which I knew wasn't true. And – he'd been stabbed.
I found him in the kitchen above the garage trying to treat
himself.'

Roper was suddenly very serious. 'Go on,' he said.

'Young Patel is obviously a man of parts,' he said when she
was finished.

'Yes, a good chap.'

Roper said, 'Katya, we're sitting here with the midnight hour approaching, the shank of the night when all things seem possible but look highly improbable, and I'm going to take a chance on you. I found out something totally devastating about Alexander Kurbsky today. It's these damn computers, you see, I have a gift for them, and if you have that, there are no secrets left in this life.'

'And how does this apply to Alex?'

So he told her about Tania and what he had discovered.

'A terrible business,' she said when he was finished. 'And to learn all that would truly open old wounds for him.'

'I saw it as a burden the moment I discovered the details. Now I've shared that burden with you and without your permission.'

'You needn't worry,' she told him. 'It's knowing what to do about it that's the problem. Whether to tell him or not, but is that so important, does he have to know?'

She suddenly shivered. 'I don't like us having to discuss him like this. Will you tell anyone else?'

'Ferguson?' He shrugged. 'I haven't mentioned the matter to him, you're the only one, but something else has come up which he does know about.'

'And does it concern Alex?'

'It concerns a friend of ours, an American called Blake Johnson.' He reached for the whisky bottle and poured. 'Listen and learn. You might find it interesting.'

* * *

It took some time, for she needed to have the whole back-ground of past events laid out for her, and of a number of individuals on both sides of the coin. When he was finished, she sat there, considering what he had told her.

'So Blake Johnson has been targeted twice in plots devised by this Colonel Boris Luhzkov. The first time he was saved by Sean Dillon and Billy Salter.'

'That's right, a couple of years ago.'

'And this time he was kidnapped by GRU operatives on Luhzkov's orders and saved by a Russian in a black hood.'

'A man in a black hood who spoke Russian, which Dillon does, and rather well, only Dillon wasn't responsible for this gig. I've spoken to him, and so has Ferguson. He's still in Cambridge with Lady Monica Starling.'

Katya said calmly, 'Are you suggesting what I think you are?'

'Blake did say the man in the hood was cut with a spring-blade knife and bound it up with his scarf. Does that sound familiar?'

'But why would he do such a thing?'

'It was a good deed in a naughty world from Blake's point of view, and a first-class professional job from ours. No police involved, no dramatic story for the media.'

'And Luhzkov and his people get away with it?'

'It never happened, Katya, it's a game we play. We know that they know, and they know that we know.'

'Does Ferguson know about Alex's involvement?'

'I'll have to tell him in the morning.'

'Yes, I can see that.'

'The thing is, there are big events happening in the next few days, things even the media don't know about. I was only told a bit about it earlier by Ferguson. Blake's involved, but I can't tell you how.'

'I see.' She got up and reached for her coat. 'I must be getting back. I've got a lot to think about. Can I call for a cab?'

'Sergeant Doyle will run you home. I insist on it.' He buzzed for Doyle and followed her to the door. 'A strange business, so many questions unanswered, including the biggest of all.'

'What's that?' she asked.

'How on earth did he know about the attempt to kidnap Blake and when it was taking place?'

It was so silly, yet so obvious, that it hadn't occurred to her. 'I see what you mean.' Doyle appeared in the van and she ruffled Roper's hair. 'You've been good to me. I'll speak to you in the morning.'

At that moment, Boris Luhzkov sat in the living room of his quarters at the Embassy with much vodka taken and angrier than he had ever been. Yuri Bounine, sitting in an easy chair opposite him, had been emptying his glass into a convenient wastepaper basket for some time.

'You know, Yuri, thank God I kept the whole damned affair from the Prime Minister. I meant it to be a surprise, my gift to him. Those idiots, Oleg and Petrovich. I'll have them transferred to a penal battalion, I swear it.' He poured another vodka and slopped it down. 'Ferguson and his damned Prime Minister's private army and that bastard, Dillon. They've done it again.'

'So you believe the man in the hood was Dillon?' Bounine said.

'Who else? Shooting off half of Oleg's ear is typical of Dillon. He's famous for it, and everybody knows that he's a linguist. Anyway, who else would it be? The history of our dealings with these people speaks for itself.'

There was a knock on the door, and a young woman with tightly bound blonde hair and a trim black suit entered, clutching a piece of paper. 'Hah, it's you, Greta, on the night shift again? What's happening?'

'Something unexpected, Colonel, so I thought you'd like to hear it straight away. It's from our Paris Embassy.'

'Well get on with it, tell me.' He poured another vodka.

'As you know, Vice-President Hardy is due to depart tomorrow for Washington. At the last moment, however, his plane will divert to London. He and the British Prime Minister are meeting with the Israeli Prime Minister and the President of Palestine to broker a deal over Gaza.'

Luhzkov almost choked on his vodka and sat up. 'Can this be true?'

'It comes from a highly confidential source in French intelligence who's on the GRU payroll in Paris.'

Bounine held out his hand and the girl gave him the sheet. 'Major.'

He read it quickly and nodded. 'Yes, exactly as Greta says.'

'There hasn't even been a hint of this, in the media, in

government circles, anywhere. What the hell are they playing at?'

'Politics, it's as simple as that. Catch your opponents on the wrong foot. Everything revolves around the Americans.'

Luhzkov's immediate response was antagonistic. 'Who says so?'

'The world says so.' Bounine suddenly felt tired, the lawyer in him sticking its head out again. Everything seemed to be run by a layer of colonels with half-brains. Where did the regime find such people? It was something to do with Communism devouring the country for all those years – had to be.

'America is still the world's greatest superpower. Sure, it makes mistakes, but it can still knock heads together and bring about solutions. Public negotiations can be endlessly time-consuming. Much better to pull a rabbit out of the hat. Everyone's watching the President because the media are like leeches on to every move he makes, so send the Vice-President on normal business to Paris, then divert him to London, and presto! Everyone gathers on a boat in the Thames and the Big Four score the public relations coup of the year.'

Luhzkov seemed to have sobered up, his eyes gleaming, his face full of purpose. 'What is this about a boat on the Thames?'

Bounine examined the message again. 'Actually, it says: "Our information is that the meeting will probably take place on a riverboat on the Thames." I presume they're thinking of the security aspect there. Make it harder for terrorists.'

'What a target, though.' Luhzkov clenched a fist. 'What a sensation the death of the four of them would make. It would rock the world.'

'I should imagine it would,' Bounine said acidly, and then he stopped. 'Major, you're not thinking of –'

Luhzkov now seemed like another man. 'Listen, Bounine. I am sixty-five years of age. I was born in 1943 during the greatest war in Russian history, when we were brought out of hell to victory by the iron will of Josef Stalin. My father, a foot soldier, died in the war, my mother took me to live with her parents. They were peasants, but the village school was good and it led to the army, which saw I had a brain and educated me further. Eventually, I was commissioned, rising steadily over the years thanks to one thing: the Communist system. It became my religion during the Cold War, and it is my religion still.'

He leaned forward.

'Then the Wall came down and Communism was kicked to the side. In its place, all the evils of capitalism flourished, the greed spilled over, touching every country in the world. Those who taught me the virtues of Communism at my village school were right then and right now. Chaos is what we must create. Chaos, disorder, fear, poverty and unrest in the Western world, because that, more than anything, will cause a breakdown in their society, working people will revolt, and Communist order will be restored!'

There was a long silence, because Bounine couldn't think of a thing to say. That Luhzkov believed every word he'd said was obvious. That the man was a dangerous lunatic was also obvious, at least to Bounine. But he dared not disagree. Better to wait and listen . . .

'What would you like me to do, Colonel?'

'This is now a priority. The moment it is confirmed that a riverboat is to be used for the meeting, I am to be notified. The moment we know *which* boat, I am to be notified. Every scrap of information must be evaluated.'

Bounine turned to Greta, who had stood almost to attention during Luhzkov's outburst, completely riveted. 'You've heard the Colonel, Greta. Do you understand what's expected?'

'Absolutely, Major.'

'Get on with it then.'

She went out, and he turned to Luhzkov. 'What next, Colonel?'

'We need a man, Bounine, to deal with our problem satisfactorily. A bad man who is also a madman.' He chuckled at his rhyme. 'A man who speaks of God, but thinks more of money. A man who doesn't care and who looks upon each day as the day he may die.'

'And you know of such a man?'

'Yes, I know of such a man. Go and get your coat, make sure you have a pistol in your pocket, and I will introduce you to him.'

13

The cab dropped Katya at the Mews and she let herself in and walked through the garden. She paused on the terrace and looked at the garage and there was no light. In fact, Kurbsky was up and watching her through a crack in the curtains. His arm felt numb, but not unpleasantly so. He wore a bathrobe and smoked a cigarette, wondering about Katya and where she had been.

He could see through the trees into the conservatory, saw her standing and talking to Svetlana. It was enough. He went downstairs, found a scarf in the hall to put round his neck and went out and walked cautiously through the trees. The door stood open to the terrace, he could hear the voices, but not distinctly, and moved carefully, keeping low in the rhododendron bushes until he was close. He had missed part of the exchange, but Svetlana's words made it plain what it had been about.

'So you say the man in the hood who saved this American, Johnson, was Alexander. Can this be true?'

'Johnson said the man in the hood was cut on the left arm and that he tied his khaki scarf about it. That was how Alex was when he came home. Hitesh will confirm it.'

'Why would he be involved in such a thing?'

'I don't know, Svetlana. Maybe just a good deed in a bad world. He saved the American from an awful fate.' Katya's voice faltered. 'But there's more, much more, and maybe I shouldn't tell, because it will hurt you terribly, but I feel that I must. It will hurt him terribly, too, but what can I do?'

She was crying so much, so very much, and the old lady took her hands. 'What is it, my dear?'

'You thought Tania died in January 1989 and was buried in Minsky Park Military Cemetery. In fact, she was sentenced to life at Station Gorky in Siberia. She was admitted on January 25, 1989. Roper discovered it.'

'Dear God, that such a thing could be. That my wretched brother should permit such a thing.' Tears were running down Svetlana's cheeks. 'She's still there after sixteen years, is that what you're telling me?'

'No, she's dead now, God rest her soul.' The tears made her choke. 'Died of typhoid in that terrible place on March 7, 2000.'

There was a groan from outside and Kurbsky appeared in the doorway. 'For God's sake, no. It can't be true.'

She went to him then, putting her arms about him and holding him. 'Oh, Alex, my dearest, it is true. Roper broke into all the files and it's all there, everything that happened to her.'

Svetlana put her hands out. 'Come to me, my dear one, come to me.'

He went to her, falling on his knees in anguish. 'You don't understand. They lied to me. She was supposed to be still alive.'

Katya crouched on the other side of Svetlana's chair. 'Who lied to you, Alex, who?'

'Putin himself, Boris Luhzkov,' and as Svetlana held him close, he told them everything.

Bounine was driving as they turned into Kensington High Street. 'Just follow my directions,' Luhzkov told him. 'It's by the river. The great and mighty Thames. I adore history, you know, it's a passion. Roman ships with slaves at the oars crept up this river two thousand years ago and made the city out of a tribal encampment.'

In between his lecturing, he managed to give Bounine instructions on their route.

'There was a time when it was the biggest port in the world, crammed with ships, queuing to get a berth. Hundreds of cranes, docks all over the place. Now it's full of penthouses on the one side and run-down estates on the other. It's a real tragedy.'

'You've been here for a long time,' Bounine said.

'Thirteen years. The best posting I've ever had. I love the

place. I spend a lot of my time sightseeing, particularly the rundown areas. It's amazing what you find. Every race under the sun, every colour, you'll find them here like nowhere else in the world, down by the river, tight racial groups, a few streets each, shops, houses.'

They were close to the river and it started to rain, as they drove down narrow cobbled streets, many of the properties around them boarded up and then they emerged onto an anchorage that had a sign *India Wharf* and was edged by tall Victorian warehouses, most boarded up. In the basin were several moored boats including an old Thames barge. The other boats had winter canvas. A curved entrance ran from the basin into one of the warehouses, and moored inside was a large orange motorboat with a huge outboard motor.

They parked the Mercedes and got out. 'That thing looks fast,' said Bounine.

'It is fast. He gave me a run in it once.'

'Who did?'

'Come and meet him.'

He led the way along the wharf. There were lights at the windows of the barge, a gangplank stretching to a companionway leading below. It was closed by two mahogany doors which Luhzkov opened.

'Ali Selim, are you there?'

'Who the fuck is that?' The voice was very Cockney.

'Boris Luhzkov.'

'Have you brought any money with you? If not you can piss off.'

'My dear Ali, when have I ever let you down?'

Luhzkov went down and Bounine followed, finding himself in a surprisingly well-ordered interior. The cabin was comfortably furnished, with padded benches down each side, pictures on the walls where there was room, small curtains at the portholes. There was a kitchen area behind a bar, an archway beyond obviously leading to sleeping quarters. The man sitting at one end of the table was of mixed blood, and looked to be in his fifties, an aggressively handsome man with a hooked nose and the look of a predatory hawk about him. He had taken an old Luger pistol to pieces, spread them on a cloth before him and was carefully cleaning them. Close to his hand was a Beretta pistol which he could have picked up in a second. His hair was very black and tied in a ponytail which hung to the small of his back, and the only Muslim thing about him was an Egyptian white cotton shirt with wide sleeves.

He paused in what he was doing and looked Bounine over. 'Who's this?'

'Major Yuri Bounine, my second in command.'

'Another one? Boris, you old bastard, they come and go, but you go on forever. I don't know how you manage to survive, your lot being the fucking maggots they are.'

'You will forgive Ali's rather colourful language. His father, an Afghan, a deckhand on a cargo ship, landed in the Pool of London around fifty-five years ago and formed a relationship with a Cockney lady from Stepney.'

'Get it right, Boris. She might have been pregnant, but they did marry in church, so my old Mum was a lady. It would displease me to think of you putting it about otherwise.'

'Heaven forbid that I should think such a thing.'

'Is this business or pleasure?'

'Very much business, my friend. This could be a very big payday for you.'

'Well, just let me fix this, and then we'll have a drink and you can tell me all about it.'

Suddenly, with incredible speed and as if it were a game, he put the pieces of the Luger together. Bounine was amazed. 'That was truly remarkable.'

'What would you know? You GRU guys sit on your arses in some Embassy office.'

'Major Bounine was a paratrooper in Afghanistan and also served in Chechnya,' Luhzkov informed him.

'Really?' Ali Selim turned to Bounine and extended his hand. 'Now that I respect. A man who went to Afghanistan and came back in one piece I truly respect. Sit down and we'll have a drink. I'll be back in a moment.'

He went out, and Bounine said, 'Quite a character.'

'A killer of the first water. Served Al-Qaeda in Iraq and Beirut. He makes big money in the drug business running heroin along the Thames. He still has family links back in Afghanistan, which helps with the poppy trade.' His mobile sounded and he answered. He held it out to Bounine. 'It's Greta. You take it on deck. I'll handle Ali.'

Bounine went up and stood under a canopy in the rain. 'Tell me,' he ordered.

'It is a riverboat, built a couple of years ago, called the *Garden of Eden*. It is very luxurious, three decks, a bit tropical in its ambience.'

'Sounds like a floating conservatory. Where will it be?'

'Cadogan Pier, Chelsea. They'll have their discussion, then their joyride past the House of Commons, and disembark at Westminster Pier. Preparations have already started.'

'Good, I'll be in touch.'

Bounine went back to the saloon and found that Ali Selim had still not returned. He quickly told Luhzkov what Greta had said.

'When we're driving back to the Embassy, we could take a look,' Luhzkov said. 'It's near Cheyne Walk.' He nodded, thinking about it. 'It wouldn't surprise me if they got their heads together before boarding the boat.'

'Who knows?' Bounine said and Ali Selim came in.

'Is everything all right, my friend?' Luhzkov asked.

'A little stomach trouble. Nothing a large cognac won't cure.' He drank one at the bar then poured another. 'Anyone else?' There were no takers. 'So, let's get on with it. What's the game?'

'The half a million pound kind of game,' Luhzkov said.

Ali Selim didn't even blink. He swallowed the second cognac, put down the glass and leaned on the bar. 'Okay, tell me everything.'

So Luhzkov nodded to Bounine.

Afterwards, Bounine said, 'I realize what a hopeless proposition this must sound. Between the British security services and the Vice-President's Secret Service men – let alone Israeli and Palestinian security – getting on the boat would be a nightmare.'

'One couldn't even plant a bomb on board,' Luhzkov said. 'They'll go over the *Garden of Eden* with a fine-tooth comb.'

'And find nothing,' Bounine said.

'Because the bomb's elsewhere.' Ali Selim nodded. 'Come with me.'

He led the way up the companionway and stood under the canopy, rain pouring down. 'Have a look over there.' He pointed to the large orange motor boat with the huge outboard. 'I call that *Running Dog* and her speed would amaze you. Some lifeboat stations use them as rescue boats and the River Police have a few on the Thames.'

'So what are you suggesting?' Luhzkov asked.

Selim turned and pointed down at the other boats moored with the canvas covers. 'One of these loaded with Semtex would do it. Sink the *Garden of Eden* like a stone.'

'Come off it,' Bounine said. 'You'd need a suicide bomber to do that. This isn't Baghdad.'

'I'd arrive while it's tacking out into the river. I'll cast off the motorboat so it can't help but collide. Since it will be carrying seventy pounds of Semtex with short-time pencil fuses, it will blow the *Garden of Eden* to kingdom come.'

Luhzkov looked at him in awe. 'And what about you?'

'What about me? I sink the *Running Dog* in some rundown dockland area, await events, and vanish if necessary with your half-million pounds to comfort me. I'll be fine. I always make out.'

Bounine said, 'And the Vice-President and the others? This doesn't bother you, not even the President of Palestine?'

'Fuck him, Major, who cares? It's a lousy world, people

live and die because these politicians push the pieces around on some gigantic chessboard.'

He led the way down to the cabin again, went to the bar, made a face, almost as if he were in pain, and poured another cognac.

'That's better,' he said. 'Was there anything else?'

'Yes,' Bounine said. 'You mentioned seventy pounds of Semtex. That's an astonishing amount. Can you get it at such short notice?'

Ali turned, dropped to one knee and pulled a khaki-coloured canvas holdall from a cupboard behind the bar. His strength obvious, he lifted it and dropped it on the bar. He unzipped and opened it and there was the Semtex neatly stacked in blocks, each covered by greasy paper. On top was a large tin. He opened it.

'Pencil timers. See for yourself.'

'Excellent,' Luhzkov said. 'Everything appears to be in perfect order.'

'Call me when you have the exact departure time. Now I've got things to do, so go.'

Bounine said, 'You haven't made arrangements for the delivery of the half-million, aren't you worried?'

'Why would I be?' Ali Selim glanced at Luhzkov. 'This old bastard knows I'll cut his balls off if he crosses me.'

'A truly frightening man,' Luhzkov said as they drove away.

'You can say that again,' Bounine said. 'Back to the Embassy?'

'Cadogan Pier, Chelsea, first and let's see if there's any action.'

At that early hour, the streets were quiet and there were many private residences around the pier area, but they paused close enough to see the *Garden of Eden* tied up at the pier, many lights on. There were men working, particularly at the main boarding point.

'That's a portable electronic arch they're putting up,' Bounine said. 'Everyone will have to pass through it for security. It'll be the same for the stern area where the crew join the ship or supplies are taken aboard.'

Luhzkov nodded. 'It will be as tight as a sardine can. I expected no less. Back to the Embassy.'

Kurbsky had gone back to his room over the garage for the moment and was sitting on the bed. It had been a couple of hours since his confession in the conservatory. It had been terribly distressing, the whole business, particularly for Svetlana, and now he had retired to think about it in the cold light of dawn.

His anger was profound, every instinct in him wishing to strike back at those who had placed him where he was. The DVD showing Tania must have been rigged from old footage when she was still alive. It was inconceivable that Putin hadn't been fully aware of that. He could not believe that his friend, Yuri Bounine, would have known, surely not that, but Luhzkov must have.

One thing was certain. Sitting here and staring at the wall wasn't going to do any good. He got up, removed his bathrobe and pyjama jacket, and examined his arm. Hitesh had done an excellent job. What a fine doctor he will make. It didn't hurt, it just felt numb, so he took two of the special painkillers Hitesh had provided, found the bulletproof vest and managed to pull it on.

He cut the left sleeve off one of the khaki shirts with breast pockets on either side, useful for his mobiles, and hurried the rest of the dressing, pulling on the French paratrooper's boots last, fitting the gutting knife in the right. He pulled on his knitted hat and looked in the mirror at the strange man he had become. He found no answer there, got his bag, went down to the garage and threw it in the Ford, then he called Bounine.

Back at the Embassy, Bounine had tried to pull himself together after his nocturnal activities by taking a hot shower and finding a change of clothes for the busy day he suspected lay ahead.

He answered his phone at once, and Kurbsky said, 'You're probably the best friend I have in the world, so prove that friendship by telling me the truth.'

'But I believe I always have, Alex. What is this?'

'What if I told you Roper has succeeded in breaking into the secret files of Station Gorky and has discovered that my sister, Tania, was sentenced to life in perpetuity in 1989?'

'Yes, but you knew that, it was in the file with the DVD.'

'The Putin file. You defended him to me, I remember, said it had all happened before his time.'

'Look, Alex, where is this leading?'

'To my sister's death from typhoid on March 7, 2000.' There was a moment of stillness. 'He lied, Yuri, our beloved Prime Minister lied and whoever put the file together lied. Was it just handed over to Luhzkov? Is it conceivable the bastard didn't know?'

'I didn't, old friend, on my mother's soul I didn't know. What are you going to do?'

'The big question is what Ferguson and his people are going to do. I've done plenty already. Killed Vronsky, the three lads on the Midnight Express, that bastard Basayev and his minder. And I sorted out Oleg and Petrovich.'

'So it *was* you?'

'I couldn't tell you before when I was still supposed to be earning Tania's freedom.'

'What are you going to do? Couldn't you do some sort of deal with Ferguson?'

'You realize I'm the invisible man? I don't exist. Theoretically, they could lock me up and throw away the key.'

'Damn it, Alex, you're still Alexander Kurbsky.'

'Whoever that is. Who does Luhzkov think shot Oleg?'

'He's convinced it was Sean Dillon. He's incensed, Alex. Packing Johnson off to Siberia was going to be a surprise gift to Putin.'

'I can see how it would upset him.'

'He's gone slightly crazy. He's been ranting like an old-fashioned Communist, talking about causing chaos and disorder in the West, overthrowing capitalism.'

'Careful, Comrade,' Kurbsky told him. 'Don't tell me too much. I'm an enemy of the State, remember.'

And Bounine, who had been on the verge of telling him of the night's adventures with Luhzkov, hesitated and drew back.

'So what are you going to do, Alex?'

'I haven't the slightest idea, Yuri, but I'd better get moving. I imagine Charles Ferguson will be sending somebody to arrest me at any moment. I'm surprised they haven't already. I'll go to ground somewhere.'

'What do I say to Luhzkov?'

'Tell the bastard it wasn't Dillon, it was me, and tell him how things have worked out. To hell with Putin and to hell with Boris Luhzkov for what he's done to me.'

He pocketed his phone and turned to find Katya leaning on the door, arms folded. 'How long have you been there?' he asked.

'Long enough. Who's Yuri?'

'My best friend and comrade from Afghanistan and Chechnya. He's one of the good guys. When I got involved in this whole mess, I asked for him to be transferred from Dublin because I wanted a friend I could trust. He's a major, and Luhzkov's right-hand man.'

'Really – and your friend?'

'He thinks Luhzkov is rubbish.'

'So where are you going now?'

'I'll hide myself somewhere and give myself some time.'

'I think you should simply walk to Holland Park, sit down and talk it through.'

'That's not on my agenda, I'm afraid. For all you know, I might decide to wait in the street one rainy night and shoot Boris Luhzkov in the head. What a wonderful thought.'

He opened the garage door and she moved and caught his sleeve. 'Please, Alex, don't go.'

He shook his head and gently removed her hand. 'Don't waste your time on me, Katya. I'm a dead man walking.'

It was a terrible thing to say and she took an involuntary step back. He got behind the wheel of the van and drove away.

Bounine found Luhzkov in his office. 'Ah, there you are, Yuri,' Luhzkov said. 'I've just had confirmation of the timing. One hundred guests will be arriving between noon and half past. Cocktails and a buffet. The four gentlemen involved arrive at one, which indicates, as we thought, that they will already have had most of their discussions. The *Garden of Eden* will slip its mooring at one thirty, sail past the House of Commons, and passengers will disembark at Westminster Pier.'

'Have you informed Ali Selim of all this?'

'I've just come off the phone. He seems very happy, but then he's that kind of man. A hunter scenting his prey.'

'Perhaps, but I've something to tell you of great importance.'

'Perhaps it can wait, this other matter . . .'

Bounine cut in, 'No, Colonel, this is far more important. I have a question to put to you. Tania Kurbsky was admitted to Station Gorky on January 25, 1989. Are you aware that she died there of typhoid on March 7, 2000?'

Luhzkov looked stunned. 'What nonsense is this?'

'Not nonsense. The Putin file, the DVD, is all fake. A plot

to persuade Alexander Kurbsky to follow the path you and the Prime Minister laid out for him.'

Luhzkov shook his head. 'She is there in the camp, she has been for sixteen years. I've seen her.'

'On the DVD, and you know these kind of things can be easily faked. Have you seen her in person? No, Colonel, because she did die on March 7, 2000, and I can assure you confirmation of that fact is in Station Gorky's files.'

'So Kurbsky has done everything for nothing?' Luhzkov said hoarsely.

'I'm afraid so. It's a good thing he's not standing here in my place. He'd probably shoot you.'

'But I didn't know, I swear it.'

With a certain pity in his voice, Bounine said, 'I actually believe you. There's one more thing you should know, however. The man in the black hood who saved Blake Johnson? It wasn't Dillon after all. It was Kurbsky. He couldn't stand the idea of someone else being shipped off to that same terrible place as his sister. I'll leave you to think about what that all means and what his mood is right now. Oh, and I think you'll find that by now, Ferguson and Roper have discovered that Kurbsky's defection is false. Their mood probably isn't much better.'

He turned and walked out.

Dillon and Monica drove down from Cambridge and made straight for Holland Park, where they were soon joined by the Salters, and then Roper.

'This is a right carry-on we've been hearing,' Harry said.

'You're saying that Kurbsky saved Blake Johnson from being kidnapped by Luhzkov's lot and shot two of them up?'

'Yes, there's no doubt about it. It was definitely Kurbsky, because he got a knife wound in the left arm and Katya found him bleeding above the garage in Chamber Court.'

'Well, all I can say is he's certainly done Blake a favour, and no bleeding mistake,' Harry said.

'And that's not all,' said Roper. 'I think he was the one who knocked off Shadid Basayev and his minder in that cemetery in Mayfair.'

Monica said, 'But why would he do that?'

'Basayev was a Chechen general, a monster of epic proportions. He butchered people left, right and centre. Amongst them were men under Kurbsky's command, tortured unspeakably. I think Kurbsky's been under a lot of stress and I think I've discovered why. He always believed his sister was wounded and then died in the rioting in Moscow, in 1989 and was buried in a place called Minsky Park. Tapping away at my computer, I discovered she was secretly sentenced to life imprisonment in the Station Gorky gulag in Siberia. And she died there in 2000.'

They had been unaware of Katya standing in the doorway behind them, listening. She said now, 'I'm afraid there's much more to it than that.'

At the same moment, Charles Ferguson appeared behind her, just arrived and unbuttoning his coat. 'What's all this then? Can anyone join in?'

* * *

Roper brought him up to scratch and Ferguson said, 'It's an incredible business. Katya, as I was coming in, I got the impression you had something important to add.' He turned to her. 'Go on, my dear, we're listening.'

'He believed the lie fed to him by his father that his sister was in that grave in Minsky Park, and you told me how sorry you were to have to tell him she'd been sentenced to life imprisonment in Station Gorky. He already knew that, he'd been told only a couple of months ago that she was still alive after sixteen years, and that he could earn her release by making a false defection that would introduce him into the centre of British security, you people. It was by the Prime Minister's decree, and he was shown a doctored DVD to prove she was alive.'

'Oh, my God,' Monica said.

'Everything, from meeting you in New York, Monica, to all that happened later, was like following a script. Those three GRU men on the train to Brest were not informed that their masters wanted him to defect. The men were ordered to kill him if he tried to. He was blackmailed, pure and simple. He killed Basayev because the Chechen was a monster who butchered his friends. He saved Blake Johnson because although he was supposed to be under Luhzkov's orders, he couldn't bear to see another human being buried alive in Station Gorky.'

There was a moment's silence, and Harry said, 'Why is it I think of cheering for the guy?'

Ferguson said, 'Where is he now, Katya?'

'He received a nasty stab wound as a result of the Johnson

affair, and he's gone off somewhere. To bury himself in London.'

'Tell him to come in.'

'I have.'

'Good.' Ferguson got up and turned to Roper. 'The computer room, and I'd be obliged if you'd get me Luhzkov. The rest of you are welcome to listen.'

Luhzkov had just called Bounine back into his office when he received Ferguson's call.

'My dear Charles, what a pleasure.'

'Don't dear Charles me, you bastard. Two things. Number one, I now know everything about Alexander Kurbsky. I held you and your master in a poor light before, but I now totally despise you. We intend to help Kurbsky in any way we can. He's already done us and the President of the United States a wonderful favour by saving Blake Johnson from a truly terrible fate. Let me make myself perfectly clear. If you in any way again involve yourself in matters detrimental to the interests of the United States or the United Kingdom, I shall personally see to it that you and at least twenty of your GRU staff at the Embassy in London are packed off to Moscow with twenty-four hours' notice.'

'Damn you, General, you can't do that.'

'Try me,' Ferguson said.

He nodded to Roper, who switched off. 'So now to the day's really important business, the meeting on the *Garden of Eden*.'

'Which gives me great pride,' Harry said, 'since it's my riverboat company that owns the *Garden of Eden.*'

'I am aware of that,' Ferguson said. 'And we're all very grateful. Now, as you would expect, the substance of the accord, the measures proposed for improvement in the Gaza situation, will be announced and signed by the Big Four aboard the boat. A certain amount of jubilation will ensue, the people on the *Garden of Eden* will then have a jolly for a while, take in the Houses of Parliament and disembark at Westminster Pier.'

'For which there will be no charge to the national exchequer,' Harry pointed out. 'I'm proud to serve.'

'You'll get a knighthood yet, Harry,' Ferguson told him. 'As to security, Lord Arthur Tilsey's seeing to our people. There will also be the Vice-President's Secret Service men, and of course, the Israelis and Palestinians have added security as well.'

'And what about us?' Dillon asked.

'I'll be there, obviously, you and Billy – and I think Monica. You'll blend in well with the great and the good, Monica, as an extra pair of eyes and ears.' He turned to Katya. 'I think you'd be better employed handling the Kurbsky situation.'

'So everybody's going to have fun but me,' Roper pointed out.

'This is a very particular day,' Ferguson said. 'No one could be more important than you, Roper, viewing the entire proceedings on your screens via the CCTV cameras. Of all people, you will be in control.'

'Now you're stroking me, but true enough.' His fingers

danced over the keys and there on screen was the *Garden of Eden* at Cadogan Pier, a hive of activity. 'There's a much better view from here, anyway. So get out of here, all of you, just go away and have an absolutely wonderful time.'

They all moved on, except Katya. 'I know I wasn't supposed to tell anyone what you discovered about him. It just all poured out.'

'A good thing it did.'

'It was Svetlana. I had to tell her, and he was on the terrace of the conservatory and overheard.'

'It's all right. 'He reached for her hand. 'It's worked out for the best, or let's hope it has.'

'But what's going to happen to him?'

'He could always seek asylum, sit around here till his hair grows back, write a truly great book and reappear on the international scene.'

There was hope on her face. 'Would that be possible?'

'Well if we wouldn't have him, the Yanks certainly would. After what he did for Blake Johnson? President Cazalet would see to that.'

'What a world.' She shook her head.

'Isn't it? Anyway, you go home and reassure Svetlana and if Kurbsky calls you, let me know at once.'

She went, leaving him there in his only true home.

END GAME

14

Kurbsky had driven around the streets for some considerable time with absolutely no idea of a destination. His Codex trembled on occasion, and when he checked, it indicated Katya. He didn't answer because he couldn't think of anything to say. He finally lost himself in a maze of side streets in the general area of the Dark Man and Cable Wharf. He found a small café on a corner and had a burger and a cup of tea while he thought.

There was a television behind the bar and a bulletin came on, the news of the day's events having leaked. Old footage of each of the Big Four came on as the reporter talked, and then some stuff showing the *Garden of Eden* and all the preparations underway. It was raining again, just to make things difficult for the workers, and it occurred to him that the men in suits should have considered the possibility of bad March weather on the Thames.

He returned to the Ford, got behind the wheel, and his Codex trembled, Katya again. This time he decided to speak to her.

'Where are you?' she asked.

'Does it matter? Back streets, the river. How's Svetlana?'

'Very upset, obviously. I've been to Holland Park and met with Ferguson and the others. They understand, Alex, they really do, now that they know everything. Ferguson wants you to just come in.'

'Really?'

'Absolutely. He told me that was what I had to tell you if we spoke, but there's something more.'

'And what would that be?'

'He had us all in the computer room while he spoke to Luhzkov on the speaker phone. Told him he was aware of his part in the whole business, from the blackmailing of you with the fake DVD and file, to the attempt to kidnap Blake Johnson.'

'What did he say in reply?'

'There wasn't much he could say.' She told him about Ferguson's threat of mass deportation.

Kurbsky actually found that quite amusing. 'It would certainly denude the Embassy of staff. There are dozens of GRU people posing as commercial attachés, economic attachés, even arts attachés. It would hit the bastards hard to be banished back to Moscow.'

'Anyway, you must think hard, Alex. They're all busy today with this conference on the Thames.'

'Yes, I saw something about that on a café television.'

'Please, Alex, I'm begging you. If not for me, then Svetlana.'

He was very touched. 'Give me a little time. I'll see how I feel. Perhaps I could come back to Chamber Court again tonight.'

'Your arm, is it okay?'

'Of course it is, Hitesh did a wonderful job. I'll be fine.'

Which wasn't strictly true, because it had been aching badly for some time. He found the bottle of painkillers Hitesh had given him. It said two, so he took four, then drove away.

Charles Ferguson's onslaught left Luhzkov in a rage. He got the vodka out, swilled it down and stamped around his office in a fury.

'That bastard Ferguson, to treat me like this.'

'I should point out that we're on his patch, Colonel. He has the legal right to do what he has threatened.'

'And we would have the right to respond, to kick people out from the British Embassy in Moscow.'

Bounine was all lawyer now. 'But perhaps Prime Minister Putin wouldn't like that, or President Medvedev.'

'I don't care about all that,' Luhzkov raged.

'It would be a pity if one or both of them came to the conclusion that you had acted unadvisedly in this matter. It'd be a great pity to lose the delights of London after thirteen years.'

It was enough and for Luhzkov obviously a sobering thought. 'Yes, Ferguson would come after me. It makes sense.' He sighed. 'Maybe we should cancel the operation.'

'I wonder how Ali Selim will take that?' Bounine said. 'Half a million up the spout.'

'He'll be sensible. We've worked together before and we'll work together again.'

Bounine nodded. 'Do you want me to stay while you phone him?'

Luhzkov was not happy, and it showed. 'A phone call, he would take badly. He is a man of uncertain temper, as you will have noticed.' He turned to the wall safe behind his desk, opened it, and disclosed stacks of cash. He took a canvas bag from a lower shelf and tossed packets of money into it. He pushed it across the desk. 'Give him this. Fifty thousand pounds, with my compliments, for his time.'

'Fifty thousand pounds for nothing?'

'Believe me, it's the safest course with that one. Take it to him now.' He frowned. 'Are you refusing to obey my order, Major?'

'Of course not.'

'Then the sooner you go, the sooner you get back.'

If I get back. Bounine took the bag and withdrew.

He left at once and was at India Wharf in little more than half an hour. Yuri Bounine was a brave man, for he could not have survived Afghanistan and Chechnya if he had not been, but in this case he was dealing with a very unbalanced human being. He had a Stechkin pistol in his raincoat pocket, which he suspected would not do him much good if it came down to a hand-to-hand struggle. So, he would just have to trust his luck.

He opened the doors at the head of the companionway and called, 'Ali Selim, it's Bounine. Colonel Luhzkov has sent me to see you. He has a message for you.'

'Then come below and give it to me.'

He was sitting at the end of the table, the Beretta pistol at his right hand beside an early edition of the *Standard*, which carried a picture of the *Garden of Eden* on the front page.

He looked up. 'I'm just bringing myself up to speed on what's happening. I was watching it on television a little while ago.' He frowned, then said calmly, 'There's something up, isn't there?'

Bounine tried a joke. 'You know what they say. Don't shoot the messenger. He wants to cancel.'

Ali Selim poured a cognac. 'Has he got a reason?'

'He thinks Moscow won't like it. It'll cause too much trouble on the international scene.'

'Why didn't he come himself?'

'Because he's afraid of you.'

'And you are not?'

'When I was in the Russian Army, I fought Afghans for long enough to learn something about them. You invited me in, I'm a guest in your dwelling.' He put the bag on the table. 'He said this is his gift to you for your trouble.'

'How much?'

'Fifty thousand pounds.'

Ali Selim laughed out loud. 'At any other time, I might have said yes, but today not only does his fifty thousand quid mean nothing, even his half million means fuck all.'

'Could you explain that?' Bounine sat down on one of the benches.

'You want to know why I've been pouring Cognac down me like it's gone out of style? Pains in my gut, started four weeks ago, and I discovered that a slug of Cognac kills the pain for a while.'

'A short while,' Bounine said.

'Exactly, so I saw the doctor, had the tests, and he phoned me up an hour ago. Wanted me to go and see him, but I'm a big boy now, so I told him to come straight out with it.'

'And?'

'Cancer in my liver and lights, already spreading like wildfire. No chance with surgery and too late for chemo.'

'How long?'

'Three months tops.' He laughed and poured more Cognac. 'And I don't fancy that, Bounine. It sounds too much like a kind of torture.'

'So what do you fancy?'

Ali laughed wickedly. 'Like going out in a blaze of glory – or should I say Semtex. Now how do you think Luhzkov would feel about that? It would be like one of those old black-and-white war movies with a title like *Torpedo Run*.'

The smile was quite mad, but he obviously meant it. 'I don't think Luhzkov would approve at all,' Bounine said.

'What a shame. He'd be getting it for free and I'd give

him all the credit.' He got up, went behind the bar and opened a cupboard. 'This is where I keep my flags.' He rummaged around and turned with the red flag. 'Hammer and sickle and God bless Mother Russia. So what do you think?'

'That Luhzkov would be so hostile to the idea that he might warn the British security services or Scotland Yard about what you intended.'

'No, I don't think so. I've handled a number of operations for him over the years, and I'll just mention one. It was before your time here, four years ago, the Liverpool shopping mall bomb that was put down to Al-Qaeda. Twelve dead, twenty-one injured. That was me. Part of Luhzkov's break-up-of-modern-capitalism campaign. Ten years ago, I arranged five different bombings in Belfast during the Troubles, also part of his obsession with causing chaos in the Western world. I could prove all this. The Russian journalist Dolishny who committed suicide from the terrace of his tenth-floor apartment in Clapham two years ago? Him, too. He didn't fall, he was pushed.'

'By you?'

'Who else? And in that case, I've got a tape of our discussions setting the thing up.'

'So everything else would be just your word? What would he have to do to persuade you to give him that tape?'

'This. He comes here and faces me, he doesn't inform on me to the British authorities, he gets the tape – and I leave at once to intercept the *Garden of Eden*. Too late for anyone to stop me.'

The smile was that of a raving lunatic, and he laughed

harshly and looked at his watch. 'You've got plenty of time. Go and speak to him.'

Bounine nodded. 'I'll do as you say.'

As he got to the companionway, Ali said, 'Bounine, just remember this: I don't give a fuck. I'm going to die and if it isn't today, it's going to be soon. So there's nothing he can do to me. Got it?'

Bounine drove back to the Embassy as quickly as he could. The whole thing was out of control, and yet some sense of military discipline and loyalty to his country still argued that his duty was to support and defend Luhzkov in any way possible. It then struck him that that must have been the argument some young SS officer had faced when his boss was Heinrich Himmler.

He found Luhzkov in his office. 'Yuri,' his boss said, 'is the matter concluded?'

'Anything but.' Bounine told him exactly what had taken place.

Luhzkov was thrown. 'But this is terrible. What can I do?'

'Well, you obviously can't warn Ferguson or anyone else in intelligence, because if they get their hands on Ali Selim, you've had it. That tape alone would ruin you, never mind his confession on other matters.'

'He's mad,' Luhzkov said.

'No, he's dying, and he doesn't care. Now what are you going to do about the *Garden of Eden?* Would you consider a phone call to the authorities?'

Luhzkov said. 'I don't give a damn about the bloody boat. My problem is Ali Selim. You should have shot him.'

'Frankly, in his unbalanced state, I consider myself lucky to have got off his barge in one piece.'

'Then you must go back.'

'And say please can I have the tape, and then shoot him? This is nonsense, Colonel. If you want the tape, you must face him.'

Luhzkov was looking increasingly desperate. 'All right, but you must come with me. You must find an opportunity to shoot him.' He poured a vodka with a shaking hand and swallowed it down. He took a deep breath. 'I order you, Bounine.'

It was a defining moment for Yuri Bounine, an epiphany. He was tired, so tired and sick of the whole business, of the GRU and men like Boris Luhzkov and Putin and the bleak prospect of a return to Moscow to serve a system which had treated Alexander Kurbsky in the way it had. This man was part of it, a man to whom others were completely un-important, who only considered his own self-interest.

He glanced at his watch and said, 'Right, Colonel, I'll do as you say, but I've things to do. We'll leave in twenty minutes.'

He went straight to his quarters, locked the door, went into the bathroom and called Kurbsky on his mobile phone. 'Please, please answer, Alex. If there's a God in Heaven, make him answer.'

And in Wapping, sitting in the Ford beside a decaying warehouse looking out over the Thames, Kurbsky was aware of the tremble and answered. 'Is that you, Yuri? What's happening?'

So Bounine told him.

When the story was finished, Kurbsky said, 'It's a hell of a pickle, Yuri. India Wharf. I'll find where it is, and you and that bastard Luhzkov make your way there, and we'll meet up.'

'Do we speak to Ferguson or somebody like that?'

'They're busy with the boat. Meanwhile, this Ali Selim is sitting waiting for you at India Wharf. We'll simply make sure he doesn't get to leave.'

At Cadogan Pier there was a kind of confusion, a build-up of traffic and people as guests started to arrive, and that bad March weather swept in across the Thames, reducing visibility considerably.

Ferguson was elsewhere, aiding the Prime Minister with the consultations being held by the Big Four at Downing Street, but Dillon and Monica were already on board the *Garden of Eden*, with Harry Salter cracking the whip over the management and crew.

Dillon left Monica in the lower lounge area, and he and Billy travelled the boat from stem to stern and deck by deck with a clutch of security and Secret Service people in tow, headed by a Colonel John Henry, who was directly responsible for the Vice-President. The three of them finally ended on the bridge, where they found the captain, Arthur Henderson, wearing an obviously brand new uniform for the occasion.

It was Billy he addressed. 'Is everything to your satisfaction, Mr Salter?'

'It bleeding well is,' Billy told him. 'A tight ship, Captain Henderson. My uncle will be well pleased.'

'And you gentlemen?' Henderson turned to Dillon and Henry.

'There isn't a door that hasn't been opened three or four times,' said Henry. 'My only regret is the weather.'

'March, you see, Colonel, and when it rains on the Thames, it rains, believe me. I'm afraid it will get worse before it gets better.'

It was already pouring, then came enough wind to drive it across the river in a grey curtain, making the view of the other side vague and ill-defined. Billy looked down to the decks.

'Well, you've rolled out all the canopies you can. They can stand out under those enjoying their drinks when it gets too crowded inside.'

Down below on the approach to the pier, limousines were delivering guests, and umbrellas were everywhere, as people pressed towards the pier, hurrying to get out of the rain. Lights from the press cameras spangled in the wet air.

'I must see how my boys are getting on,' Colonel Henry said, and left.

'Big day, Captain,' Billy said. 'My uncle takes it very seriously.'

'So do we all, Mr Salter.'

Billy led the way, Dillon followed, and they arrived at the deck lounge and bar. There was music playing, a jazz quartet set up on a dais in one corner, plenty of roving waiters on hand in white monkey jackets already offering champagne to early arrivals. Monica came towards them.

'Is everything okay?'

'Tight as a drum.' Dillon took two glasses of champagne from a passing waiter's tray and handed her one. 'Here's to smooth sailing.'

'Here's to the Big Four producing an accord that's really going to make things better in Gaza,' Monica said.

'Well, it would be nice to think so.' Dillon managed a diplomatic smile. 'Here's to us anyway.'

Harry arrived and he was agitated. 'Look at it, the bleeding weather, and where are we going to put them all?'

'Don't worry, that's why we have deck canopies,' Billy told him. 'They can stand outside.'

Harry reached for a glass of champagne. 'I suppose so if the worst comes to the worst.' He looked thoughtful. 'I was wondering,' he said, 'do you think I ought to put up one of those plaques commemorating today?'

Dillon laughed out loud, and Monica reached over and kissed Harry on the forehead. 'I've said it before, Harry, you are a one-off.'

At Chamber Court, Katya and Svetlana sat in the conservatory discussing what might happen to Alex. 'Do you really think he will return to us tonight?'

'I desperately hope so.'

'A new beginning for him perhaps?' Svetlana nodded. 'Or should I say another new beginning. When you consider his life, his childhood, his time with Kelly and me here in Belsize Park must have been a special experience for him, a release from the Communist regime that had damned his life.'

Katya sighed. 'All snatched away by his father's wickedness.'

'No, my dear, that's too simple. Yes, my brother was corrupted by his political beliefs, and his position in the KGB was more important to him than his children, but everything in this sorry business stemmed from Tania's behaviour. She was a wild child who was indulged by her father, and became even wilder as a student. The consequences we know. If she hadn't involved herself in the student uprising of ninety-two, had stayed home, Alexander would have carried on here, would never have gone into the military and had the appalling experiences of Afghanistan and Chechnya.'

'Yes, I can see that.'

'But enough, I think. Let's turn on the television, and see what's happening with the Big Four.'

Kurbsky found India Wharf with no trouble, in a decaying area of dockland just twenty minutes downriver from Wapping. He braked on the edge of the basin, taking in the situation quickly – the barge, the motor boats and the *Running Dog* berthed inside the archway.

He already had a Walther in the right hand pocket of his coat. He quickly opened the secret compartment in his bag and found the .25 Colt. He couldn't put on an ankle holster, the French paratroop boots were too high, and he had the gutting knife hidden in the right one. He slipped the Colt into his belt at the small of the back and got out.

There was the roar of an engine and the *Running Dog* reversed out of the archway, a man was standing at the wheel. He smiled. 'Hello there, what can I do for you?'

This had to be Ali Selim, Kurbsky knew, because Bounine had mentioned the orange boat and its strange name.

'I seem to be lost, it's like a maze back there.'

The *Running Dog* taxied in beside the barge, and Ali Selim cut the engine and looped a line on a stanchion. He stepped across to the rear deck of the barge and from there to the wharf.

'Where were you looking for?'

Kurbsky couldn't think of a thing to say except Wapping High Street.

Ali had taken a pack of cigarettes out and was lighting one. 'Hah, you couldn't be more out of the way, man.' He walked forward two steps very fast and pushed Kurbsky off the wharf into the water.

He went down maybe ten feet, struggling, his left arm clumsy, and rose, pulling with his right, and surfaced to find Ali Selim squatting on his haunches, holding the Beretta and pointing it straight at him.

'Do exactly as I say or I'll blow your fucking head off, do you follow me?'

Half-choking, Kurbsky nodded, 'Yes.'

'Just come up those few steps and join me.'

The ladder was ancient and rusting, and stretched from the water three or four feet to the wharf. 'I can't,' Kurbsky said. 'My left arm is injured.'

'Hmm. All right, you look like a serious man. I'll believe you.' Ali tossed the end of a line down. 'Loop it round and I'll pull.'

Which he did, demonstrating his enormous strength, and Kurbsky ended up on his knees, spewing up water. Ali stood him up and did a quick search and discovered the Walther. 'You've got taste, my friend, but a man like you would always have an ace in the hole. Ankle holder maybe?' He bent down and patted. 'No? Let's have a look at your waistband at the rear.' He found the Colt .25. 'I approve, especially with hollow-point cartridges. I take care, my friend, I take care.'

'I can see that,' Kurbsky told him, thinking of the two mobile phones Ali had missed in his shirt breast pocket.

Ali said, 'So your arm's fucked? Take off your coat and prove it.'

Kurbsky did awkwardly, disclosing his heavily bandaged left arm minus a shirt sleeve. Ali nodded. 'I see what you mean. What was the problem?'

'I didn't duck fast enough. It was a knife.'

'I knew I was right about you. You can tell a fellow pro instantly, at least I can. A man like you would only be here on business.' He shrugged. 'So I suppose I'd better put you back in the water permanently.' He raised the Beretta and paused, because Kurbsky's woollen cap had come off in the water. 'There's something funny about your skull. You look like one of those Buddhist monks. Are you into Zen or something?'

Kurbsky saved his life, at least for the moment, 'No, I'm into the death business. Chemotherapy.'

'You've got cancer?'

'Of the lung.' He started to shake from the bitter cold, standing there in the pouring rain, the visibility so bad on the Thames that you couldn't see the other side, confronting this dangerous madman, and he knew that his life dangled from a thread.

'Lung cancer?' Ali Selim said. 'That's a bad deal. I've got cancer, too.' He paused, looking at Kurbsky. 'Oh, hell, let's get you below and find you something warm to wear. If I'm going to shoot you, at least you'll be comfortable. Right? Right?' And he started to laugh.

I was right, Kurbsky thought, he's crazy as a loon. He took his time going below, clutching the banister with his right hand. There was still the gutting knife in his paratroop boot and the two mobiles in his shirt pockets. Any attempt to use one of those would lead to instant death, he had never been more certain of anything in his life.

Ali Selim followed close behind, shooed him down to the end of the table, went behind the bar and found a towel, which he tossed to him. 'Go on, dry yourself a little,' which Kurbsky did. 'When I'm hurting, I find cognac helps. What about you?'

'Vodka.'

'Ah, so you're another Russkie? I might have known, with

that bastard Luhzkov involved.' He put a bottle of vodka on the table and three glasses. 'Help yourself.'

'Three glasses?' Kurbsky said.

'We're expecting company, aren't we? Come on, you wouldn't kid a kidder.' Kurbsky had a large one and poured another. 'Were you an army man?'

'That's right, Afghanistan and Chechnya.'

'Heh, I'm half Afghan and half Cockney, isn't that a hell of a mixture?'

'Yes, I suppose it is.'

Ali Selim opened a long cupboard in the corner by the bar and rummaged, without his eyes leaving Kurbsky for a moment. He produced a navy blue linen sailing smock with wide sleeves. 'Help yourself.'

Kurbsky said, 'Thank you, I will.'

He pulled it on, then poured another large vodka and swallowed it down and it started to burn and it suddenly occurred to him that there was absolutely nothing he could do about his situation.

Ali Selim said, 'That Major Bounine who was with Luhzkov, is he a friend of yours?'

'You could say that.'

'I thought so, but I don't think he likes Luhzkov.' He poured a touch more cognac in his glass. 'They are coming, aren't they?'

It would have been pointless Kurbsky denying it. 'Yes, that was the general idea, Luhzkov is coming.'

'Well, he would be, because he wants something from me, something very important.'

'So I believe.'

Ali nodded. 'You interest me. I'm not sure how you fit in.'

'Just helping a friend out.'

'Bounine. I can't see a man like you finding much to interest him in a worm like Luhzkov.'

There was the sound of a car engine outside. 'So here they are.' He poured vodka into Kurbsky's glass and cognac in his own. 'Here's to you, my friend.' He emptied his glass. 'In the end, all roads lead to hell.'

'You could be right.' Kurbsky swallowed the vodka. 'We'll find out soon enough.'

'Up on deck and we'll greet them properly. You first.' And Ali Selim pushed him to the door of the companionway.

15

At Belsize Park, Katya and Svetlana sat watching the tele-vision, and the weather was even more disastrous than ever. The Thames was totally shrouded. The congestion at the Cadogan Pier had been reinforced by the rain and the motor cavalcade bearing the Big Four had arrived a little while ago. The cameras were covering the boat, but also roamed over the river, and as the commentators kept saying, it was impossible to see a thing.

'It's a washout, if you ask me,' Katya said.

'It would appear so. I'm glad we're not there.'

Roper was glad, too, high and dry as he viewed every-thing on his screen. He spoke to Billy, who was wearing an earpiece.

'All the world and his wife there.'

'And all putting the booze away like there's no tomorrow. The Vice-President just made an announcement that everything's been worthwhile and we look to the future with hope.'

'Where have I heard that before?' Roper said.

'And he remembered to thank the Prime Minister for the use of the hall and his warm support.'

'Did he remember to thank Harry for the use of the *Garden of Eden?*'

'Piss off, Roper. We'll be leaving downriver in half an hour. See you later.'

The Mercedes was parked at the end of the wharf, Bounine got out and stood looking at them. Kurbsky said, 'I can't help, Yuri, he's already had me in the water.'

Ali Selim said, 'Don't stand there looking at me as if this is the Gunfight at the OK Corral or I just might shoot you.'

'He means it, Yuri, I'd do as he says,' Kurbsky called.

'Get your boss out,' Ali Selim said. 'And keep in front of the Mercedes so I can see you and watch your hands.'

Yuri opened the passenger door and Luhzkov got out. He stood there looking terrified, and Ali walked to the other side of the wharf, paused for a moment, as if daring someone to shoot him in the back, then turned.

'So you don't want me to blow up the *Garden of Eden*. Have you spoken about it to anyone?'

'Before God, I have not, I swear it.'

'I can vouch for that,' Bounine said. 'He couldn't care less about the boat and the people on it, he told me so. It's his future he's worried about, both here and in Moscow. That tape could destroy him.'

'What tape?' Ali Selim turned to face Luhzkov and barked that harsh laugh. 'There is no tape, you maggot. If there were, it would have me on it, I'd be condemning myself. Do I look stupid?'

His arm swung up and he shot Luhzkov between the eyes, hurling him back over the edge of the wharf into the water. It was so instant, so brutal that it took the breath away. Bounine didn't make a move.

Ali Selim said, 'If you'd pulled a pistol, old son, you'd have been swimming with him now, but I'll keep you a bit longer because you could be useful. Ease your piece out and throw it in the water, and use your left hand.'

Bounine did exactly as he was told. 'Now what?'

'Back down to the cabin. Walk in front of your friend.' Bounine led the way and they paused at the end of the table. Selim said, 'Sit down for a minute.'

They did, and Kurbsky said, 'What happens now?'

Ali Selim opened another wardrobe and pulled out three yellow and black fluorescent jackets. 'Each of you put one on, and help him with his arm,' he told Bounine.

He retreated and put one on himself quickly. Then he found a life jacket, pulled it over his head and tied the tapes at his waist. They had done as they were told and now he took some plastic ties from a drawer.

'Wrists, both of you, behind the back. Do your friend,' he told Bounine again.

Bounine struggled, but Kurbsky's left arm wouldn't bend. 'It won't work.'

'Then tie them in front of him and I'll do you.'

It was finished and they stood looking at him and he produced the bag from behind the bar, put it on the table and opened it. He leaned over and sniffed. 'I love that smell, Semtex. I've blown up parts of Belfast in my day with this stuff and the IRA got the blame. Mind you, it's no use without these.' He took out the tin box and opened it. 'Pencil timers. If you'll excuse me, gentlemen?'

He went to work, quickly and deftly, to do what needed to be done, and finally zipped up the bag. 'I'm going to blow them all to hell, so let's get on with it.'

Bounine led the way, followed by Kurbsky, who said as they went up to the stern deck, 'Tell me one thing. Why the lifejacket, you won't need that in hell.'

'But it's what some nosy River Police patrol boat would expect me to wear, a legal requirement.'

'You think of everything. What are you going to do with my friend?'

'I could shoot him, but I wouldn't like him down there in the same water as Luhzkov. You and I want to go all the way, and together.' He turned to Bounine. 'He's got cancer like me. It's better this way.'

'He hasn't got cancer,' Bounine said. 'You're crazy.'

'Don't say that. And he does have cancer, he told me. You only have to look at him, anyway.'

Kurbsky said, 'Of course I've got cancer, Selim, but he hasn't. Let him go.'

'That's perfectly correct, so I'll tell you what I'll do. Just before we turn to run into the *Garden of Eden*, I'll roll him over the side.'

'With his bloody hands tied?'

'Who knows? If he kicks and struggles enough, he might float. It's all in the hands of God, though I'm not sure which one. Now, down the steps and sit side by side in the stern. Go on, do it.'

Bounine went first and Kurbsky followed gingerly and they got themselves settled. Ali Selim followed, put the bag containing the Semtex close to the prow and cast off. They drifted out a little, the body of Luhzkov in the water a few feet away. Ali Selim crouched down.

'This is it, the big moment. The *Running Dog* does forty knots tops, so when I turn it up, we fly. It's all going to happen very quickly, do you understand? I'll be at Cadogan Pier in fifteen minutes. You'd better believe it.'

'I think by now you've made your point,' Kurbsky said, 'No Russian flag?'

'Fuck the hammer and sickle. Attempt anything out of order and I'll just give you each a bullet in the head.' He stood up, the rain pouring on him, and said cheerfully, 'What a terrible day to die in.'

He went and sat behind the wheel, switched on the engine and moved out into the Thames then turned upriver.

And fly *Running Dog* did, at an incredible speed, particularly considering the weather, the rain like a lace curtain obscuring everything. The *Garden of Eden* had cast off and was moving out into the channel to proceed downriver towards the House of Commons when Captain Henderson, on the bridge beside the helmsman, saw the moving dot on the radar screen.

Ferguson, Harry Salter, Dillon and Monica were below, but Billy, who didn't drink and found most social gatherings boring, had joined the Captain.

Henderson said, 'What the hell is that?'

The helmsman said, 'By God, it's shifting, I've never known such a speed on the river.'

Billy reached for a pair of glasses and focused them, 'It's one of those orange jobs like the police and customs use. I think it could be the police. They're wearing the right jackets. There's one guy at the wheel and two in the stern. It's difficult to work out what's happening. It's bouncing about, and with all that spray and the rain you can't see much.'

'I don't like it,' Henderson said. 'It's already veering off centre. I'll try the hooter.'

The warning blast echoed in the rain, and Ali Selim laughed. 'There they are. Already working out, ready to proceed downriver. Too late. He won't have time to manoeuvre.'

On the *Garden of Eden*, there was no alarm, no panic as the music played and people enjoyed themselves and the Vice-President of the United States glad-handed his way through the crowd, followed by Blake Johnson, but on Roper's screens it was different.

'What in hell is that?' he said to Sergeant Doyle, who was

standing beside him. He tried for a close-up, but the curtain of rain and spray defeated him.

Ali Selim, standing up at the wheel, howled with delight. 'There she is, ready and waiting.'

Kurbsky and Bounine had been drenched with waves engulfing them and it had taken time for Kurbsky to wrestle the gutting knife free with his bound hands. He showed it to Bounine, who half-turned, holding up his wrists at the rear, and Kurbsky sliced through. He held out his hands, Bounine freed him and gave the knife back to him.

Kurbsky stabbed into the thwart of the *Running Dog*, the razor sharp blade doing terrible damage, and it swerved and immediately started to slow. Ali Selim turned, hanging on to the wheel, trying to keep his balance. Bounine and Kurbsky tried to stand up. Everything seemed to happen at once. Ali Selim held on to the wheel with one hand and drew his Beretta, loosing off a shot wildly as the boat swerved. Bounine was hit in the right shoulder and knocked back in the stern seat.

'You bastard,' Ali Selim cried, and shot Kurbsky twice, once in the nylon and titanium jacket, the second round passing straight through the left hip. He turned back to concentrate on the steering, the boat slowing down, and Kurbsky flung himself against his back, sliding his right hand round and cutting his throat.

Ali Selim fell to his knees, bowing his head across the steering wheel as his life ebbed away. Over to the left, the *Garden of Eden* was virtually invisible in the rain and mist. The engine suddenly died, and the *Running Dog* drifted, half full of water, pushed by the current.

Bounine was trying to sit up, Kurbsky sliced the waist tapes of Ali Selim's life jacket, removed it and went and looped it over his friend's head.

'Hang on, old lad, we're going for a swim.'

'The bag, Alex,' Bounine croaked. 'The Semtex.'

'Of course.' Things seemed to be happening in slow motion for Kurbsky. 'I think we'll leave it to go down with the ship.'

He was knee-deep in water as he helped his friend over the side and followed him. The tidal current pulled them away, Kurbsky holding on to a strap on Bounine's life jacket. The *Running Dog* had disappeared completely now. It was quiet, distant city sounds, the rain muffling everything, and then the surface of the river heaved, and an enormous fountain jetted up, the sound echoing with a curious flatness.

In the computer room, Roper said, 'And what in the hell was that?' to Doyle, and hurriedly called Ferguson on his mobile, connecting with him instantly. 'What's going on?'

Ferguson said, 'Don't know. It wasn't us. There was some craft proceeding very fast mid-river and then it stopped and there was a muffled bang. The River Police are investigating.'

In extreme conditions, a five-knot current can be found on the Thames, but three knots is relatively common and it was enough to push Kurbsky and Bounine at some speed downriver. There was a certain amount of traffic, but visibility was so poor they simply weren't seen.

They'd been in the water at least forty minutes, hypothermia kicking in, when their luck changed and a strong eddy in the water swept them in towards the shore. They drifted in towards an entrance between two wharfs. A notice board, paint peeling, said Puddle Dock.

Bounine said, 'What the hell does that mean?'

'English humour, Yuri, who cares? We're alive.'

'Only just,' Bounine gasped as they were swept in between stone piers and ended up at broad stone steps leading down into the water.

It was only when attempting to scramble out of the water on to the steps that Kurbsky realized how serious his wound was. He sprawled on a step in considerable pain.

'The bastard got you twice?' Bounine said.

'I think I'd have been dead if I hadn't been wearing a bulletproof vest, but the other one's in the right hip. It's bad, Yuri. What about you? Now we're out of the water, I can see you're bleeding like crazy.'

'Left shoulder.' Bounine looked about him at the decaying building, the rotting barges, the total desolation. 'Well, I don't know what we're doing here at the backside of the world, but we're alive, Alex, at least for the moment. What do we do?'

Kurbsky took out a mobile from his right breast shirt pocket. 'Waterproof. I think we'll hand ourselves in.'

Roper answered at once. 'Good God, Alex, where are you?'

'In a bad way, Roper, with my good friend, Yuri Bounine. Luhzkov's dead at the hands of a very bad article named Ali Selim, who was going to blow up the *Garden of Eden* using a fast orange rescue boat with seventy pounds of Semtex primed with short-time pencil fuses in a suitcase. Bounine and I were his prisoners, we managed to break free, I cut his throat, the boat went down and blew up. In the process, Bounine and I got shot to pieces. We must have left a quart of blood each dissolving downriver with the current, and let's get one thing straight, in case I die on you. Bounine's one of the good guys in this. Treat him right.'

'Where are you?' Roper demanded again.

'Don't laugh, but according to the sign it's called Puddle Dock. I can't go on, I think I'm going to pass out.' Which he did, dropping the Codex on the step, and Bounine picked it up.

Roper was saying, 'Hang on, Alex, hang on. We'll send a helicopter.'

'Bounine here. Whatever you send, it better be quick, he's out of it and I'm not feeling too good myself.' He leaned against Kurbsky, tried to put his good arm around him, and fainted.

Katya and Svetlana had moved back to the conservatory after turning off the television, when the buzzer sounded and Katya discovered Billy Salter on the screen.

'Let me in, Katya, it's important.'

She did, and was waiting at the front door when he appeared in his Alfa Romeo. He got out and she knew from his face it was bad news.

'What is it, Billy?'

'I'd rather keep it for both of you.'

'That bad?'

'I'm afraid so.'

He followed her in and along to the conservatory, where they found Svetlana sitting on her wicker throne. 'Why, Mr Salter, it's you.'

'And my news isn't too good.'

'Then let us hear it.'

'So the helicopter found them half dead at this place Puddle Dock and rushed them straight to Rosedene. It's in the same area as the safe house in Holland Park, local people assume it's a nursing home, but it's a very private hospital maintained for security personnel, run by Professor Charles Bellamy, the finest general surgeon in London. I should know, he's put me back together again twice.'

'And he's operating now?' Katya asked.

'He and his assistants are taking care of both Alex and this Bounine guy as we speak. The very best of treatment, and by God they've earned it. The Prime Minister, the Israeli Prime Minister, the President of Palestine and the Vice-President of the United States. If this guy Ali Selim had managed to bring it off, it would have shaken the world.'

'To put it mildly,' Katya said.

'So, can we go now to this clinic, Rosedene?' Svetlana asked.

'That's what I'm here for. Ladies, your carriage awaits.'

It was late evening at Rosedene, and dark outside, and they sat in the lounge with Dillon and Monica, the women talking in low voices. The matron, Maggie Duncan, looked in. 'We've two teams working away, Professor Bellamy alternating. Both patients have lost phenomenal quantities of blood, but that's down to the time they were floating downstream in the river. Bounine took a shoulder shot that passed straight through, so he isn't too bad.'

'And Alex?' Katya asked.

'Much more serious. His bulletproof vest stopped the first round, but the second caught him in the hip and fractured the pelvis. He's going to need a plate and that's being attended to now.'

Katya said, 'That's not too good, is it?'

Surprisingly, it was Svetlana who said, 'He's alive, which, considering his activities in past years, is a miracle. The hip will mend, there is excellent therapy available these days.' She shrugged. 'The love of a good woman. Who knows?'

Maggie Duncan said, 'He isn't going to die. We specialize in desperate cases here, so I'm an expert. I expect you'll want to be here for the long haul? We have accommodations available if you'd like.'

Katya glanced at Svetlana, who nodded. 'Thank you, we'd like that.'

Dillon and Monica got up. 'We'd better be off.'

'Me, too,' Billy said.

They went, and Maggie Duncan said, 'I'll have one of the girls bring you some fresh tea.' She turned to go, and Professor Bellamy came in wearing theatre scrubs, Maggie made the introductions.

'I won't pretend it isn't serious. It is and it will take time, but he will respond to the right treatment. His friend is a happier story. He'll be up and about quite soon. But let me say this about your nephew, Mrs Kelly: he has been wounded many times. He can't continue like this.'

Svetlana smiled. 'We'll try to see that he doesn't.'

'Give it an hour, then you can look in, but don't stay too long,' and he left them there.

They had more tea and a sandwich, and about an hour later the outer door opened and Roper appeared in his wheelchair, followed by Ferguson. The General was in excellent spirits.

'I've just had Bellamy on my phone telling me how things stand with our two heroes. We've played the whole episode down, so there won't be any media follow-up. I think we can get away with it. We've put out a cover story on the boat exploding. An overheated gas tank, pure accident. No one could see or hear anything, anyway, so I think we'll be all right there, too.'

'And where does that leave Alex?' Katya asked.

Roper answered. 'Remember what I said? That he could always sit around somewhere, let his hair grow, write a truly great book, and reappear on the international scene when it suited him? The Americans have agreed to give him asylum, so he can start that process whenever he wants to – wherever he wants to.'

'And this friend of his?'

'Bounine? Asylum, from us, too. He can work for me.'

Maggie looked in. 'He's stirring. If you want to take a quick look, do.'

Katya turned to Svetlana, who shook her head. 'I can see him any time now, thanks be to God. You go, my dear.'

Katya opened the door and stepped in. The light was dim and he was propped up, a cage over him from the waist down. He looked very frail lying there, his head bald, the eyes closed. She moved closer, filled with an incredible tenderness.

His eyes flickered open. 'Katya, is that you?'

'Yes, Alex.'

'Good.' His eyes closed again.

She went out, full of energy, dazzled by hope. Ferguson and Svetlana were talking and stopped and Svetlana said, 'How is he?'

'He's well, I think, and he'll be better.' She turned to Ferguson. 'What you were talking about, Alexander's future? Is that a definite offer, slate wiped clean?'

'Absolutely, my word on it.'

'And you can do that?'

General Charles Ferguson smiled and, for a moment, there was a touch of the wolf there. 'My dear lady, I can do anything,' he said.